OUT OF THE WOODS

KATE WILEY

Storm

Ebook ISBN: 978-1-80508-451-8
Paperback ISBN: 978-1-80508-453-2

Cover design: Blacksheep
Cover images: Shutterstock, Depositphotos

Published by Storm Publishing.
For further information, visit:
www.stormpublishing.co

ALSO BY KATE WILEY

Detective Margot Phalen Series

The Killer's Daughter

Her Father's Secret

The Killer Instinct

In the Blood

Margot Phalen FBI series

Tell Me Her Name

As Sierra Dean

The Secret McQueen Series

Something Secret This Way Comes

A Bloody Good Secret

Deep Dark Secret

Keeping Secret

Grave Secret

Secret Unleashed

Cold Hard Secret

A Secret to Die For

Secret Lives

A Wicked Secret

Deadly Little Secret

One Last Secret

The Genie McQueen Series

Bayou Blues

Black Magic Bayou

Black-Hearted Devil

Blood in the Bayou

The Rain Chaser Series

Thunder Road

Driving Rain

Highway to Hail

The Boys of Summer Series

Pitch Perfect

Perfect Catch

High Heat

As Gretchen Rue

The Witches' Brew Mysteries

Steeped to Death

Death by a Thousand Sips

The Grim Steeper

The Lucky Pie Mysteries

A Pie to Die For

To Jennifer Martin, without whom I would never have come this far. You were the first to make my dream a reality, and you've never stopped cheering me on since. Thank you.

ONE

One of the traits Margot, like most homicide detectives, had learned after years of standing over dead bodies, seeing the evil that one human could do to another, was to shut off your emotions at the door.

There was no room at a crime scene for sadness, for repulsion, for anything that might cause a detective's mind to veer away from what was important. Facts. Evidence. Detail. The things that could help solve a crime.

But this time, as Detective Margot Phalen looked down at the pretty brunette in the ferns, her skin purple from the early stages of decomposition, and her eyes milky white, unseeing, Margot *felt* something.

She felt *angry*.

The woman was clothed, but barely. Her skirt had been hiked up over her hips, her shirt torn to show a lacy black bra. Her dark brown hair had been in a high ponytail, but strands were pulled loose, bits of leaves and twigs now tangled within.

The woman, who couldn't have been much older than twenty, had been wearing acrylic nails, and several were missing, one on her right middle finger broken in half.

Scrapes and cuts adorned her knees, elbows and forearms. At some point there'd been a struggle and she'd tried to get away.

She hadn't made it.

On the other side of the woman's body, Margot's partner Wes Fox was looking down at the victim, taking in all this same information. His brow was deeply furrowed. After a long moment, he looked up and met her gaze across the crime scene. They shared an unspoken understanding that what they were seeing was familiar.

Too familiar.

They'd known that before they came, though, based on the location, based on what they'd been told. They'd been called in early for their evening shift just because the location had told the day crew everything they'd needed to know.

Margot could already see tomorrow's headline in the *San Francisco Sentinel*. "Redwood Killer Strikes Again—Police Stymied By Psycho."

Well, Sebastian Klein would probably try to give them a nicer headline, but he didn't always get final say.

And maybe they deserved it.

Because the woman at their feet, half hidden by large ferns and tall grasses, looked very much as if she was the fourth victim of a serial killer.

A serial killer that they were no closer to catching now, than they had been eighteen months earlier, when he'd first left a body in Muir Woods for them to find. They were no closer to knowing who he was than they'd been with Rebecca Watson. With Leanne Wu. With Frederica Mercado.

And Margot was pretty sure he knew it, too.

Detective Leon Telly, the case lead, came to stand beside Margot. For the first two victims, he'd been able to pretend this wasn't a serial killer. But now that they were up to four, and Margot had found a connection between them, there was no way to deny that these women were being targeted.

"Looks like our guy," Leon admitted, grudgingly.

Margot nodded. "Stab wounds to the torso, pelvic area, and chest, consistent with our previous victims. Looks like some bruising around her throat as well. Likely choked her to incapacitate her before he went to work."

Margot's tone was clipped, clinical.

Inside she was so filled with rage she wanted to scream.

She was angry not only because this woman was dead, and had died horribly, though that would have been reason enough.

She was angry because she *knew* that there was more to these cases than met the eye, and her hands were tied from exploring all the angles she wanted to.

This woman was going to have a tattoo on her, Margot was willing to put money on it. It would be of a small bird, so tiny it might be mistaken for a birthmark.

Because two of the others had.

Because they all worked for the same escort agency.

And that agency was run by a man Margot couldn't touch.

And not being able to do her job was pissing her off.

Margot crouched down beside the body then looked up at the tall redwoods towering so high that they seemed to be mere spindles at the top, though their bases were so wide it would take three people to reach around one.

From this angle, the forest was serene in shades of russet, green, and brown. The birds were singing, the ever-present call of the chatty Pacific wren. Wind rustled the leaves and made the trees creak and groan like an ancient choir.

Margot hoped this was what the girl had seen when she took her last breaths. That there had been a fragment of peace in her final moments.

Margot turned her attention back to the body beside her, looking at the woman's broken acrylics, hoping there might be some useful DNA under them. So far, all the Redwood Killer victims had shown signs of fighting back, of struggling to get away. They all wanted desperately to live.

A theory had started to percolate in Margot's mind that perhaps that was part of the thrill for this killer. Give the women a sliver of hope, the illusion that they might get away if they fought hard enough, only to turn around and snatch it all back again.

A sick, twisted little game. She hated that she thought this way.

That was where her theories started to conflict with what she knew about the case. The man who ran the escort company had his fingers deep in organized crime. He had dirt on some very important people, people who were in Margot's direct chain of command.

The way these women were killed didn't read like a hit.

If they were being eliminated for some reason, there were aspects of the crimes that didn't make any sense. Why such elaborate, brutal murders? Why only women from one "team"? The escort agency operated a website that was meant to look like a women's rec soccer league. There were multiple teams—which Margot had surmised meant the women's willingness and availability to do certain activities—and so far, all their victims had belonged to the Larks.

If Margot removed the connection to the agency boss, Emmanuel Riga, and just focused on each homicide individually, they were dealing with a sexual sadist serial killer. Everything about the case suggested someone who was getting his thrills based on the way he butchered these women.

What Margot needed to figure out was how both of those things could be true.

She stood up, looking around the area they were standing in. It seemed as if their killer had learned a thing or two about the difficulty of bringing a body right into Muir Woods park, because his most recent victims, including this Jane Doe, had been left on the periphery of the park. On hiking trails nearby.

This woman had been discarded near the rocky shore of a creek a little way downhill from the park. By car they were less than five minutes from the front gate.

This new victim hadn't been hidden particularly well, either. She was at the bottom of a six-foot slope that rolled away from the road. Her placement made her hard to see from the road itself, but she'd been easily spotted by a cyclist who paused on the narrow shoulder to check his tire.

He'd gone down the hill, thinking she might have had an accident, but on seeing the stab wounds all over her, he'd called in the police. As usual, it led to a moderate jurisdictional headache, but Margot was grateful that the Marin County sheriff seemed to recognize when a case belonged to them.

And this one certainly did.

The thickness of the trees themselves had helped to hide the woman's body from view, but it wasn't as thorough a job as he'd done with the others. There was no effort made to cover her, and he hadn't placed her off the trail in a location where she'd be stumbled across by hikers.

Margot was no expert in lividity—that job belonged to the chief medical examiner Evelyn Yao—but she'd been a detective a long time. Even she could tell this body hadn't been here for more than seventy-two hours or so.

It was as if their killer had just taken this victim to the side of the road and pushed her off, letting nature and bystanders take their course.

Was he trying to get caught?

If so, Margot was more than happy to oblige.

TWO

Margot loved many aspects of her job, despite its sometimes grisly nature. She liked that she was able to constantly use her brain, being forced to work out complex puzzles and put together all the pieces that helped solve an investigation. She liked being able to help families sleep at night. She *loved* taking killers off the street.

There were, of course, complicated reasons for that. The most obvious was that she had grown up sitting across the table from a serial killer.

Coming of age with Ed Finch—The Classified Killer—as a father hadn't seemed strange to Margot at the time, because back then he had just been *Dad*. But ever since his arrest when she'd been fifteen, she had started to see the world in a different way.

Everyone she crossed paths with had the capacity to kill.

It made her very slow to trust, but in turn it had also made her an excellent homicide detective.

And while Margot loved to be a detective, there were aspects of the job she could have done without. Right now, she was experiencing one of them.

"We're going to go through it one more time, OK? And I know it's a serious matter, detective, but you're coming across quite stiff. Do you think you might be able to relax your face a little?" The prosecutor's name was Hildy Shaw, and while Margot knew she was a very good lawyer, she was also not Margot's favorite person at the moment.

"I'm not going to smile," Margot said tensely. "It's a murder trial."

"I'm not asking you to smile," Hildy replied, clearly trying to be patient and kind. Margot knew she was probably being a pain in the ass, but she didn't understand why anyone cared if she was stiff. "Only... maybe don't clench your jaw as much, OK?"

Margot unclenched.

"Great. So, let's go over this from the top. Detective Phalen, you were one of the responding officers at the scene of Shuye Zhou's murder, that's correct?"

"Yes." Margot knew better than to elaborate—it was a sure-fire way to fall into lawyer traps. Just the facts, nothing else. She *hated* appearing at trials, and she *really* hated that she would need to participate in this one. Wes should have been the one they called—he was right there with her every step of the way, and no one would need to tell him to lighten up.

"Can you describe the crime scene for us?" Hildy asked. There were large blown-up photos of it leaning against the wall of the room they were sitting in. They'd been adjusted to make the blood look more red, Margot noticed, but she didn't say anything about that. The goal of the photos was to shock the jury. They would serve their purpose.

Margot recounted her arrival at the Chinatown apartment of Shuye Zhou that February. She didn't talk about how neat the apartment was, how it was filled with toys for when Shuye's grandchildren came to visit. How there were little red envelopes on the dining room table so Shuye could hand out blessings of wealth to her neighbors for Lunar New Year. Margot didn't talk about the wounds on Shuye's forearms that told them she had tried to protect her face and head from attack.

That wasn't what she was being asked.

"We discovered the victim, female, Asian, mid-seventies in her bedroom. She had been stabbed twenty-two times." The number *twenty-two* caught in her throat, and she paused to take a sip of water from the glass in front of her.

"Everything OK?" Hildy asked, mistaking Margot's response for an emotional reaction to remembering the crime scene. Margot didn't correct her.

"I'm fine."

"When did you first hear about Ethan Willingham in connection to the case?"

"Willingham was Mrs. Zhou's next-door neighbor. We heard him mentioned by workers at a nearby restaurant who described him as spending time in the alley behind the apartment complex. We later interviewed both Mr. Willingham and his mother separately."

"That alley where he spent time, was that the same alley where the murder weapon was discovered?"

"Yes."

"Why did you interview Ethan Willingham alone?" Hildy asked. While Margot knew these were prep questions, she still didn't like the tone of accusation in Hildy's voice.

"He chose to speak to us willingly. When he was remanded into our custody his mother chose not to come."

"Ms. Phalen—"

"Detective."

Hildy gave her a look. "Margot, there's no room for grandstanding in front of the jury. If you come across as hostile, they're not going to listen to what you're telling them."

"If you don't want me to be hostile, don't ask stupid questions." Margot crossed her arms over her chest and gave Hildy a challenging stare. "Why are you even bringing me in on this? You know Detective Fox plays better to the crowd, especially the ladies. Put him up there to charm everyone and you don't need to worry about me being a bitch to the defense team."

"We can't ask Wes, he's tied up with another trial that overlaps and has to be available for them. Believe me, Margot—and I mean no offense by this—you were not my first choice."

Margot let out a sigh, but she felt a little kinder toward Hildy as a result.

"Do you think this will actually go to trial? He all but confessed to us, he was *proud* of what he did. He should take a plea deal and go rot in San Quentin." Margot chewed on her thumbnail. She didn't like to be reminded of the time she'd spent with Ethan Willingham, the seventeen-year-old psychopath who had murdered his elderly neighbor.

"I don't know, but we need to have you prepared in case it does happen."

Margot wasn't sure how prepared she could ever be for this particular trial.

The biggest issue was that this crime was committed as an homage to Margot's own father. Something that was bound to come up at trial now that Margot had decided to out herself in a documentary on Ed's crimes.

She kept waiting for Hildy to sneak an Ed question into the mix, but so far it hadn't happened. The mounting tension she felt waiting for it was contributing to her less than sparkly mood.

"Are you comfortable discussing the details of the case?" Hildy asked her.

"Of course."

"Do you suppose you could do it without sounding completely detached from human emotion?"

Margot set her hands in her lap. "A woman was slaughtered in her own home, by a boy she invited in because she trusted him. I'm not sure what emotions you want me to convey that aren't rage or horror. Do you want me to smile when I tell them he stabbed her in the skull?" Margot mimed a stabbing motion beside her own temple.

Hildy blanched. She was no stranger to this level of detail, but it was never easy to be confronted with it.

"Sorry," Margot said a moment later. "I can't do both. I can do detached and thorough, or I can show them what I really think of this little prick."

Hildy pulled out a chair and sat down across the table, folding her hands neatly in front of her. She stared at Margot and didn't look away.

"I need the jury to feel you have the capacity for empathy. Because if you go out there and coldly detail the killings, *if* the defense team brings up your personal connections to the case, the only thing the jury is going to be able to see when they look at you is Ed Finch."

The words hit Margot like a punch, stealing all the air in her lungs and causing her to physically recoil from the table.

She knew it wasn't personal, she *knew* Hildy wasn't saying she was like her father, but she couldn't help but hear the implication in the words. An implication that the defense might well use to their benefit to make her a less reliable witness.

Margot braced her hands on the edge of the table and pushed her chair back, the wood legs scraping loudly against the tile floor. She grabbed her bag from where it was slung over the back of the chair and headed toward the door without a word.

"Margot," Hildy said, wheeling around. "Don't just leave."

Margot looked back at the lawyer, working her tight jaw free of its tense lock and choosing her words carefully.

"If you didn't want to deal with the daughter of a serial killer, Hildy, you should have found someone else to help you." And she slammed the door on the way out.

THREE

Margot often wished there was a way to turn her brain off. When she woke up the next day, as she showered and laid out her clothes for the day, she was still thinking about Hildy, and regretting her bad behavior. She felt bad enough about it, she accidentally conditioned her hair twice.

It wasn't Hildy's fault that the public now knew Margot was Ed Finch's daughter.

Margot had only herself to blame for that.

She hadn't *wanted* to be a part of the docuseries.

She had been perfectly fine living under her new name, with her new nose, her new life. But there was no escaping her past, no getting away from the person she'd been, and she'd known it was only a matter of time before someone put the pieces together and outed her against her will.

She'd felt certain it would happen in the wake of the Ethan Willingham case. Ethan's mother—Toni—was, it turned out, actually married to Ed Finch. And that had given Ethan direct access to talk to—and learn from—a killer.

Ethan and Toni both knew who she really was thanks to their connection to Ed. They had used the murder of Shuye

Zhou as bait; as a way to get Ed her new name. And Margot had been shocked that neither of them had done anything else with that information.

For months, she waited for a newspaper story to drop, for a camera crew to be waiting outside her apartment. It hadn't happened.

And then her brother had arrived on her doorstep, drunk and desperate, begging for her to participate in the series. He needed it for closure, he told her. He laid on a heavy emotional guilt trip about Margot being able to see Ed in prison while Justin—now David—was left to deal with the trauma on his own.

He didn't seem to care that Margot didn't *want* to visit their father. That she was only doing it to help close more cold cases. To find and unmask Ed's accomplice. To bring justice for both of their misdeeds.

She wasn't just catching up with her old man.

The documentary, Justin said, would give him peace. And so Margot talked to the producers. She talked to Andrew Rhodes, the FBI agent who had caught Ed and was now working with her to find his previously unknown victims. She had listened, and she had decided, after much heartache, it was time to stop hiding from who she had been.

The truth was now out in the world, and she'd been both surprised and relieved to find that not that many people cared. At work, there was a certain coolness in the air around her as her fellow detectives processed the information. But she was a good cop, her record was flawless, and since they learned that their captain had known, and so had both Wes and Leon, they seemed to be handling it with more acceptance.

Her address was not publicly searchable, her phone number private, but her lawyer said there had been an uptick in mail to his office. She had him shred it all. There had been requests for more interviews. A few literary agents were making their cases to her lawyer for book deals. Margot told him she wasn't interested.

Admittedly, for a woman who lived in a small apartment furnished entirely in second-hand items, a seven-figure book deal offer had been hard to ignore, but she didn't *want* the notoriety. She'd only come out publicly with who she'd been so that the information was no longer a threat.

She wasn't Megan Finch.

She was Margot Phalen.

But she couldn't ever be completely Margot with Megan lurking like a shadowy monster waiting to come out and destroy the life she'd worked so hard to build.

Making money off of that, and off her father, didn't feel like the right thing to do.

Plus, she couldn't write a paragraph to save her life, let alone a book.

That was Andrew's thing.

The one saving grace of the whole experience was that the docuseries did what it had promised. It focused a huge chunk of the narrative on Ed's victims, both old and new, and really made sure to emphasize who they had been and what their loss had meant to those around them. Margot had felt a surge of emotion seeing the women's faces on screen, edited together with old home movie footage, and hearing their families talk about who they were. It was as if the documentary made the victims immortal, in a way that Ed could never ruin.

Margot didn't want pity for herself or her family, though she knew in a sense they were victims as well. But she wanted to be a voice for her mother, who was no longer alive to try and explain how they never knew who Ed really was.

"You always look under your bed and in your closet for monsters before you go to bed," Margot had said. "You never think to look right across the dinner table."

That quote had been used in every piece of promotion for

the show. She wasn't on social media, but someone told her it was a viral soundbite on some platforms where people were turning it into a humorous trend, putting it with videos of their pets knocking things off the table, or of their boyfriends looking up from dinner with confused expressions on their faces.

Margot didn't really know how that worked, but she hated the very notion that she was a meme. If that was the worst thing that came out of this, however, then she was better off than she'd expected.

Justin seemed more at peace now, though Margot suspected he was secretly frustrated that she'd been given more airtime than him when she hadn't wanted to participate in the first place.

That was just sibling rivalry coming through, though. He'd always been a little petty about her successes.

Now, a few months on from the release of the series, Margot was relieved that the interest was dying down; it might soon be nothing more than another blip in her history. Except that Hildy Shaw was hinting that the worst was yet to come.

And maybe it was.

There was a part of Margot that always believed that, because it had proven to be the case historically.

She hadn't always felt that way. For fifteen years she'd been one of the most optimistic people alive.

But optimism can't last long in the face of the total destruction of one's life.

Margot took a moment before she left her apartment, putting everything in order. While nothing she owned was new or fancy, she had come to realize lately that keeping her home in order did give her some semblance of having her life together. Coming home after an exhausting shift of hunting down killers and looking at dead bodies was hard, it didn't need to be made harder by walking in to see dishes in her sink or yesterday's underwear still on the floor by her bed.

So she was trying.

There were so few things in life she had control over, folding a throw blanket and putting an empty bag of Doritos in the trash was a small price to pay to claim a little sliver of peace.

She made the drive to work in silence, not because she wanted to be alone with her thoughts—perish the notion—but because radio DJs made her want to rip off her own ears and she didn't have the patience for it today.

At the office, Margot slid behind her desk, tossing her bag on the floor, and stared at the empty place by her mousepad where there would normally be a coffee waiting for her.

Wes wasn't there.

Wes normally arrived before her, no matter if they were on the morning shift or the late-night rotation. His punctuality was borderline passive-aggressive, like he was competing with her to always be the first one at the precinct, the first one at a crime scene if they weren't going together. He was so irritating about it.

But he softened the blow with coffee, always.

There was no coffee on her desk now.

She peered over her shoulder out into the main bullpen, but there was no sign of Wes's long, lean figure. Margot frowned and checked her phone but there were no missed calls or texts from him, either. The sudden wave of anxiety she felt was surely misplaced, but anxiety wasn't something that responded to logic.

Wes was just running late, or he'd been caught up in a meeting. He didn't need to tell her everywhere he went. They were partners, not a couple.

Still, she was accustomed to his presence, and the lack of it was sending the darker recesses of her mind into an unwelcome spiral.

Wes was dead.

He'd been hit by a car on his way to work.

Someone had followed him home last night.

He'd crossed a woman with an angry husband who decided to take it out on Wes.

Maybe he was in a hospital and no one knew. Should she start calling hospitals?

As she mentally went through all the steps that the police department insisted other people take before filing a missing person's report, Wes came through the door, his coat flapping and cheeks flushed. He set a coffee down in the usual spot on her desk and let out all his breath in a *whoosh* as he slumped down into his chair.

Margot breathed out through her nose so he wouldn't hear her sigh of relief. "You're late," she said coolly.

Wes grinned. "You worried about me?"

Margot sipped her coffee. Perfect as always. "I was enjoying the quiet, actually."

He shucked off his coat and re-settled in his chair. "Nah, you missed me. You came in and were like, *oh no, where is his beautiful face?*"

Margot stifled a laugh, shaking her head. "Your face isn't that beautiful." Her lips quirked upward.

Wes was ignoring her. "You were going to pack up and go home without me."

"I did miss my coffee," she admitted.

"That's all I am to you, isn't it? Your caffeine concubine."

"Your words, not mine, Wesley. Why *were* you late?"

"See, I knew you cared." He entered his password on his computer and sipped his own coffee. "I got a goddamn flat on Washington. Have you ever had to change a tire on Washington?"

"I can't say that I have." She pictured the intense slope of the hill. She wasn't even sure how a car jack would work at that angle without sending the car rolling back and crushing someone in the process.

Wes seemed to read her mind. "You can't. It can't be done. Had to have the fucking thing towed to a shop."

"Man, what karmic gods did you piss off?"

He threw his hands up in the air. "All of them. So, anyway, you're Bullitt for the day, kid."

"No one is Bullitt in a Honda, Wes."

"Don't sell yourself short."

She rolled her eyes and pulled up a now too familiar website. Women's faces beamed out of the screen at her. The Larks.

This was her victim pool. The women the Redwood Killer kept returning to time and time again. She didn't need to be a detective to know that their new Jane Doe would be here somewhere.

The biggest issue with finding her was that the website had professional quality photos of flawless-looking women, while their victim was in early decomp. The second issue was that even if Margot found their Jane Doe in the Larks directory, none of the names on the website were real. She'd probably be listed as Cindy or Bethenny and not whatever her real name was. It would give them a tie, but it wouldn't give them her identity.

Still, while they waited for Evelyn Yao to run dental records, all they could do was look through the resources they had. The woman's fingerprints had been a bust, so she'd never been arrested before.

The woman had no identification on her, no purse, no wallet. All of the initial signs from the crime scene indicated she'd been killed somewhere else and then dumped at the scene, which aligned with their killer's previous victims. Margot was beginning to assume he must live near the park, because otherwise he was making a lot of effort to drag the bodies all that distance. It was a risky thing to do.

But this was also a man who wanted his work to be found.

Whether that meant he wanted to be caught, or he just liked to follow the stories of his work in the press, Margot couldn't decide.

A tap at the door drew their attention. Leon was standing there, his jacket on and a grim expression on his face.

"What does that look mean?" Margot asked warily.

"Means I hope you're ready for a familiar drive." Leon's voice sounded tired, mirroring how Margot felt.

Her brows knit in confusion. "They find something we missed at the scene?"

Leon shook his head. "Found another scene."

Wes let out a low whistle across the desk. "Same guy?"

"We'll have to see it to be sure, but they think so. Only half a mile from Jane Doe One. They think she's been freshly dumped, but she also looks like she's been dead longer."

Margot got up and grabbed her coat. Wes followed behind her, handing her the coffee she'd forgotten on her desk.

As they drove back to Muir Woods Margot's mind was racing. They'd had victims discovered close together before. Rebecca Watson and Leanne Wu had been found within a week of each other. Leanne's body had been out longer, it was just harder to find.

Every victim after Leanne had been dumped somewhere it would be discovered quickly.

Two body dumps on the same road in two days was a very bad sign in a serial killer case, especially one who had seemed to be slowing down his pace up until recently. Something had set him off if he was starting to kill with this frequency.

Margot felt a heavy sense of déjà vu as they pulled up to the crime scene. The same Marin County sheriff SUVs waited for them that had been there the previous day, and the same local cops lingered by the roadside waiting. Same damn stretch of road.

Though they were far enough down the road she couldn't

see the previous crime scene from where they stood, they had passed the yellow tape only moments earlier, and there was still a patrol car parked there to keep the scene monitored.

How ballsy was this guy? Would he come past a police car then stop only yards around the bend to dump another body?

While the actual National Park of Muir Woods wasn't open at all hours, this stretch of road was certainly well-traveled. Even at night Margot wasn't certain a passing car would have stood out at all. But it was unbelievably risky for him to have dumped another body this soon and so close to the last one.

He was getting reckless.

And reckless men made mistakes.

Margot felt an unexpected thrill go through her. The last thing in the world she wanted was to be standing at another crime scene, but she also knew that this killer's new haste was going to be the thing that finally brought him down.

She *had* to believe that.

The sun was dipping low behind the trees and Margot followed closely behind Wes and Leon as they moved down the embankment, using thin young trees to keep their balance with the loose rock underfoot.

It was a sharper incline here than it had been at the previous scene, the side of the road dropping off sharply. There was no water running along this side of the road, though Margot could hear the stream trickling from the opposite side. It should have been a comforting, idyllic sound, but it wasn't helping take the edge off.

Much like yesterday's Jane Doe, this victim appeared to have been dumped off the side of the road with no attempt made to hide or bury her body. There were scrapes on her arms, legs, and face that would make sense given the rocky tumble, whether the victim was alive or not when she died.

Margot could see right away that the visual assessment that this body had been dead longer had been made with good reason. The woman's skin had taken on a greenish hue, and the smell that wafted up the hill toward them was very distinctively that of a decaying body. The fly activity around her was incredible, even with the warmth of the day fading.

One of the Marin PD plainclothes officers was standing next to the body. His hands were shoved deep into his pockets and he was staring down at the woman like he couldn't believe it was his dumb luck to be here twice in one week. Margot knew the feeling.

She momentarily felt grateful that poor Ranger Abbott hadn't been involved in finding these victims. The poor man was probably traumatized every time he went out on a hike to check the park paths now, having been present for three of the victims.

This scene was unique, however, because, for the first time, with a stab of realization, Margot recognized the victim.

She knew her face from the hours and hours she'd spent on the rec soccer website looking at photos of the Larks. The shock of red hair and the round cheeks jogged Margot's memory. Her eye had repeatedly been drawn to this woman's headshot in her previous searches. She had looked so different from some of the others, the blondes, the brunettes.

After a while all those smiling faces had blended together. But she remembered the redhead, her eyes wide, cheeks cherubic. She'd been a sweet-looking girl.

Now she was another name on a list.

But that name meant something to someone. It had to mean something to Margot, too. She needed to remember that these women, no matter how many of them piled up along this stretch of road, were important, even if society wanted to write them off because of the work they did. Even if someone wanted them dead.

The stigma of sex work was a vicious thing. It turned victims into targets, as if, because of what they did for money, they were asking to be murdered. The thing about that mindset was that the agency these women worked for catered to very wealthy people, people that these women had assumed were vetted and safe.

Yet they were all winding up dead in the woods.

And Margot, for one, wanted to find this guy before another young woman's life got cut short.

FOUR

Their new Jane Doe had a name. Or at least what they suspected might be her name.

Around her neck was a gold pendant with a nameplate that read *Steph*.

Margot wasn't sure if this was going to help lead them to their victim—it could be the name of a child, or lover—but it was more than they had for their other victim. They could run her prints and also start checking the missing persons' database to see if there were any Stephanies in their early twenties who had recently been reported missing.

The woman's body was far gone enough that someone was likely to have noted her absence by now.

The light was fading fast as they searched the area around the body, but, as with their previous scenes, there was nothing that stuck out as being potential evidence. Bits of garbage were bagged and tagged, but in Margot's gut she knew how unlikely it was that any of this would be meaningful to their investigation.

Margot borrowed a flashlight from one of the Marin deputies and fanned it back and forth over the ground, looking for anything that might give them the slightest edge in this case. When nothing popped out, she returned to the body and trailed her light over the woman, practically begging the crime scene gods to give her something.

Like their previous victims, this one had been stabbed multiple times, the slashes and cuts appearing almost black under Margot's beam of light. She was dressed casually, a pair of denim leggings and a crop top from Tulane University. That might give them another clue to the girl's identity if the other searches came up blank.

Margot also spotted something she'd known they would find eventually. A tiny tattoo, so easy to miss that if she hadn't been looking for it, she would have written it off as a mole.

The little bird was behind the woman's left ear.

The tattoos had bothered Margot for a while. She knew they represented the group the women belonged to on the website, but there was something more sinister to them. What kind of agency required their girls to get tattoos that effectively branded them as property of that one group?

Or, if it wasn't the agency forcing them, why had all these women felt compelled to get tattoos that connected them to dozens of other sex workers? Was there something about this agency Margot wasn't fully grasping?

She was so engrossed in the woman's tattoo, she almost overlooked something else, but a little flash of color caught her eye as her gaze skimmed the woman's head.

She crouched down, shining her flashlight closer to the woman's neck, squinting against the glare of the light, wondering if maybe she had only imagined seeing it because she'd been hoping so hard to find anything at all.

But no, tangled in the fine hairs at the base of the woman's neck there were a small number of blue fibers.

"Wes, I need an evidence bag over here," Margot called out, worried that the moment she looked away the fibers might have vanished. She pulled her phone out of her pocket and snapped a few pictures on her phone before remembering the scene photographer had arrived.

As she called for the photographer, Wes came to her side, a bag in hand. Margot pointed out the blue fibers, needing someone else to see them to prove they weren't wish fulfillment on her part. The photographer squatted down beside her, and using the light from her flashlight for additional illumination, snapped several photos of the hairs before Margot felt comfortable pulling them free and depositing them in the plastic evidence bag, which was then marked and added to the others.

"What do you think?" she asked Wes.

"Hard to say. Too long to be from a car interior, I think, but maybe a rug?"

Margot nodded, his thoughts mirroring her own. They hadn't found any similar fibers on the other victims. Maybe this guy really was starting to get sloppy.

So far, none of the women had been killed in their own homes. There was no reason to believe this victim would be any different. So there was a real chance the carpet the fibers came from belonged to her killer.

A bit of carpet fiber wasn't necessarily a signed confession, but it was stuff like that they *loved* in the jury box. It helped get killers convicted.

Margot needed to be careful about putting the conviction cart before the arrest horse, though. All they knew now that they didn't know before was that their killer *might* have a blue carpet.

That narrowed things down, but not in a useful way.

Margot didn't want to move the body and risk losing any additional fibers that might be present, but she did a longer, closer inspection to make sure there was nothing else.

And lo and behold, it was her lucky day.

Their victim was wearing a bracelet, and as Margot lifted her wrist, she spotted a dark hair tangled in the bracelet's clasp.

Carpet fibers might not point them to a killer, but a good DNA sample just might.

Margot held her breath, terrified that the slightest puff of air might send the single hair drifting off into the dark, never to be found again. It was a silly thing to think, of course The hair had held on this long, all the way down the hill. Like it had been waiting for them to find it.

Wes opened the bag for her and held it under their victim's wrist as Margot unclasped the bracelet and let everything fall together into the waiting bag.

Margot wasn't an optimistic person by nature—she didn't like to get her hopes up about things, or really have hopes to get up—but there was a nagging feeling in her chest as she looked at the bag under the light of her flashlight, and she knew that stupid feeling was hope. Optimism. The idea that this *might* be the piece they'd been looking for all this time.

She knew more likely than not it would be a dead end, an unusable sample, any number of things that could turn good evidence against them. But she couldn't help but feel a little excited, as dangerous a feeling as that was.

Maybe she was setting herself up for disappointment, but she didn't want to talk herself down from the ledge.

Margot felt like a shark that had smelled blood in the water.

She wasn't going to stop until she found where it had come from.

FIVE

Evening shifts had their benefits, though they were few and far between.

It was easier to drive places with no rush hour to contend with. People were generally home when Margot went to talk to them. All good things.

The bad part was that the number of bodies that were found at night versus the daytime tended to feel unfairly skewed. Margot was just grateful nothing new was currently being piled on their plate, because she and Wes were busy. Leon was pulling in overtime with the two new bodies being discovered so close together, and the department was *finally* giving them some extra manpower now that news was starting to spread about two new Redwood Killer victims.

The only problem with a task force was that they didn't know squat about the case, so Margot suddenly felt like both a detective and a preschool teacher; people kept coming into her office to ask her the most asinine questions.

As Margot was settling down to start her report on the most recent case, a young detective peeked his head into the office she and Wes shared. He hovered near the door as if afraid to step over the threshold, like Margot might be one of those sphinx statues that forced people to answer riddles before letting them pass, otherwise she would kill them.

"What do you want?" she barked without looking at him. His presence alone was enough to set her teeth on edge. She hated it when people *lurked*.

"Oh, I, um..."

Margot shot a look across the desk to Wes, who was trying desperately not to laugh, but also wasn't doing anything to help her get rid of the guy. Margot spun her chair around to face the man in the door, but her direct attention evidently didn't do anything to help this man's confidence. The guy quickly looked at Wes, then realized the error of his ways and turned his focus back to Margot.

"I was reviewing some of the earlier case files. Looking at Rebecca Watson specifically."

"OK," Margot replied.

"I saw that no one ever interviewed the owner of the house where Watson lived."

Margot's expression shifted from annoyed to actively unfriendly. "We did interview the owner. He was living outside the country at the time of the murder. He was interviewed by phone, and I think you'll find a complete transcript of that conversation if you dig a little deeper into the file.'

The man's cheeks flushed red and he took a moment before he spoke again. "I'm sorry, I should have phrased that differently. No one interviewed him in person."

"We couldn't. He wasn't in the country."

"Oh, well... I checked with his maid—I saw you interviewed her as well—and she said he's back. I mean... if you think that lead is worth looking into."

Margot twisted around to look at Wes. She had honestly almost entirely forgotten about Richard Downey, the man who owned the plush mansion in the Sausalito hills where Rebecca

Watson had lived. He'd been written off as a suspect because of an airtight alibi, but now that they were investigating the links Rebecca and the others had to the same escort service, and that service's connection to Emmanuel Riga, Downey seemed like a person she would very much like to talk to again.

She checked her watch. It was early still, only eight, and while it would take them some time to get back out to Sausalito, she didn't want to let this opportunity go. Who knew when he'd split town again, taking his information with him.

The young detective had a good instinct, if no backbone to support it. In-person interviews were always the best if you could get them.

"You want to take a drive?" she asked Wes.

"I could go for a drive." He pulled his coat off the hanger then jerked his chin in the direction of the young man in the doorway. "Should we adopt him for the night?"

Margot made a face at him, knowing the other man couldn't see it. No, she didn't want to absorb a tagalong for the night. But she also knew people in the kid's situation—new to the department—needed a guiding hand, someone to show them a little kindness until they got their feet under them. Being a detective was a whole different beast to being a beat cop, and it often took people a while to adjust.

Some didn't adjust at all.

She wasn't sure if this one had the mettle for it, but they'd never find out if he wasn't put through his paces.

Margot spun back around in her chair.

"What's your name?"

"Branson," he answered slowly, uncertainly. "Riley Branson."

His name alone made her feel ancient. Riley felt like such a late nineties name that she almost wanted to check this kid's ID before letting him into her car. Had he even seen a body in person yet?

She scolded herself for that unkind thought. Of course he had. No one ended up in homicide without some exposure. You had to *want* this job to take it. No one ended up in homicide by accident.

"Branson, you have a coat?"

He looked so confused Margot almost felt bad for asking. She knew she wasn't being very nice, but she also didn't know how to be anything else. "A jacket, kid. You might want to grab one."

When he still didn't seem to understand, she got up and put her own coat on, like demonstrating it might help.

"Because you're going to come with us to follow this lead of yours," she explained finally. "So go get your coat."

It finally seemed to click, and he bolted out of the room so fast she imagined cartoon dust in his shape was still lingering in the door. She looked back at Wes and rolled her eyes as she pulled her long ponytail free from the collar of her jacket. "I can't believe you're making me bring a twelve-year-old with us. Do we need a permission slip from his mom?"

Wes smiled at her and put an arm around her shoulder, pulling her close against his side as he gave her a playful shake.

"Be *nice*, Margot. The freshmen are terrified of you."

"Good, then they can start putting their stupid questions to someone else."

"If you don't think Leon is sending them to you intentionally, I think you're kidding yourself."

Margot groaned and fished her keys out of her bag. Branson had returned, still looking flushed, and now a little breathless.

"I want you to observe, that's all," she told him as they left the precinct together and headed for her car. "I will let you know if I want you to talk, OK? Otherwise just eyes and ears. Mouth is not equipped for tonight. You understand?"

Branson nodded mutely. Wes patted his shoulder. "Smart man, you catch on quick. Took me a good six months of working with her before she let me have the jar with my balls back."

Margot smacked him in the chest. "Don't give him false expectations, Wesley. You know you only have part-time custody."

They got into the car and she could see the conflict warring on Branson's unlined face. They were being funny. They were telling jokes. Was he allowed to be this light and relaxed, too? He looked too scared to try.

Probably for the best; it took time to fall into the same rhythm as the team, and who knew how the other veterans at his precinct behaved? She didn't want to set this poor kid up for a nightmare when he returned to his squad.

The drive out to Sausalito was a pretty one, the kind of drive that tourists might rent a car to take. Unfortunately for Margot it was the same drive—in part—that took her out to San Quentin whenever the FBI arranged for her to have chats with her father. It was a reminder that she had another one of those coming up this week—her first since the documentary had released—and she was dreading it.

Ed had been in a sulky mood since the series came out. She wasn't sure how he'd been able to see it—the prison didn't exactly offer streaming options on death row—but he seemed keenly aware of what she'd said about him, and how his victims had been given center stage, and it had made him a bit petulant.

She was almost disappointed. After she'd gone to visit one of Ed's accomplices and the meeting had gone disastrously wrong, ending with their target's suicide, she had wanted to see his face when he found out. She'd wanted to know if that had been his goal all along.

Wes pointed out a turnoff that took them up a sloping hill in Sausalito until they turned a corner and the view of the city unfolded before them, San Francisco twinkling like a jewel. This was a vista of the city Margot rarely saw, and for a moment, she let herself enjoy it. The Bay Bridge was lit up, and the city had never looked cleaner or more perfect. No wonder people paid millions to be on the outside looking in.

Margot thought the view from her own North Beach apartment was decent enough, but this was exactly what people were talking about when they said *room with a view* Branson was staring out the window looking at the city like he'd never seen it this way before, and maybe he hadn't. It was rare for anyone who lived in the city to make their way outside just to take in the tourist views, but Margot supposed there *was* a good reason people loaded onto tour buses simply to look back the way they'd come.

Margot remembered the house from their visit the previous year, after finding Rebecca Watson. That case felt like a million years ago, but also like it was yesterday. Somehow, Rebecca had led them to everything that happened after. She wasn't the Redwood Killer's first victim, but she was the first one they had found.

She was also the only victim so far who *hadn't* been on the Larks website, even the archived versions Margot had scoured. They'd connected her to the service through a photo of her wearing the same logo as the other girls had tattooed.

Rebecca was a bit of an enigma. Margot didn't think she was working for the agency in the same capacity as their other victims; her connections to those surrounding the case pointed to a role that might have been more about grooming new girls or acting as something of a madame. No one had said those things about her, but it was a vibe that Margot was getting as other pieces of evidence fell into place.

The entry to Richard Downey's home was a brightly lit modern gate with a buzzer and camera mounted to the side. Margot pulled up and pressed the buzzer. For a long moment there was no answer, then a male voice gruffly asked, "What do you want?"

"Mr. Downey, I'm Margot Phalen, a detective with the San Francisco Police Department. We spoke last year regarding the murder of Rebecca Watson."

A long pause, then, "Yes, and...?"

"We'd like to speak with you regarding that ongoing investigation."

A soft curse was nearly covered by the sound of the gate buzzing and sliding open to allow them access.

"This is going to be super fun," Margot said dryly, and Wes raised an eyebrow in response. Unwilling witnesses were almost worse than unwilling suspects, because there was no way to barter with them. They had what she needed—information—and there was nothing they wanted from her, except for her to leave them alone.

They parked in front of the brightly lit mansion, its front entirely made of concrete and glass, showing off the posh, modern interior. Why did rich people feel the need to have every single light on in their home at all times? Did this guy really need the whole hilltop to see how fancy his house was?

Also, wasn't it a pain in the ass to turn off all those lights before bed? Or did he have a special timer that did that for him? Margot was a blackout curtains and lamps kind of girl. Anything to keep notice from traveling up to her space. The less that people knew and wondered about her the better.

Wes looked wholly unmoved by the gratuitous splendor of the house, but Branson's mouth was hanging open as they approached the front door. The interior had a honeyed glow to it thanks to a metric ton of polished white oak that had certainly been used to balance the masculine brutalism of the concrete. It was all a little too modern for Margot's taste, but then, *Architecture Digest* wasn't pounding down her door to do a feature on her thrifted couch and mismatched side tables.

She looked back at Branson and snapped her fingers in his direction to wake him up out of his wealth-induced stupor. She hated being the kind of dickhead who snapped at people, but it was the only way to get his focus without yelling at him and it worked. He fell into line behind her and Wes.

She was about to reach for the doorbell when the large front door swung open, and a man stood at the threshold. He held a lit cigarette, and wore lightweight sweatpants that looked to Margot like cashmere, and a long-sleeve gray Henley button-down. In the background, classical music played softly throughout the house.

"Detectives, are you aware of the time?" he drawled before taking a long draw from his cigarette and blowing the plume of smoke almost directly into Margot's face. She wasn't sure how to explain it, but the man sounded rich, like if he'd been born fifty years earlier there would be a Transatlantic rasp to his voice and he would call everyone sport. His words were annoyed, but his tone was bored.

Margot wrinkled her nose at the smoke, but she didn't give him the satisfaction of waving it off. She just stood her ground and smiled at him.

She'd been told her smile was more unsettling than it was soothing, and she hoped that was the case today. "Good evening, Mr. Downey. Yes, we are aware of the time, we took a chance hoping you might be available to speak with us. We know how busy the schedule of a man in your position can be."

Downey's eyes scoured her from the top of her head to the tip of her scuffed boots. He made no indication whether or not he found what he saw there acceptable or lacking. After a moment he let out a snort and then stepped out of the doorway, ushering them in with a dramatic wave of the arm.

Margot led the trio of detectives inside, where they followed Downey into an office Margot only vaguely remembered from her first visit. There was a large wooden desk in the middle of the room with two wingback chairs facing it. A fire was in the fireplace on the wall beside the desk, though it wasn't really cold enough to warrant it.

Downey sat behind his desk and Margot indicated Branson should sit in one of the two chairs. The younger detective looked to Wes, as if making sure this was all right with him, and Wes gave him a nod. Wes loved situations where he was forced to stand during interviews. He would wander the room making observations. He often learned as much as Margot did by speaking to someone.

"We really appreciate you taking the time. I'd like to find out if you know any of these women or recall ever seeing them visit with Rebecca when she lived here." Margot withdrew a slim envelope from her interior jacket pocket and arranged the photos inside on the desk facing Downey.

At first, he was more interested in looking at Margot and Wes—Branson barely seemed to register to him—before he looked at the photos at all.

"Well, this is obviously Rebecca," he said tersely, moving one of the pictures aside. He cast a quick glance over the others and shook his head with a shrug. "What exactly are you hoping to learn? I believe I shared all the relevant information I had with you when we spoke on the phone. I don't know who killed her, and I most certainly did not, as my alibi verified."

Margot sighed. He was already on the defensive, which wasn't good.

"We're not here to accuse you of anything, but you knew Rebecca, and we were hoping you might have some insights into the people she spent time with."

Downey gave her a thin smile, then looked down at the photos again. "Rebecca seemed to have a constant coterie of young women around her. They were all very lovely, but if you don't mind my saying, they were all too similar to really tell them apart."

"Similar how?" Margot nudged.

"I'm sure this will make me sound ungrateful, and perhaps dull, but have you ever really looked at a room full of models? It's all the same bodies, the same faces, and it seems like sometimes the only way to tell them apart is by hair color, but even then, you see too many blondes and they all start looking alike to you. Beauty is in the eye of the beholder, but if you walked into a room of Picassos and it was the real deal and a hundred copies, even the real one would lose its luster." He shrugged.

Oh, the hardship of seeing too many beautiful women.

Margot resisted the urge to roll her eyes and gave herself mental points for the effort. She wasn't sure what it was about rich men that made them almost universally unbearable to be around, but this one was proving to be the rule and not the exception.

"Can you double-check and see if you recognize any of the others?" she said gently, nudging the photos forward. "It would really be beneficial to us."

He glanced at them again, though there was obviously no real effort in the gesture, then he shrugged and shoved the photos back at Margot.

"I think I explained when we spoke on the phone that I wasn't often here when Rebecca hosted her friends. I spend a great deal of time abroad, you understand." His tone was icy, and Margot could tell this had been a sore subject between the two.

"Do you think you could give me a better idea of what your relationship with Ms. Watson was like? When we previously spoke you referred to her almost like it was a renter-landlord situation, but I get the feeling there was more to it than that. Were you and Rebecca romantically involved?"

Richard Downey sat back in his chair, his hands folded over his stomach. His cashmere sweatpants did little to hide the fact he wasn't wearing any underwear, and Margot wondered if his posture was incidental or if he was intentionally trying to make her uncomfortable.

Or perhaps it was pure male primate behavior at its root and he was "presenting" himself. Whatever it was, she would have preferred he was wearing some more structured pants.

If Branson, sitting beside her, noticed anything unusual about the display, he wasn't showing it. When she glanced at him, he looked tense and pale.

Eyes and ears only.

After a long pause, which Margot knew was likely more about mind games than actually thinking of a reply, Downey spoke, his voice low, almost like he was telling a secret. "Have you ever heard of a sugar baby?"

Margot cringed. She had obviously heard the term before. A sugar baby was a kept woman, usually young, who received gifts and an allowance from a wealthy benefactor—usually male—who would expect some kind of physical affection in return.

It wasn't prostitution, but it wasn't far off, either.

"Are you saying you were Rebecca's sugar daddy?" God, she *hated* that those words had come out of her mouth. Hated even more the sly little smile that appeared at the corner of his lips when she said the word *daddy*. Margot wanted gin and mouthwash.

This interview was making her feel significantly more uncomfortable than she had anticipated at the offset.

"We had a mutually beneficial relationship," he said finally. "I wouldn't have called her my girlfriend, I don't think she would have called me her boyfriend, but neither of us was dissatisfied with what we got from each other." He gestured to the house. "I mean, it wasn't like she could afford something like this on her own."

Margot took the photos from the desk and slid them delicately back into the envelope. There were six photos, though only five were victims of the Redwood Killer. The sixth, a young woman named Angela Gromand, hadn't been one of his kills, but she was peripherally connected to the case, and Margot had kept her photo in the mix because it wouldn't have surprised her if someone who recognized one of the other girls from their work might recognize Angela as well.

She also kept it there to remind herself how carefully they needed to tread with this case. Only she and Wes knew that the people involved went all the way to the top in terms of police connections, and they were going to need to make their case so airtight that no amount of corruption could undo it.

They were nowhere near that right now.

Angela's death was a reminder of just how dangerous this could get for everyone involved.

Margot tucked the envelope back into her jacket pocket.

"Were you aware of what Ms. Watson did for work?" she asked, leaning back in her own chair and trying to mirror his laissez-faire posture.

If he was trying to get a rise out of her, she simply wasn't going to engage.

He chewed the inside of his cheek and leaned forward on his desk again, fixing her with a cold stare.

"I'm not a foolish man, Detective Phalen. Nor am I a romantic man. I'm a realist and a pragmatist. I am aware of the types of people Rebecca consorted with, yes. I'm not responsible for what Rebecca did when we weren't together. And if she did anything in my house, I have no knowledge of it. I can't be held accountable for her actions. She was a grown woman."

Compared to the other victims, this was true. Rebecca was older, more established.

Margot tried again. "I'm trying to figure out what her role was in the service. Was she finding the girls or was she only there to monitor them in party situations? Make sure everyone was playing by the rules."

Downey fanned his hands out, palms up, and gave a little

shrug. "We didn't talk much about the semantics of her job, because when she was with me, she didn't want me to feel like I was one of *those* men. I know she was a bit miffed when they put her out to pasture. Not a lot of demand when the crow's feet start coming in. She did her best to keep things tight. On my dime. So, I didn't mind much. Since I was bankrolling her regimen, I got to make requests." His gaze openly drifted to Margot's chest.

She hadn't thought Wes was paying much attention to the conversation, but from somewhere near the fireplace she heard him clear his throat loudly, and the sound seemed to do the job; Downey shifted his gaze.

As much as Margot didn't want or need anyone to defend her against creeps like this, there was something very sweet and protective in the small gesture. Anyone else she might have given an earful to afterwards for stepping in.

Wes wasn't anyone else.

She gave Downey a thin smile. "We appreciate your generosity. Without some of her... enhancements it would have taken us considerably longer to find her."

Downey raised an eyebrow. "How so?"

"Well, since no one had bothered to file a missing person's report for Rebecca, we identified her using the serial numbers on her breast implants."

This statement was slightly unfair to him. A missing person's report wouldn't have necessarily helped them ID Rebecca any faster, but she *did* want him to feel guilty for not caring enough to make one.

If he was capable of feeling guilt at all, that is.

"How interesting. I had no idea those had serial numbers. A shame, though, that I can't send them back for a refund after the fact. They cost me a fair sum."

Oh, how she hated this man.

"Sir, that's a person you're referring to. Someone you had an intimate relationship with," Branson interjected, his tone tight. It was evident he was as sick of Downey's bullshit as Margot was. He hadn't had the experience to learn how to ignore it. "Show a little respect."

Downey gave the kid a long look, and Margot wasn't sure if it was because he was a man or what, he just gave a nod and said, "Yes. Apologies. Poor form."

If Margot had spoken up, she knew she would have gotten a *lighten up* response.

She looked over at Branson but there wasn't anything chastising in her expression. She wasn't mad at him. In fact, she was glad he'd said what she was thinking. It wasn't going to change what Downey was, wouldn't make him question his own actions in any deeply reflective way, but maybe he'd stop being such a douchebag in this interview.

"How did you and Rebecca meet?" Margot asked. When she'd originally asked this question a year earlier, he'd told her it had been on a website for renters. Back then they hadn't known about Rebecca's connections to the Larks, nor Downey's relationship with her. They had no reason to doubt him.

He had obviously already forgotten this lie, or wasn't going to insult her intelligence by dredging it back up again.

"We met at a party."

"Like one of the parties Rebecca hosted here?"

"Something like that."

"Who was throwing that party?"

"An acquaintance. I'm not even sure I know who owned the house. I was invited and it sounded like a fun evening."

"Do you remember the address of the party?"

"Somewhere in the Marina District. Couldn't tell you much more than that. It's been several years."

Marina District meant money, which didn't surprise Margot one bit. She was hoping he might be stupid enough to point her to Emmanuel Riga, but maybe there were a few brain cells bouncing off each other in that thick head of his, because he wasn't giving her anything useful.

"How long did you see Ms. Watson professionally before your arrangement changed?"

"Up until her role with the agency pivoted. She wasn't one of their working girls anymore, so I just adjusted the terms of our agreement. I wound up saving myself some money in the long run because those greedy bastards weren't giving the girls more than a fraction of what they were being paid, I can tell you that much."

What a guy. He was patting himself on the back for having the entrepreneurial mindset to become his own pimp.

Margot tried—and likely failed—to keep her real feelings from showing on her face. Downey didn't seem to care, his smug demeanor remained unchanged. He knew he was untouchable as far as this case went—he had a rock-solid alibi for more than one of the murders, considering he was out of the country at the time and had witnesses and flight records to back it up.

Margot knew that, unfortunately, not liking someone wasn't enough to make them guilty of things.

She shifted in her seat and decided to try a different tactic. "Now that we're being a little more honest with each other, do you have any ideas about who might have wanted to hurt Ms. Watson? The agency, perhaps?"

Downey shook his head without hesitation. "No, they liked her too much for that. She was great with the girls and had good relationships with the long-term clients. She knew how to keep everyone happy."

"Perhaps she knew more than she should have." Margot thought of the tape she had watched not long ago, where one of the Larks had found herself with some very incriminating evidence of an assault. An assault that had involved none other than the current police commissioner.

People with that kind of knowledge often didn't live long

enough to share it. That was what had happened to the girl in the video.

Margot had to wonder what kind of secrets Rebecca Watson had after all her years with the agency.

Downey seemed to be considering her theory for longer than she might have expected before he gave his head another shake and leaned back in his chair, like this was the most casual conversation he'd ever had.

"Here's what you need to remember, detective. Wealthy men want to keep what they have, their money, their power, their respect. They learn to know who they can trust with that information, with their... proclivities. The agency worked very hard to only employ girls they knew they could trust, and Rebecca—when her role changed—was responsible for maintaining that trust. You don't get rid of good people."

"Then who do you think was responsible for Rebecca's murder?" She kept it specific to Rebecca because she knew none of the other girls mattered to him. While Rebecca had earned his affection, the other girls were mere sex workers to him, and she doubted he would ever see any of these victims as human beings deserving of justice and attention.

At least Rebecca represented a personal loss to him, and that was something Margot could work with.

After some consideration, he spoke again. "I believe you're going on a pointless witch hunt if you're looking for her killer among her former clients. No one would want to risk that kind of heat. These are men with far too much to lose to muddy their hands with the kind of thing you're talking about. Not to mention, these men, for the most part, wouldn't even know how to order their own coffee at Starbucks, let alone perform multiple homicides without leaving behind some kind of evidence. No, you want to look at the people who *worked* the parties."

He must have seen the confusion in Margot's face because he leaned forward, forearms resting on the desk.

"Parties like this, you don't want people to find out what goes on. Can't have a loose-lipped waiter or bartender talking about a US senator who likes to have his asshole fingered, can you?" He held up a pinky and crooked it.

That was more information than Margot needed, but she nodded for him to go on.

"The agency has strong working relationships with certain vendors. Vendors they trusted. You'd see a lot of the same waiters and bartenders working these events because they were reliable. Vetted. But those waiters and bartenders also saw the same girls at all these events. Got attached, you see?" He raised an eyebrow at her.

"You're saying you think one of the service staff who worked at these parties killed those girls?"

Downey shrugged and settled back in his chair. "I'm not here to point fingers, but I know that wanting something you can't have has made people do some bad things throughout history. So, if you were to ask me where to look, that's where I'd tell you to start."

Margot stared at him. His live-in girlfriend had been killed over a year earlier and he was only now deciding to offer them a tip on where to find her killer.

Margot could never, and would never, understand the moral vacuum that the rich lived in.

"Thank you so much for your help," she said as she got to her feet. Her words were laced with sarcasm.

Downey either didn't hear or didn't care; he looked done with the whole thing.

"You and your friends can show yourselves out."

SIX

1994

Ed had fucked up.

Royally fucked up.

There was one thing Ed prided himself on most when it came to his work and that was his ability to plan. He was careful, he was thorough. He watched, he waited, he knew every possible flaw before he made a move, and *that* was how he had gone so long without getting caught.

But this time things hadn't gone according to plan, and if Ed didn't think of something *fast* this was going to be the absolute fucking end of him.

He was hiding in a closet, a dead body lying no more than ten feet away from him, and he was listening to another person milling around outside the bedroom door.

This had never happened to him before.

This woman—her name was Bethenny—lived alone. He knew that because he had been following her for weeks. He'd watched her carefully, making sure that he knew her routines, if she had a boyfriend, a dog, anything that might get in his way.

She didn't. He *knew* she didn't. He'd taken the information for her classified ad himself when Susan at the desk was out sick. He'd made her repeat things just so he could hear more of that too-sweet voice of hers, the way she giggled when he intentionally spelled her name wrong.

She was always by herself at night. No one else lived here.

So who the *fuck* was wandering around her apartment right now, and why were they acting so completely at home?

For a moment he considered whether or not it might be a burglar. Another nighttime opportunist who wanted to rifle through the jewelry box and steal Grandma's best earrings. But as he listened, he heard the fridge open and close and the microwave hum. Soon the entire apartment was filled with the smell of popcorn.

Then a light knocking on the door. "Bethy?" A soft female voice, sweet and high, like he remembered Bethenny on the phone.

Bethenny's voice hadn't sounded so sweet when she was begging him for her life only a half hour earlier, but Ed could still remember the way it was the first time he spoke to her.

"I made popcorn, Beth." A pause. "You awake?"

Ed glanced down at the body slumped at his feet. Her eyes were open, transfixed on him as if she was staring at him even now. But he knew she wasn't looking at anything.

He waited, his breath held, praying to a god who did not exist that the owner of that sweet voice wouldn't open the door to check the room. He'd left the covers tossed half off the bed in his haste to move the body when he had heard the key rattle in the lock. It was an instinct—an act of pure panic. Had he been a smarter man he would have tossed a blanket over her instead, so anyone being nosy would think she was asleep.

Instead, if someone were to peek in, they would find the bed empty, pillows knocked to the floor. If they turned on the lights, they would see the white sheets were painted red with fresh blood.

All of this would destroy him.

Everything he'd worked so hard for. His legacy. His life's work. It would all be undone because he hadn't known that someone else would be here.

After an agonizingly long pause the voice said, "OK, well, if you wake up, I'm just going to watch a movie. Let me know if the volume is too loud."

Ed groaned internally. A fucking *movie?*

He'd come in via the fire escape outside the living room window, something he hoped the woman beyond the bedroom door wouldn't notice or think too hard about. The only window in Bethenny's bedroom was a small square high in one corner. Barely enough to qualify as a window, and certainly not enough to get out through.

The muffled sound of music came through the wall, then voices he couldn't quite make out. He rested his head against the clothing dangling behind his back, and waited

SEVEN

Margot half expected Branson to start asking a million questions as soon as they were out of the house, but instead the three of them headed back to the city in a shared, tense silence.

Finally, before they hit the Golden Gate Bridge, Margot looked at the kid in her rear-view mirror. "What do you think, detective?" she asked him. There was no sarcasm or malice in her voice. She was glad he had brought Richard Downey to their attention. Tonight's interview had yielded better results than she had anticipated.

They weren't much closer to their killer, but a new avenue to approach would give them something fresh. Unfortunately, Margot couldn't call up Emmanuel Riga and ask him for his preferred vendor list.

If being a homicide detective were that easy, everyone would do it. But it wasn't like solving a game of Clue. Every time she thought she got a little closer to her guy, the goalposts moved in another direction, onto another field. It was beginning to feel impossible.

Branson seemed surprised by her attention. He shifted in

the back seat, leaning over so he was in between Margot and Wes. "You think he was telling the truth?"

Margot sighed. The question felt almost innocent to her, like honesty was black and white. "I think the truth is a moving target, and there are aspects of what he said we should listen to. We know this guy didn't do it, as much as I'd love to arrest him for being the world's most obnoxious douchebag. Alibi was airtight, no way around it. I don't think he respected Rebecca Watson very much, but I know he didn't kill her. And if I'm being totally honest, I think if he *did* know who killed her, that he has connections with people who could deal with that in ways that the police never could."

"You think he loved her?" Branson asked.

Wes scoffed, but said nothing.

Margot waited a beat, then answered. "I don't think a man like that loves anything other than money and himself. And for a while, Rebecca was good for him. But no, I don't think he loved her. I think she was another thing he thought he owned, and rich men don't like to lose their favorite toys."

Branson took this in. She waited to see if he would offer up any insights of his own, hoping that he'd learned something from all of this to make it worth bringing him along.

"That's an awfully cynical way to look at things," he replied, his tone low.

"It's a cynical world, kid, I don't know what to tell you. If you want to cling to some kind of optimism, you're in the wrong business." She kept her eyes on the road, the winding highway requiring her undivided attention lest they go careening off the side of a cliff. She was aware of intrusive thoughts telling her to turn her steering wheel toward the guardrail. But the intrusive thoughts rarely won.

Margot wasn't suicidal, she was just tired.

Branson was quiet for a beat longer. "If you think he cared about her as an object, then one would also have to assume that he would want some kind of justice for losing something he liked to own. Rich folks don't tend to take it lying down just because they can afford to replace something that was stolen from them. If he did think of Rebecca the way you suggest he did, then I don't see any reason why his suggestion about the party servers isn't a relevant lead to follow."

"Unless protecting himself matters more than getting justice for her," Wes cautioned. Margot caught his eye briefly. "There are some very powerful people involved in this, people who don't want their names getting out there and who would do pretty shocking things to keep their secrets on lockdown. If Downey didn't want to be on the bad side of those people, then I could see him lying to send us in the wrong direction."

Margot looked in the rear-view mirror. Branson was frowning, but it seemed more like he was deep in thought than frustrated by their input. Maybe he was willing to listen and learn after all.

"What does your gut tell you?" she asked.

She couldn't keep looking at him, so she waited through his silence to see what might come next. It was important for a detective to learn to trust their gut. While it wasn't a perfect rule, it was good to trust yourself, because after a long enough time, there came a point where you could sniff out the liars a lot better than you could on your first day.

"I believe him," Branson said finally. "I think he's being honest when he says he thinks one of the staff at those parties was to blame."

Margot nodded. While she was sure Downey had plenty to hide and more than a few skeletons in his closet he'd like to keep them from finding, she had also got the feeling he had been telling them the truth, at least as far as it was true to him. Perhaps he wasn't willing to accept that one of his cronies might have a hand in it, and would rather point a finger at the working-class waiters, but even if it was his own prejudice that got him there, Margot believed that *he* believed.

And it was a good lead at a point where they had precious few of those.

While Emmanuel Riga wasn't going to give up the names of his service staff, Margot did have one idea of where they might be able to start looking.

About forty minutes later they pulled up in front of the station. She let Branson and Wes out at the corner and found parking about a block away. She sat in the car by herself for a few moments, listening to the engine tick as it cooled and watching pedestrians pass by her without registering her presence.

She thought of Ed in that moment, even though she didn't want to. Sometimes her father crept into her mind at the most inopportune times. As the people walked by her car, seemingly without a single concern in the world, she wondered how often Ed had sat in his car like this, watching the object of his fixation, waiting for his moment to strike and knowing that he could do it with so little difficulty.

So many people went through life blind to the risks around them. Margot wondered if there was something to the old saying that ignorance is bliss, because she knew all too well what the dangers were lurking around every corner, and sometimes she wished she could live her life like they weren't there.

Would it be nice to be able to walk down a sidewalk at night without being hyper-aware of every footfall behind her? Would it be freeing to take a back alley shortcut or not have a can of pepper spray at the ready because your mind couldn't escape the *just in case* of it all?

A girl no older than twenty walked past her with bulky headphones on and music so loud Margot could hear it through the car window. Yeah. It must be nice.

She sighed and got out of the car, making her way the short distance back to the station along the brightly lit sidewalk, but even then she was keenly attuned to the sounds around her and everyone that passed by, from the kid on the skateboard to the couple arguing about something that happened at a party.

Back in the station there was no sign of Branson, but in her office, Leon was sitting at her desk, chatting with Wes. Leon looked *tired*. It was something she was noticing more frequently these days, like all the time spent on this case was slowly chipping away time from his life. He wasn't young, but Margot had never thought of him as *old* until the last couple of months when the dark circles under his eyes seemed to become a permanent fixture and he had lost some of the twinkle that made him such a uniquely lovable man.

Margot wanted to solve this case to get her old friend back, because she was certain the Redwood Killer was doing his damnedest to drive them all into an early grave.

"Hey, kid," Leon said with a smile, moving to get out of her seat.

Margot quickly waved him away and shucked off her coat before sitting down in the decrepit love seat against the back wall of the room. She didn't want to count the number of times she had fallen asleep on this couch, or know how many sweaty detective asses had sat on it before it had come to live in their office.

See, ignorance really *was* bliss in some cases.

Leon settled back into the chair and Margot noticed the slight wince as he did, like something was pinched in his lower back, causing him pain. It was a feeling she knew well herself after many late nights in that very chair, but it was also one more thing reminding her that none of them were all that young anymore. Her evening with Branson had made her wonder if there might be a few new gray hairs staring back at her in the mirror when she got home later.

"Wes tells me you took one of the newbies out for a little interview," Leon commented.

Margot hadn't been outside all that long, so she doubted Wes had gotten very far into the story of their interview with Richard Downey.

"Yeah, he's a real piece of work. Makes me understand why people joke about eating the rich. Except I'm sure he'd taste like bullshit and terrible cologne."

Wes snorted.

"We cleared this guy already, right?" Leon asked. "Any chance we missed something?"

Margot shook her head. "No, his alibi is airtight, he's not our guy. He's a grade-A asshole who was less than forthcoming with us about his relationship with Rebecca Watson, but he'd hardly be the first person to leave out details when speaking to the police. And he did give us a crumb to follow, so it wasn't a totally wasted trip to Sausalito. At least the newbie got to feel involved."

"And the crumb?"

Margot explained Downey's theory, and Leon nodded along with it.

"I figure maybe we go back to the Odyssey nightclub, see if another grade-A asshole wants to give us a little information." They had previously visited the nightclub thanks to a tip about Emmanuel Riga running some of his girls through there, and while they hadn't learned *much*, the club's owner and manager, Jesse Simcoe, had copped to being involved with Rebecca in the past. If he knew anything about Riga's business—like who he hired for his parties—perhaps he'd be willing to share that information with them if it meant doing a small kindness to Rebecca's memory.

"Oof," Leon said, wincing again. "You can do that one on your own, I think. I'm worried that even stepping onto a dancefloor right now might tweak something permanently."

Margot smiled at him. "You just don't want to talk to the owner again, admit it."

"I think if we're being really honest with each other right now, you're the one person in this room who is the most likely to get that... charming gentleman to divulge any information."

Margot leaned back in the love seat and kicked her legs out in front of her. For such a hideous piece of furniture it really was ridiculously comfortable.

"You know, I'd say that was sexist, but you're probably right."

"We all know I'm right," Leon scoffed. "And it can't be sexist if it's true, isn't that how those things work?"

"Careful, old man," she teased, but she was smiling.

The fact was, even based on her limited experience with Jesse, she knew she was the right person for the job. It wasn't that he respected women, but he wanted to appeal to them, and if he wanted to appeal to her, he'd need to get chatty.

When she'd last met him, Jesse had seemed about as warm and caring as Richard Downey. *Come to think of it, Rebecca really seemed to have a type, didn't she?* Margot thought to herself, somewhat uncharitably. When Jesse had first learned about Rebecca's death, he hadn't shown much empathy about it. Richard had been similarly blasé.

Still, if Margot knew one thing, it was that you couldn't count on people to mourn in logical ways. Everyone wanted people to sob and cry endlessly, but that wasn't the way it went a lot of the time. Some people cried, others got stoic. Some got angry. Some shut down entirely and gave no emotions away, but despite what armchair sleuths and media talking heads thought, being quiet didn't mean guilty.

Showing no empathy didn't necessarily mean Jesse didn't *care.*

And she was hoping Rebecca had meant enough to him that he might give her one more crumb in the trail.

All she needed was a name.
Sometimes that was all it took.

EIGHT

When Margot got home the sun was already starting to come up and though she was dying to climb into bed and pass out, she still had things to do.

First, there was Betty to think about.

The ancient dog had not been Margot's idea. No one sets out to bring home a blind Maltese that sleeps twenty-two hours a day and needs help getting up onto the couch. But Margot had watched Betty's owner die, and had known deep in the pit of her soul that if she'd left this old lady in the hands of a local shelter that she would have been euthanized.

Margot had seen too much that day to let another living creature down, so she'd brought Betty home with the notion that she could find a better, more permanent home for the dog. It turned out that permanent home had been with Margot.

She wasn't a dog person. She *might* be a cat person if she allowed herself the idea of a long-term pet. But Betty was sort of the best of both worlds; a dog that was small and slept a lot was *basically* a cat anyway.

When Margot unlocked her front door and stepped inside, Betty lifted her head up and turned in the direction of the noise.

The dog might not be able to see anything, but her sense of smell was still as sharp as ever, and once she realized it was Margot her little tail thumped happily.

"Hey, lady," Margot greeted her warmly, collecting the leash that was hanging next to the door. "You ready for your walk?"

Betty's *hearing* was also just fine because her ears perked up and the tail thumping became more expressive. Betty could really only manage a single block before she needed to be picked up and brought back home, but she *loved* that one block.

Margot fastened the leash to Betty's collar, pausing to look at the battered nametag the dog sported. Margot should really get her a new one, something with the correct phone number on it. She'd never quite got around to changing it, no matter how often she noticed the oversight.

After Betty had done her business and sniffed every sniffable item on the block, Margot went back inside to let the morning people do their morning things. She, unfortunately, had a call she'd been putting off returning, and it was time to bite the bullet on at least *one* thing she'd been avoiding.

It wasn't quite eight yet, but she knew Andrew Rhodes, and she knew he would be up.

Sure enough, he answered on the second ring.

"You never struck me as an early bird, Margot."

"I'm whatever bird I need to be, Andrew."

He chuckled at this, and Margot helped Betty up onto the couch where she had an old blanket folded up to provide a bed for the old girl and help corral her shedding. She had been relieved to discover that, despite Betty's abundant white hair, she didn't shed much at all.

Betty immediately put her head down and started to snore softly, leaving Margot to focus on her conversation with Andrew.

"So, you've been trying to get a hold of me?" This was an

understatement. He had called daily and sent her several texts, all of which she had ignored.

Margot had worked alongside the FBI on her father's ongoing case, because the only person Ed would confess his dirty deeds to was his daughter. She knew it was his way of exercising control over her even when he was locked away, and she hated every minute of it, but they had been able to find several previously missing women, and had also been able to bring closure to the families of several other victims Ed hadn't taken credit for before she was involved.

There was some reward in knowing she had helped, but she often wondered how long he could drag this out for.

And after he'd sent her to find Jimmy, his former friend and someone he had apparently committed several murders with, she wasn't in a huge hurry to run back to visit her father.

Jimmy, Betty's former owner, had sensed the end was running up to meet him and decided he didn't feel like spending his final days in jail with Ed. Margot couldn't really blame him, but she also could have done without seeing his suicide whenever she closed her eyes.

There were a lot of things that haunted Margot. Jimmy just happened to be the current ghost she couldn't shake.

Andrew cleared his throat, bringing Margot back to the present. Her mind tended to drift a lot these days, something she was going to need to get a hold on before it became a real issue.

"There are two things I wanted to talk to you about, and I'd hoped to do one of them in person, but I can tell that pinning you down is going to be a real battle of wills right now, and it's one that I suspect you're going to win, given how damn stubborn you can be."

Margot felt like he was trying to goad her into an argument, but she was simply too tired to deal with that at the moment, so she let the barb go without a fight. He was probably right, if she was being honest with herself.

"Fair enough. Let's hear it."

"Ed's lawyer reached out. Says he's got one last case to tell us about."

This sent an unexpected shiver down Margot's spine. For some reason she had imagined Ed was going to drag this interview process out until either he or Margot kicked the bucket—or until he pushed her buttons so much she stopped coming.

"He said it like that? *One last?*"

Though she couldn't see Andrew, she could almost sense him nodding before he spoke again. She thought of all the photos hanging on the whiteboards in the FBI task force office. All the women they had believed could potentially be Ed's victims.

So many of those cases would go back to being cold. But Margot realized, with a flush of relief so intense she felt guilty for it, that they would no longer be *her* responsibility.

"One last case. His exact words. At least as told to Ford Rosenthal."

Margot let her head fall back against the couch and she looked up at the slightly yellowed ceiling of her apartment, feeling a rush of unexpected joy. Did that mean she was almost free of her father? She could finish this off—certainly he would drag it out—and then never have to see him again? The mere idea of it was a thrill to her.

"There's a catch."

Margot let out a sigh, and all the relief that had come over her washed back out, leaving her feeling as heavy as ever. "Of course there is."

"Ed has told us that there's no way we're going to find these bodies without him. That he needs to take us to them."

Margot waited for the punchline, or for Andrew to scoff at

the very notion of this suggestion, but neither of those things came. He seemed to be silently waiting for her to reply.

"Well, we can't possibly do that."

Again, a tense silence.

Margot sat upright on the couch, the swiftness of the motion enough to make Betty lift her head and turn her milky eyes in Margot's direction before deciding nothing worthwhile was happening and putting her head back down on her paws.

"Andrew, you can't seriously be considering this."

The silence was so thick she could hear the moment he licked his lips before speaking again. "Look, I don't love the idea of it either. But every bit of intel Finch has given us up to this point has panned out. We've closed a bunch of cases, given a lot of families closure. If this really is Ed's last hurrah with us, and he can help us close this chapter of his history once and for all, then I think we have to consider it. But I want you to talk to him first; we need to decide whether he's jerking our chain or if there's some merit to this before we decide how we're going to proceed. The logistics of getting a death row prisoner out for a day trip are monumental, and I'm not going through all that paperwork if he's just dicking us around."

"Of *course* he's dicking us around," she said, her tone sharp and annoyed. "Haven't you been sitting in the same room with me for the past two years? Haven't you heard the same bullshit that I have, over and over again? Yeah, he eventually lets it pay off, but only after he's had his fun with us. This isn't going to be any different. He's looking for an excuse to get out, you know that."

"Ed isn't a young man anymore, Margot. He's not a threat."

Margot actually laughed out loud at that, because whenever she imagined someone lurking in the shadows of an alley, someone testing the locks on her windows, someone hunched in the back seat of her car, it wasn't a faceless, nameless killer.

It was her father.

No, just because Ed was old Margot didn't believe for a second he wasn't still lethal. Men like that never lose the broken thing inside that makes them tick. Even a grandfather can still be a killer.

"You'll talk to him?" Andrew asked, ignoring her laughter.

Margot let out a long sigh, frustrated with herself and with Andrew because they both knew what her answer would be.

"Yes." One last time. "I'll do it."

"I'll set it up and let you know. What days are you off this week?"

"Thursday and Friday. Unless this killer decides to drop more new victims, then who knows?" she replied.

There was another pause, and Margot wondered if maybe he had hung up, but after a long moment, Andrew spoke again.

"There's the second thing."

"I thought Ed wanting a day pass for a walkabout was the second thing," Margot said.

Andrew chuckled. "All right then, consider it a bonus third thing. And before you answer me, Margot, I want you to actually take some time to think about this, because I wouldn't be asking you if I didn't think it was a good move for you."

With that preamble, Margot had no idea what Andrew was about to say next, and found herself both nervous and curious. It wasn't about Ed, so what could he possibly want from her, aside from her connection to her father?

"Working with you over the last couple of years on this has been remarkable. I've never met someone with your ability to get to the truth with a killer like Ed. Whether you believe it, or even recognize it, you have a gift for this. It's probably what makes you an exceptional homicide detective."

Margot, at a loss for what else to say, simply murmured, "Thank you?"

Andrew continued. "There's been a lot of discussion here about what comes next, when we're no longer a dedicated Ed

Finch task force, and the work we've been doing has gotten a lot of positive attention up the chain of command. Attention that wonders if we can't take what's working here and apply it to other situations. Other places where we believe incarcerated killers might have unknown victims."

Her palms got sweaty, because now she knew where this conversation was headed, and she wanted to hang up the phone before he had a chance to say what he was going to say. She didn't want to hear it. But maybe the bigger issue was that part of her—a part she didn't recognize—*did* want him to finish his spiel. And that part of her won out, letting him go on.

"Carter is taking an internal promotion, he'll be leaving the team. But Alana and Greg want to continue on with this work, and I've discussed it with them and with my supervisors, and..." A long pause, like he was steeling himself for her rejection before he even asked. "Margot, we want you to join us. Officially. You'd need to go through a standard application process, but we already screened you before allowing you in as a special contractor. I want you to join the FBI."

She took this in, processed what he was asking, and said, "I'm too old."

This wasn't a commentary on her achy bones, her growing intolerance to alcohol, or the gray hairs she kept finding mingled in with her signature red. It was just a fact.

The age limit to apply to become an FBI special agent was thirty-six. If you weren't already an active agent before your thirty-seventh birthday, you were ineligible.

Margot, on the cusp of thirty-nine, was two years too late.

Andrew chuckled softly on the other end of the phone.

"If your age is your only concern about this, then let me put your mind at ease. There are always exceptions. And this is a situation where the Bureau wouldn't think twice about making one."

When she didn't answer him, he went on, "Does that mean you're willing to consider it?"

Margot wanted to say no.

But she also *didn't* want to say no.

"Let's finish with Ed, first," she said. "I can't think of anything else until that case is done and I never need to look at him again. *Then* I can decide if this is a good offer or the most insane thing you've ever suggested to me."

She heard the smile in his voice when he asked, "Can't it be both?"

NINE

Margot sat in front of the Odyssey club and wondered why it was that night clubs looked so depressing in daylight. It was like seeing an aging showgirl without her makeup and feathers on—the shine just wasn't there.

She sipped her coffee and wished she had waited to do this until she could bring Wes along with her. Wes offered not only an additional officer for support, but he also always brought her good coffee. What she was currently drinking was mediocre at best, but a girl did what she had to do to caffeinate.

She wasn't technically on duty at the moment. After a restless morning with little sleep thanks to Andrew's phone call, she had gotten out of bed much earlier than she would have liked and tried to burn off her energy by cleaning her apartment and taking Betty out for a quick walk, but neither of those things managed to do much to take the edge off.

By noon she was pacing the apartment and her stir craziness was getting to both her and the poor dog, so she decided rather than sitting still at home with the massive question of joining the FBI looming over her like a cloud, she would go to Odyssey and wait to see if Jesse showed up. She had a funny feeling he might be a bit more willing to open up to her if it was her by herself.

Margot wasn't above using whatever limited feminine wiles she had if it meant getting them a little further ahead on this case. She was no pro at flirting, but she knew she was still attractive enough that some exposed cleavage and direct eye contact could make up for whatever other skills she lacked.

At this point she'd sell a kidney or punch a toddler if it meant finding out who killed all those women. Wearing a low-cut shirt to talk to a sleazy club manager hardly seemed like a sacrifice.

She also wasn't an idiot.

She texted Wes to let him know what she was doing, since she'd be seeing him at work in about two hours anyway. His reply was almost immediate.

You want backup?

> No, this guy isn't a threat. I'm just going to see if he knows anything about who Riga used for parties.

Bubbles danced at the bottom of the screen.
Instead of a lecture, Wes wrote,

Be smart, he's not a stupid guy, he knows what you're after.

Margot had almost expected him to try to talk her out of going alone, but after so many years together, Wes seemed to know her better than anyone on the planet. He knew she was going to do what she wanted, no matter what anyone said.

She wondered what he would say about the FBI offer.

A pang hit her directly in the chest, knocking the breath out of her. As flattering as the FBI offer was, it would mean losing one of the things that meant the most to her in her life. She wasn't exactly going to be able to make Wes part of her transfer agreement. He'd never mentioned an interest in joining the FBI, and she highly doubted the Bureau was going to waive *two* over-thirty-six clauses.

No, a move to the FBI would mean leaving Wes behind.

She tried to imagine not seeing him every day. Not sitting down to the cup of coffee on her desk that he brought with him like clockwork, her favorite blend as second nature to him as his own.

Who would make bad jokes with her to cut through the tension of a hard scene? Who would understand her, no matter what she said? Wes had been with her when no one knew who she was. He'd been by her side for years now, and was one of the few people in her life she could trust without question. That commodity was something she didn't take lightly.

She couldn't leave the department.

But...

A voice in the back of her head that she had been trying to ignore for months, maybe longer, spoke up.

If you aren't working together, then there's nothing to stop you from being together.

This was an over-simplification, and not entirely true. Professional ethics weren't the only reason that Margot had avoided getting into bed with Wes, despite their obvious mutual attraction and emotional connection.

She wasn't only worried about fucking up their work relationship if she crossed that line. She was worried about losing him entirely.

Margot let out a long sigh and looked at her watch. It was shortly after one, and while the hulking bouncer wasn't outside yet, she suspected there would be life inside the club, even this early. She needed a good distraction from her own thoughts, and figured Jesse could offer her that.

Crossing the street, she eyed the gray building warily,

making sure she was aware of the doors—there were two—and scanning the exterior for any cameras—there were several. Someone would see her coming, and she wasn't surprised. She wondered if anyone was going to tell Emmanuel Riga about her visit.

She sort of hoped so.

She recalled the way he'd looked at her when they first met in person, the way his human mask had slipped away for a moment, showing her the monster that lurked below the surface. Had she not been something of an expert in monsters, that one moment would have shaken her.

But Margot knew all too well how to lock eyes with evil and not flinch.

She'd been doing it most of her life.

She smiled up at the camera near the door, hoping to give the man she was hunting something to think about.

Before her hand was on the buzzer, the front door opened with a heavy, metallic click. A short woman wearing all black, her blonde hair pulled into a high ponytail, and her blue eyes sharp and assessing, looked out at Margot.

"You here to talk to Jesse?" she asked.

Any doubts Margot might have had that the cameras were attended went out the window. She recalled all the monitors sitting on the club manager's desk the last time she'd been here. He'd been watching her since the moment she stepped up to the building.

Good.

"I am." She didn't bother to flash her badge and the woman didn't ask. She simply held the door open and let Margot walk through.

As Margot passed her, she caught a whiff of a sweet perfume, like cotton candy, that seemed oddly out of place here, and on a woman with such an icy stare. Margot didn't comment on it.

"You know where to find him?" the woman asked, pushing ahead down the hall and not looking back, like she already knew the answer and the question was merely a formality.

Margot wasn't sure if the woman had an issue with her specifically, or if she simply didn't appreciate being made to do Jesse's bidding. Whatever it was, she made no secret of her disdain.

"I do," Margot replied to the retreating back.

The interior of Odyssey was as jarring as the last time she'd been. Nightclubs weren't meant to be seen with the lights on.

Margot barely gave the black-and-white striped walls a second look. She did give a passing glance to the disco ball in the ceiling overhead. Without it spinning to reflect light, all she could see was a thousand smudged duplicates of herself and not a single one of them looked happy to be here.

She passed by the main bar, where the woman who had let her in was hard at work mixing up various juices and blends that would serve as the base for the club's numerous sugary cocktails. She didn't bother to look at Margot again.

There was a long hallway beside the main bar, with door-ways marked for the club's bathrooms, and two swinging doors leading into the club's small kitchen. Beyond that was the door to Jesse's office.

She knocked and a moment later his gruff voice bid her enter.

He was sitting behind his desk, pretending to be looking at something on the screens, but Margot suspected he'd been following her progress, and now he wanted to look busy and disinterested.

Jesse Simcoe was a handsome man if you liked men who looked like they had a criminal record and a bad temper. He had a nose that would have been the Roman ideal if it hadn't been broken at least once, and his brow furrowed in a way that Margot could only call *cranky caveman*.

But he was a club owner, and she suspected a wealthy one at that given what he was probably making off of his connection to Riga, so Margot figured he probably didn't have a hard time getting women to fall for his minimal charms.

"Detective Phalen, right?" he asked, glancing up from the monitors to look at her.

"Good memory." She took a seat across from him without being invited.

"I don't meet a lot of attractive detectives, if you don't mind me saying. Made you more memorable than most."

Margot allowed him a smile at the compliment. "Well, thank you."

"Just saying what I see, detective." He smiled back at her before returning his attention to the monitors. There couldn't possibly be any activity worth watching at the moment, but she let him stare. Normally she liked to look people in the eye when she was speaking to them, but if he was distracted, it might work in her favor.

"I thought you might like to know that we have a potential lead on Rebecca Watson's death."

Jesse's hand stilled, eyelid twitched, but he still didn't look at her. "That's good, considering it's your job to solve murders."

The barb didn't land. Margot simply smiled. "That's true. Even when people don't seem to want to help us, we still manage to find the truth. Because it's what we do best."

A thin smile crossed Jesse's lips, and he clicked on something, the sound of the mouse almost deafening in the small, quiet space.

"Did you come here to tell me you *might* be able to find Rebecca's killer? Because it seems like an awful lot of effort, given how little I cared about her during our last discussion." His gaze cut to her and he rested his hands on his stomach, no longer pretending to be busy with anything else.

Margot held his stare for a long moment, wondering which

of them would feel uncomfortable first. She found, much to her frustration, it was her. She blinked, and shifted her focus to the space between his eyes.

"Actually, I'm here because I think you cared more than you let on. And I think you're exactly the right person to help me figure out who did this to her."

"I hope you're not saying that because you think it was me," he replied with a chuckle.

"No, your alibi for several of the murders proved to be rock solid. I don't think you're charming enough to get *that* many women to corroborate your story."

He lifted one hand to his heart. "You wound me." He was grinning.

Good. She wanted him in a good mood for what she was about to say.

"How did you meet Rebecca?"

His big grin faltered a bit, and he gave her a questioning look. "I thought you said you'd ruled me out as a suspect."

Margot clucked her tongue. "Jesse, if I thought everyone who had fucked Rebecca Watson was a suspect, I'd have to spend the rest of my goddamn life questioning people. I think we both know that. I'm allowed to ask you questions without thinking you're a killer."

He raised an eyebrow at her, then leaned forward in his chair, resting his arms on his desk. "You're an interesting woman, detective, you know that?"

"I've been called worse."

"You seeing anyone?"

Margot was taken aback by this. She'd anticipated she might need to flirt a little to get Jesse to warm to her, but to this point she'd only been slightly bitchy, and apparently that had worked better than her meager flirting skills. The game had changed since the last time she'd made any effort.

"How about you help me out, then we can talk about whether or not I'm single?"

"So you *are* single." He smiled, his gaze fixed on her. "I can work with either, honestly. I'm not into complications, but it's usually only complicated for the other guy." He tilted his head to the side, assessing her. "Or the other girl."

Guess she had worn her most bisexual jacket that day.

"Let's focus," she said, not bothering to give credence to any of his guesses. "I think you met Rebecca at one of Emmanuel Riga's parties."

Jesse's jaw ticked and he was quiet for a moment. "Man, you go straight for the hard shit right up front, don't you? I bet you're a saucy thing in the sack."

Margot rolled her eyes. There was no point in telling him to tone it down, he would only use that as an invitation to push the envelope further.

"Just answer the question," she said.

"Yeah. I mean, I think it's fairly obvious you know what's up with Riga. I bet he talked to you once already, didn't he?"

"I'd ask if I have you to thank for that, but I think he was probably a bit ticked off that I spoke to his son," Margot replied coolly.

Jesse whistled, a low sound that made the hair on the back of Margot's neck stand up. "Damn, detective. You're made of sterner stuff than I thought if you crossed that line. He loves the fuck out of that little piece of shit."

Well, obviously Riga didn't have *ears* in this office if Jesse was willing to let his feelings be so known.

"So did you meet Rebecca at one of his parties?" Margot urged.

"I didn't, actually. I met her when she was one of his prize girls. He brought her into the club one night; I got to talking to her when she wasn't otherwise occupied, and gave her my number. I did see her a few weeks later at one of his parties, though, one he hosted here, a private event."

Bingo.

"Then I think you really *can* help me. Do you remember anyone working at that party who might have stood out? Maybe some of your staff might have complained about them being a bit odd, or intense?"

"My staff don't work those events. Riga doesn't like outside eyes on those parties, likes to use people he can trust."

"But you attended them?"

"Well, sure. This *is* my club. And I suspect you are smart enough to know that I'm not a stranger to Riga's work."

Cleverly phrased. Not admitting he was complicit in said work, but acknowledging that he was aware of it. Margot was impressed with Jesse in the way only a cop can be impressed with a criminal. He was well aware of how to toe the line and keep himself out of trouble, something he may very well have learned from watching Riga.

"Look, I'm going to cut through the bullshit here, and I hope you'll do the same," Margot said bluntly.

"I can do that."

"I think there's a possibility that one of the service staff who worked Riga's parties could be responsible for the death of Rebecca and those other women. I know I can't ask Riga for help, but I'm asking *you*. Tell me how I can find those people so I can help put Rebecca's case to bed."

Jesse's eyes flashed as if she had tempted him by the phrase *to bed*, but he kept his composure and didn't make the obvious joke. Instead, he opened his desk drawer and pulled out an honest-to-God Rolodex, something Margot hadn't seen in person in at least a decade, and flipped through it. It looked as if each tab had a business card paperclipped to it, rather than having the names and numbers written out. He paused after a moment and withdrew a matte black card with metallic silver writing.

No name on the front, just a phone number.

Sure, that level of pretentiousness fit with what a guy like Riga would be into. Jesse offered her the card, but when she went to take it, he held tight, keeping her locked in place as he met her eyes. "I know you think none of us care about what's happening, but we do. If you think that the law can't reach these guys, and you figure out who did it, you let me know, OK?"

Margot's eyes searched his, unpacking the meaning of those words.

She thought about the video she and Wes had secreted away, the one that showed the chief of police, Pressley Boyd, assaulting a now-dead woman who had worked for Riga. A video so important, so explosive, that it was eating away at her day after day to not be able to share it. But if this lead from Jesse was good, she was one step closer to letting that bomb go off.

That was a mighty big *if*, though.

"That's a nice offer, Jesse. But if the law can't bring this guy down, then you and I have much bigger problems. And I think you know that."

He stared at her for a long time, and it felt to Margot that they were both trying without words to gauge how much the other person knew.

Finally, he relented with a nod, letting go of the card.

"Good luck, detective."

As she stood, she looked at him one last time. "You, too."

TEN

Margot's investigation into the mystery caterer would need to wait. As soon as she hit the street and her phone got consistent service again—why were night clubs such a vortex of cell service?—she got a message from Wes.

> Hey, let me know when you're out. Leon just
> got a call from Evelyn and the two new Park
> Does have been autopsied.

Wow, Evelyn Yao, the chief medical examiner, had to have worked overtime to accomplish that. She most certainly had to put their victims ahead of a lot of other bodies to have finished both autopsies in such a short period of time.

Not that Margot was complaining.

Glancing down at her phone she saw there was a missed call from Leon Telly and a voicemail notification. Leon was old school, he preferred calls to texting any day of the week, whereas Wes knew that Margot didn't love to chat on the phone, and he defaulted to sending texts.

Margot didn't bother heading to the station first; she texted Wes that her interview with Jesse was over and she'd meet them at the morgue. While it was still technically a few hours before the evening shift began, none of them wanted to put this off until then.

The building that housed the morgue was relatively utilitarian-looking by San Francisco standards, and the morgue itself was situated below ground. Because of San Francisco's heavily angled streets, most buildings had a base level that was half-basement, half-first floor, with windows overlooking the street, but most of the level being built into the hill. For a state that didn't have a lot of basements, San Francisco seemed paradoxically filled with them.

The morgue itself was a chilly, sterile space. Thanks to the plants that Evelyn had positioned in the basement-level window, the space had a permanently greenish hue. The temperature was always much too cold for comfort, but Margot understood the necessity. She kept her jacket on.

She managed to get to the morgue before Wes and Leon, and that gave her some rare one-on-one time with Evelyn.

"Margot, my darling girl, how have you been?" Evelyn greeted as Margot entered the morgue, the blast of cold air making her shudder even though she'd expected it.

Evelyn was wearing a simple black dress with a lab coat over it. Her short, dark hair currently sported bright orange streaks. She was in her sixties but didn't look a day over forty, and she was a voracious flirt, something that would become obvious when Leon and Wes arrived. She was not at all discerning about which direction her flirtation was aimed. If there was a man within ten feet of Evelyn, she was going to say something to him. Her flirtation was always light-hearted; Margot was fairly certain someone would have to be an absolute villain to report Evelyn to HR for her banter. The environment and situations they all worked within on a daily basis needed that kind of levity to keep everyone sane.

Margot's hands felt empty and cold without a coffee cup in

them, but she hadn't thought to grab anything on her way thanks to Wes being her ever-present coffee-bringer. She had a pang of guilt as she added that to the list of reasons she shouldn't consider the FBI offer.

Then she scolded herself for being so ridiculous. The FBI *had* coffee, she knew that well enough. It wasn't *great* coffee, but it was a hell of an improvement over the swill served at the police station.

You could buy your own, a little voice in the back of her head said.

She shook it off, tamping it down with any other suggestion that she form a habit that might become routine. Someone could get accustomed to her going to a certain Philz every morning. A barista might start to know her order. Most people wouldn't think about that, or if they did, they'd be flattered by the familiarity.

But what if that barista was like Ed?

What if that barista was like the Redwood Killer?

Statistically speaking it was unlikely, but Margot had encountered more killers in her life than the average person. It would be just her luck that the moment she decided to support her own coffee habit, she would get the one sexual psychopath barista in all of the Bay Area as her regular guy.

"I'm living the dream, Evelyn. You?"

"Oh, you know. Armpit-deep in guts, but I guess that's what they pay me the medium-sized dollars for. Where's that handsome partner of yours?" She leaned over to see if the six-foot-plus form of Wes was somehow hidden behind Margot.

"What am I, chopped liver?" Margot chuckled. "He and Leon should be here any minute. How's that new grandbaby of yours?" This was an effort for Margot, who very rarely let her questions dip into the realm of the personal. Asking Evelyn about her life was inviting Evelyn to ask about Margot's and Margot *hated* talking about her personal life.

Evelyn hadn't mentioned seeing the Ed Finch documentary, but it seemed reasonable to assume that she, like almost everyone else Margot worked with, knew about it. Sebastian Klein, Margot's friend at the *San Francisco Sentinel*, was begging her to let him write a feature, but Margot thought the documentary was plenty of exposure, and so far, Sebastian had let it go.

If Evelyn knew Margot's deep, dark secret, she wasn't bringing it up, and Margot loved her for that.

"Ohhh, he's so cute," Evelyn squealed delightedly. "Do you want to see a picture?"

Margot understood social expectations well enough to know that this was not an optional request. "Sure, I'd love to."

While she didn't particularly understand the allure of babies herself, she did know how to make the appropriate noises of delight when looking at the chubby-cheeked baby. Evelyn flipped through several photos on her phone before Leon and Wes arrived to rescue Margot and save her from being grilled on anything horrific like her dating life or her biological clock.

And Wes was holding a still-warm Blue Bottle coffee for her, bless his beautiful soul.

She took it, smiling gratefully at him. "You save the world from my uncaffeinated wrath on a daily basis. A true hero among men."

Wes smiled, his gaze lingering on her just a moment longer than polite, and it made her heart skip a beat.

There'd been so much going on the past few months with the discovery of the video, the ongoing work on the case, and through it all, Wes had been patient. He'd waited. But she had promised him that as soon as there was a lull in their lives, they could talk about things.

She knew he wanted more from her, knew that their friendship was on the cusp of something bigger, scarier.

She'd been avoiding that conversation, not because she

didn't *want* to be with him. More and more each day she couldn't imagine herself with anyone else. But because she was a disaster of a human, and disasters tended to ruin the things around them.

If Margot agreed to be in a relationship with Wes, it could end.

It could end horribly.

And then what would she have left, if the one person in the world she could imagine herself loving didn't love her back anymore?

She sipped her coffee—perfect—and pushed that fear way, way down inside her. No matter how much her therapist, Dr. Singh, told her that she had the tools she needed and the self-awareness to make a relationship work, she still felt like saying yes to it would be the biggest risk she could take.

She and Wes were both notoriously terrible with commitment. What made them think that loving each other would be enough to cure them of those habits?

Evelyn was busy chattering away to Leon, showing him the baby photos, and once the friendly banter had wrapped, they turned their attention to what they had all been avoiding looking at. The two bodies draped in clean white sheets laying on metal worktables in the center of the room.

Evelyn, her expression now serious and professional, moved to the table closest to them, the one on the right. She removed the sheet, exposing the naked body of the first of their two new victims.

"We were able to put a rush on checking the dental records of both victims, and thankfully came back with hits on both no more than an hour ago. I had already texted the names to Detective Telly, but since we're all here together, I'd like to introduce you all to Sabine Keller." She indicated the body she was standing next to. "Our other Doe is one Diana Prince."

"Wonder Woman," Wes said, almost reflexively. His cheeks

colored as soon as he realized that he'd said it out loud. "Sorry. Diana Prince, that was Wonder Woman's name."

Margot patted him on the arm.

Evelyn smiled at him, a kind look to let him know the outburst hadn't bothered her. "Ms. Keller was an Oakland resident, twenty-five years old. Ms. Prince was from Palo Alto, she was only twenty-one."

Margot recalled the redhead's rounded cheeks in her profile image, the sweetness that had radiated out from that single photo. Twenty-one was so young to be doing this kind of work, and to be lying dead in a morgue because of it.

Not that there was ever an age that made it OK, but sometimes the young ones felt a little harder than others.

Evelyn brought their attention back to Sabine Keller. Sabine had the physique of a swimmer, toned muscle all over her body. She was short—only five foot three according to Evelyn—and where most of their other victims had long hair, hers was cut in a close-cropped pixie style that made Margot think of Audrey Hepburn. It also made Margot realize Sabine must have been wearing a wig when they had found her, because she vividly recalled the high ponytail. Perhaps long hair was better for business?

While her wounds had all been cleaned, it was easy to see even at a glance all the deep cuts that marked her torso and pelvis. Margot had seen enough from this killer's previous victims that the location of the wounds didn't surprise her, they were almost identical to what she'd seen previously. She suspected that, once Evelyn removed the sterile sheet covering Diana Prince's body, the patterns would be almost spot on.

Their killer seemed to focus his efforts on the chest and torso for the killing blows, but he also put in a good amount of effort on the pelvic area, stabbing his victims in the region around their genitals, but not in the genitals themselves. It was an unusual distinction.

Margot was no stranger to the tell-tale signs of a sexual sadist. While the media would love to have the world believe that most serial killers fell into that category because it was the most shocking and compelling for books and movies, it simply wasn't the case. Sexual sadists were actually exceptionally rare, but since Margot's own father had been one, she had long ago learned what the signature of one looked like.

People incorrectly assumed that a sexual sadist would sexually assault his victims, but the truth was, they got their pleasure and power from the act of the killing, not from any physical penetration of the victim's body. Much like her father with his victims, this killer seemed far more interested in getting his rocks off through the act of stabbing than through any other violation he could enact.

Not that that was any relief for the victims, obviously.

"—the wounds are consistent with what we've seen on the other victims. Even in terms of the number. He's not so meticulous to have an exact count, but he seems to fall in the range of about fifty wounds with each of his victims. Both of our young ladies here are in that range. Ms. Keller had forty-two stab wounds, with the largest concentration being on her torso and then a reduced number on the groin. We did determine that the wounds on the groin were deeper, more aggressive. There was additional tearing on the skin, and when we did an X-ray, it was clear that there were some knife marks on the pelvic bone."

Margot grimaced. While she understood the need to have this information, sometimes it was an unwelcome gift she had no way to return. She *knew* all this, but hearing it again and again never took the edge off it. She'd heard some of the older detectives say that they got desensitized to the violence at a certain point, but the best Margot could do was soften her focus, let the visceral nature of it just turn hazy and red.

She needed to know the details, but that didn't make them something she'd ever get used to hearing.

She figured the moment she accepted that kind of violence as a norm, that was the day she needed to quit her job.

Margot listened but also didn't listen as Evelyn went over Sabine's body, pointing out the wounds, the marks that would indicate the young woman tried to defend herself, and the lividity that confirmed she died somewhere other than where she was found.

"What about the tattoo?" she heard Leon ask, bringing her focus back into check.

"Yes, both of them have one," Evelyn confirmed. She gently took hold of Sabine's chin and turned her head to the side, where a little bird tattoo was visible behind the girl's ear.

Like all their other victims, the mark was so small it could have looked like a birthmark at a passing glance. But they'd learned early on in the case that these were actually marks to indicate they were all part of the same group of escorts. The Larks.

While she leaned toward the branding option, she also knew these were smart women, based on everything she'd learned about them, and she didn't want to strip them of their autonomy just because of her own assumptions.

Evelyn completed her review of Sabine's autopsy, but Margot mainly heard her own pulse beating in her ears. A few times Wes or Leon asked questions, but for the most part it was Evelyn reciting her grim soliloquy.

They moved over to Diana's body, and when Evelyn removed the sheet Margot let out a long sigh. No one seemed to notice or if they did, they didn't acknowledge it, but it was all so *depressing*. Another young woman, this one *so* young, and there again were the same stab wounds, the same patterns, the same defensive marks, the same tattoo.

There were now so many girls and so much similarity between them that they ran the risk of becoming known as *his victims* rather than being remembered for the people they were.

Whenever that risk started to become too real in a case, Margot repeated one name to herself.

Georgeann Hawkins.

It was strange, because Georgeann's case had nothing to do with Margot's past, nothing to do with her work, yet it stuck with her. Georgeann was one of Ted Bundy's victims. A college co-ed who said good night to her boyfriend and went to take the one-block walk back to her own home, and was never seen alive again. There was something about that story that Margot could never quite get out of her mind, that someone could simply vanish like that in the time it took to walk down a back lane.

Whenever she felt there was a risk that she might start letting all the victims in her caseload start to blend together, she remembered that name. Remembered that one person *can* just vanish into the night, but that it didn't diminish the life left behind.

It was like a mantra that kept her grounded.

That, and knowing that Georgeann's killer did eventually face justice for what he'd done to her, even though they could never officially confirm whether Georgann's body was among those they uncovered.

And if Bundy could face justice, then this sick monster would, too.

Margot's attention sharpened with Evelyn's discussion of Diana's remains. She felt tired and angry, but most of all, she felt a renewed sense of righteousness that these two young women would be the *last* bodies the Redwood Killer left for them.

His time between kills was speeding up.

Which meant they were going to need to put this puzzle together before he killed again.

ELEVEN
1994

Ed could try to leave.

He could tempt fate, slip out of the bedroom and through the front door. There was a good chance this unexpected interloper would see him, but perhaps she might think Bethenny had a male guest over. While he'd been watching the apartment long enough to know this wasn't typical behavior for the girl, he also knew having company stay over wasn't in her routine either.

There was a chance this newcomer might just have a laugh at her friend's one-night stand and think nothing of it until the morning when Bethenny never woke up. And then what would she be able to describe? His rough height? The color of the hair at the back of his head? His jacket? He could ditch the jacket, that was no problem. And what was he if not the model of average in terms of height, build and even his brown hair.

Yes. He could try to slip out.

He'd paid attention to the layout of the apartment before entering Bethenny's bedroom. The front door was immediately outside her room, and the furthest point away from the fire escape where he entered—and where his new foe was situated—meaning she likely wouldn't get a very good look at him as he ducked out.

Otherwise, he was stuck, waiting. Waiting for her to fall asleep. And he hadn't been watching her, didn't know her habits, had no idea how late of a night owl she was. She was out there watching a goddamn movie. For all he knew, she might be up for hours more, and he couldn't risk getting home too late. Kim was away with the kids for her mother's sixtieth birthday, but he knew she would check in. There was a fine line between how late he could claim to be out with imaginary friends from work and a point where Kim would start to get suspicious about another affair. She was already pissed at him for not coming along, and her paranoia would be heightened. Him being out all night wouldn't help that.

He groaned inwardly and risked stepping out of the closet. It was too cramped, too uncomfortable. His muscles were beginning to ache, and he didn't need to get a cramp that might prohibit him from making a run for it if the opportunity presented itself.

Whatever movie she was watching in the living room, she wasn't being quiet about it. The volume was up, which emboldened him to move around Bethenny's bedroom, stretching out his legs. He took a moment to sit at the end of the bed, then leaned down and sniffed the rumpled sheets. The scent of sweat, fear, and blood filled his nostrils and Ed smiled to himself, awash with a renewed sense of purpose.

No, this wouldn't be his last stand. This wouldn't be the final kill, or the moment that broke him. He'd experienced the unexpected before. He'd had near-misses when the girls he was following sensed something was up; he'd had moments of approaching women in the street and being rebuffed. There were plenty of points in the past where someone with a little more self-preservation, or with the wherewithal to call the police and mention a man behaving unusually might have been the thing that brought him down.

But it hadn't happened. Because most people couldn't be bothered to make the effort for something like that. Most people just wrote off an unpleasant encounter as someone being weird, or someone with no social skills, or some creepy loser making a pass at them. When they should have listened to that voice deep in their guts. A voice that was screaming *predator* at them.

Except these days people didn't seem to believe there were literal predators out there who might mean them harm. They saw weirdos, or men with no charisma. They didn't listen to the voice, because they had unlearned how to speak the language of fear.

Ed could teach that language with the fluency of a master.

So why was he in this bedroom hiding? From what? Some woman? What could she do?

He had proven time and time again that there was nothing a woman could do when he wanted to exert his will on her, so why was this one any different? Because he hadn't planned for her?

He was looking at this all wrong. She wasn't a problem.

She was a gift.

Ed smiled, his fingers caressing the smooth material of Bethenny's bedspread.

He'd never had a two-for-one before.

TWELVE

Back at the police station, Margot's hope of doing research on their two new victims was dashed when the captain called the three of them into a conference room the moment they walked through the doors.

The captain was sneaky—he usually didn't cross paths with the overnight shift, but with the three leads in the Redwood Killer case being on night rotation at the same time, he had apparently decided to make time to see them face-to-face.

And he wasn't alone.

As Margot entered the conference room, she stopped dead in her tracks, forcing Wes to walk into her back with an unexpected *oof* sound.

"What the hel—" His voice stopped mid-sentence as he realized why she had stopped.

There were two people sitting with Captain Tate. One was an exhausted-looking young woman with her laptop out, fingers poised as if she was ready to record every single word of this exchange. A thick day planner sat beside her on the table, and her pantsuit was creased, indicating this was the tail end of an already long day, not the start of a new one.

Beside her was Pressley Boyd, chief of police.

Margot had only been in the same room with him a handful of times, and even then, those had been significantly bigger rooms than this, where she never had to speak directly to him.

She'd been fine with living a life where Pressley Boyd didn't know she existed.

That was especially true these days, considering what she and Wes had on him, which was evidence that would ruin not only his career, but likely send him to prison. The only reason they hadn't shared it yet was because it was so closely tied to the Redwood Killer case that the disruption could theoretically stall the case or derail it entirely.

But being in the same room with him, she felt like there was no way for her to hide what she knew.

She darted a quick look at Wes, who appeared almost queasy.

She had to assume he was wondering the same thing as her: why was Boyd here? And were they about to lose any shot they had at bringing him down?

Margot swallowed hard and tried to project an aura of confidence, but in actuality she worried the moment she opened her mouth she might throw up.

Boyd was a weaselly-looking guy, with sallow skin, a balding head, and ears that were slightly too big to look right with his otherwise pinched features. He was perfectly capable of turning on the charm in public settings, and Margot had watched him woo media and politicians alike. But he evidently didn't think it was necessary here, because there was no smile on his face and his dark eyes were clouded with something unpleasant.

"Have a seat, detectives," instructed Captain Tate.

Margot eyed the captain carefully. She'd always liked Tate, considered him to be someone who was both fair and understanding. He'd always been supportive of her. But sitting next to

Boyd, she had to wonder how in the dark he truly was about Boyd's after-hours habits. Were there rumors about the chief of police? Hints of any impropriety he might be aware of?

The thing about scandals like the one Margot and Wes were poised to break was that they never happened in a vacuum. There was always someone who said afterwards, "You know, I'm not surprised, I kind of suspected he was doing something like that."

There were always people who knew things, if only by deductive logic, and did nothing about them.

Was Tate even a little bit aware?

And if so, could he be trusted when the time came to reveal the truth? So far, Wes and Margot hadn't told anyone about the video, because they couldn't widen that circle of trust without fear of consequences. Margot wanted to tell Leon, but she also knew he would insist on blowing it open immediately, and she and Wes agreed they needed the leverage to stay quiet at least a little longer.

They couldn't risk a single thing going wrong when they brought their evidence forward, because one misstep would be the end of their careers, while Boyd would get away scot-free.

And with Boyd being tangled up with the Rigas, it wasn't only their careers Margot and Wes had to worry about, it was their lives as well. So they needed to be completely certain they could take Boyd down and not risk the murder case going haywire in the meantime.

It was a delicate tightrope to walk, and there were days Margot just wanted to send the video to Sebastian Klein at the *Sentinel* and wipe her hands clean of the whole mess.

Margot sat at the table across from Tate, Boyd, and the woman who hadn't yet been introduced. It felt as if they'd been called into the principal's office for some infraction they didn't know they'd committed.

Margot hated that feeling, because if there was anyone in

the room who should be feeling guilty, it was the sweaty man sitting across from her. She wanted to bore a hole into him with her gaze, but knew that looking at him directly was only going to give away that she knew something, and she didn't need his attention on her.

She needed to get through whatever the hell this meeting was so she could get back to doing her job.

She looked over to Wes, but he seemed to be pointedly refusing to look at her. His jaw was tight and his whole body was tense, like he was trying to keep control over something inside himself.

Captain Tate cleared his throat. "I don't want to keep you too long. I know you just got back from the morgue, and you'll want to focus on the case. But Chief Boyd wanted an update on the case progress for a morning press conference, and with all three of my primaries on this case working evenings, we had to pin you down when we could."

Margot's gaze flicked to Boyd, and she knew she looked annoyed, but she couldn't help it. He was disrupting them so he would have a good soundbite? Wouldn't it be better to let them do their jobs so he might have an actual solved case to talk to the press about?

Margot chewed her inner cheek and turned her focus to Leon, who was the lead on the case and should be the one talking.

"Things are moving along since my last report. Detectives Fox, Phalen, and Branson re-interviewed an old witness—"

"A suspect?" Boyd interrupted.

Leon took a deep breath. "A *witness*. He had some new insights on the case that we are following up on, but no leads we can publicly share yet."

Since they'd gone right from the morgue to the station, Margot still hadn't had a chance to tell them what she'd learned from Jesse, and she would need to get into the card he'd given her as soon as they were out of here.

Now she was more anxious than ever to be done with this sham of a discussion.

She knew Boyd was under pressure from the mayor, from the general public, and heaven only knew how many other outside sources. She honestly wouldn't have been surprised if he was getting pressure from Riga to put this to bed. No businessman wanted to lose their investments, and Riga was losing a lot of girls to this maniac. He hadn't done anything to solve the case himself, and his son's behavior proved that Riga didn't care about the safety of his girls, but he couldn't be enjoying all this media attention. Certainly, he wanted this finished just as badly as anyone else, even if it was just to keep prying eyes off his business.

Though not badly enough to actually be of any use to them, because that would simply make their lives too easy.

Margot let out a sigh, and Wes jammed his thumb into her leg, letting her know she hadn't been silent.

Leon continued explaining their progress, but now Boyd was looking at her, his focus sharp and unpleasant.

"Detective Phalen?" he said, as if not sure precisely who she was. She would have been fine without him ever knowing.

"Yes, sir."

"I wasn't aware you were involved in this case."

Margot felt her back go rigid. How could he not be aware? She'd been on the case since it was her and Leon alone. Her name was all over the files. Either he'd chosen not to notice it, or he was only now realizing who she was.

"Yes, sir. Since day one."

His mouth formed a thin line. She could see he was struggling with something, and she was pretty sure she knew what it was. He didn't want her name attached to this, not with the recent documentary and general interest around her still lingering. But how could he take her off a case she had been on for over a year without having to explain that decision? He was trying to figure out what the lesser of two evils was

She stared him down, challenging him to just *try* to take her off this case.

Whatever it was Boyd had been considering saying, he seemed to recoil at her expression, and Margot wasn't sure which of her hereditary looks she was giving him. Her mother's stern no-nonsense look of challenge, or the dead-eyed shark stare she'd seen on Ed's face looking back at her from across a prison table.

Either way it seemed to do the trick and he changed tack.

"Heard you might be giving evidence at the Willingham trial. That's going to be a doozy."

Margot swallowed down a lump in her throat. She had almost entirely forgotten about Ewan's upcoming trial, and the part she might need to play in that. She gave a one-shoulder shrug. "I think we'd all prefer that it was Wes giving a statement about that trial rather than me, but I drew the short straw."

Boyd watched her carefully. "Yes, well. I suppose we can always hope there is a plea deal before then."

Fat chance. Ewan-slash-Ethan was too high on his own horse to turn down the attention of a trial, especially now that he was eighteen and he wouldn't be hidden by the protections afforded to minors. He wanted to show Ed how impressive he was, and going to trial would be the ideal way for him to peacock.

No, that trial was an inevitability, and so was the unwelcome requirement of her being badgered by two sets of lawyers when she had helped get that little psycho off the street. She truly hated appearing in trials. By the end of it she wanted to throttle someone.

She recalled a time only a year or two prior when the defense lawyer had spent hours grilling her, trying to make her crack, trying to find flaws in her police work and making every possible effort to belittle her in front of the jury, only to find her after the proceedings ended for the day to ask her out for a drink.

There were plenty of good reasons for Margot to hate trials, but lawyers were probably the main one.

She had put the trial out of her mind, and aside from trying to kick her off the Redwood Killer case, it was about the worst thing Pressley Boyd could have said to her today.

They continued to discuss the case, and the unnamed woman—Margot assumed she must be his assistant—typed at speed, recording every detail of the conversation. There likely wasn't much that this silent observer missed.

Margot watched her carefully, and as with everyone connected to Boyd, she wondered what his assistant knew, how much she had seen. What she was aware of.

There was an ingrained sense of distrust that went along with knowing such a big secret, and Margot found that as a result she was starting to question everyone, to doubt everyone. It wasn't a very nice feeling, especially considering how shut off her life already was.

Maybe, once all of this was done, she really *should* consider a change of pace. Something new. Not that the FBI offer was so different or new from what she was already doing. She'd still be investigating murder, she'd still be facing the worst of humanity on a daily basis. But she found herself disillusioned now with the life she had built.

She'd become a cop because she wanted to do good, to make up for the things her father had done.

Now she was wondering if the work she was doing was really enough to make up for all the bad she saw as a by-product. Could she be proud of being a San Francisco police detective if the person who was at the head of that organization was so corrupt that his exposure would create a scandal so big it could taint the department for years to come?

Margot didn't know if she could be a part of that.

But she also knew that there was a chance she was looking at the FBI's invitation as an easy out. While it wasn't like her to take an easy out, this entire situation felt so unprecedented. The past months she had been questioning—both to herself and with her therapist—if the reason she'd gotten into this line of work hadn't been misguided from the beginning.

The deeper she got into Ed's history, the more literal skeletons they pulled from his closet, the more Margot thought that a lifetime of bringing killers to justice wouldn't be enough to undo the things Ed had done.

Ten lifetimes wouldn't be enough.

And when did she start to live her life for herself?

She'd been so lost in the haze of self-reflection she didn't realize things were winding down until Pressley Boyd's hand was in front of her face, an offer for a handshake waiting.

She didn't want to touch him.

She wanted to slap his hand away.

Instead, she got to her feet so she was standing taller than him and took his hand in hers, squeezing it firmly and never letting her eyes move from his. She wanted to let him know she was watching. Let him know she wasn't fooled by the charm he worked on others.

I'm coming for you, she thought to herself.

And *that* made her smile for the first time since they'd come into the room.

THIRTEEN

Margot arrived back at her desk with a cloud following over her head. Thankfully, Wes was also on her heels because his very presence could cool her down before she erupted.

The funny thing about that was, given a different scenario, Wes could also wind her up so much she thought she might explode.

She slumped into her desk chair with a loud huff of a sigh and sipped her now-cool coffee, which thankfully still tasted delightful, and booted up her ancient computer.

Wes took her jacket, which she had flung on her desk, and along with his own, hung them on the coat rack in the corner of their small office. Wes was like that, neat, efficient. Somehow Margot had been surprised to find his apartment meticulously tidy and welcoming, rather than being a messy bachelor pad with cold, masculine finishes.

She shouldn't have been surprised.

Wes had always been more than he appeared to be on the surface. It had just taken her a while to open up to seeing it. To seeing him.

"What a prick," Wes grumbled, settling into his own chair,

pushing it back from his desk so he could kick his long legs out in front of him and focus on her. His gaze was heavy, she could feel it even without looking at him. Not that she minded looking at him, but she was trying to cultivate a bad mood at the moment and being around Wes when he was being charming—which was pretty much any moment he was awake—made that very difficult.

"I wanted to wring his neck," Margot huffed, pulling out the black business card Jesse had given her and sticking it in her keyboard.

"I know," Wes said, wheeling his chair closer so he was sitting next to her desk, his thigh almost touching hers. He smelled good, expensive, the kind of cologne that probably advertised itself as being *sensual* and *woodsy*. He always smelled good, like he had showered only minutes before seeing her and had then rolled around in whatever scent romance novelists doused their conflicted bad boy heroes in that they described as *the smell of a man.*

Margot wrinkled up her nose, trying to chase away the distraction of clean linen, pepper, and sandalwood.

Didn't he understand that she wanted to be mad?

"How did your meeting with that sleazeball at Odyssey go?"

Finally, Margot sat back in her chair and looked at him, coffee cup still in hand. He'd long ago stopped pointing out to her when coffee had gone cold, because Margot was the kind of person who drank iced coffee in the dead of winter. She didn't care what temperature her coffee was as long as it sent a jolt of caffeine right to her heart.

But Wes, damn him, had succeeded in shifting her attention from her Pressley Boyd-shaped annoyance. She was just going to have to be irrationally angry a different time.

"He was actually quite forthcoming. For him."

Wes quirked an eyebrow. "Yeah, go figure he'd be chummy when you went by yourself. Real shocker there."

Margot bit back a smirk. Was that... jealousy?

"Whatever gets results, Fox, whatever gets results." She handed him the business card, which he turned over in his hands, looking baffled by its simplicity.

"You know, if I didn't know how these women advertised their services, I'd say you had just handed me the card for an escort service."

"Close, it's for those who serve the escort services."

Wes raised an eyebrow. "He actually told you who works those parties?"

"Unless that card is a sham, in which case he gave me something useless to get rid of me. But I think he knows I'd come back to bother him endlessly if he did that, and despite his attempts at flirtation, I don't think he really wants to see me again any time soon."

"He flirted with you?"

Margot snatched the card back, returning it to the keyboard. "Jesse Simcoe would flirt with a brick wall, Wesley. I wasn't exactly flattered by the attention."

Wed made a small *mmm* noise in the back of his throat and then wheeled himself back to his desk. "Looks like we got an email from DeAndra," he said, looking at his monitor.

DeAndra Leggit was the new lead CSI, she'd been with the department for about two months at this point and Margot found her to be smart, efficient, and excellent at her job, though her incredibly personable attitude was often a bit more than Margot could handle. She was just so damned *nice*. How was anyone that upbeat after looking at crime scenes and grisly evidence all day? Nothing seemed to keep DeAndra from smiling, so Margot could only handle the woman in small doses, lest her positivity risk rubbing off.

"She get anything on those samples?" Margot was already opening the same email, looking over the high points from DeAndra and her team. They *had* been able to get a DNA sample from the hair, but it would take some time before they were able to locate any matches. If there were any.

The blue fluff had come back matching a low-pile carpet, one that was frequently used in Nissan cars from 2000 to 2006.

Margot and Wes locked eyes over the top of their computers, sharing the same thought without saying it out loud.

If they could talk to the service staff who worked for Riga's parties, and could compare their DMV records, there was a chance—a slim but real chance—they had enough evidence to figure out who their killer was.

Margot let out her breath in a *whoosh*. After more than a year of effort, of looking for this guy without a single real lead, they might *finally* have what they needed to pin him down.

All thanks to a bit of fluff.

And if they could match the DNA, that would be the icing on the cake in terms of a trial. A tidy little bow to wrap things up and put this fucker away for the rest of his life.

But first they needed to find someone who fit the bill. They were relying very heavily on Richard Downey's suggestion that he'd gotten some bad vibes from service staff, and that in and of itself was no smoking gun. What rich asshole *hadn't* cast judgment on someone working class?

Yet, as Branson had said in the car, there was something believable about his theory, and more than that, it seemed obvious that *he* believed his theory. And now they had tangible, physical evidence to back it up.

Despite the late hour, Margot picked up the card and dialed the number. She had a feeling that this wasn't the typical kind of company that would stick to standard business hours.

A moment later a woman answered the phone, her voice as low and smoky as a phone sex operator as she said, "Elite Party Planning, this is Yvonne."

"Yvonne, I got your card from Jesse Simcoe over at the Odyssey."

The woman was silent for a beat then Margot heard a soft sigh. "You're the detective, I assume."

Ah, so the moment Margot had left the bar, Jesse had given them a warning. Margot was miffed, but at least she didn't need to dance around the topic of her being a cop. That cat was already out of the bag.

"Yes, Detective Margot Phalen. Do you think you might be able to talk to my partner and I for a few moments about a case we're working on?"

"I'm going to tell you right up front that I won't discuss any of my clients with you. I sign an NDA with every client, and you'll need to have better lawyers than the city can afford if you want me to break those."

Not a *no*, just a *don't waste my time*.

"We don't want to talk about your clients," Margot said. "We want to talk about your staff."

Another beat passed, but Margot could hear Yvonne breathing, could practically hear her thinking, trying to figure out a way to make it so this didn't have to happen. Eventually, though, she must have decided that the easiest way out was through. To get rid of the cops she would need to talk to them.

"Fine." She rattled off an address in Russian Hill, a nice area, though not overly affluent. "You can come by in forty minutes if you want to talk. I have things to do tonight, so be prompt or don't come at all."

She hung up the phone before Margot could reply.

Catching Wes's eye she said, "You want to go on another field trip?"

FOURTEEN

The address Yvonne gave them was for a tidy-looking Victorian in Russian Hill, the facade painted in a fresh mint green with lilac trim, something that wouldn't work on anything other than a stately old painted lady.

The street parking was slim thanks to the hour, all available spots filled with residents, so Margot parked a few blocks away and they hoofed it back to the house at a quickened pace in order to make it in Yvonne's strict visitation window. Margot's calves were burning from a steep incline hike by the time they reached Yvonne's front door.

When they rang, a woman with her hair in a slightly frizzy bun opened the door and gave them a quick once-over. She was holding an iPad and wearing a wireless phone mic over one ear.

"You're the police?" she asked, peering at them over the top of her tortoiseshell glasses.

Since everything about this woman screamed *assistant*, something Margot was learning to spot after their meeting with Pressley, she nodded. "Detectives Phalen and Fox." She held out her badge which the woman gave a cursory glance before opening the door wide to let them in.

"Please take your shoes off," she announced.

Margot glanced down at the woman's own feet, which were clad in slippers that looked to be made out of felted wool and had probably cost more than all of the furniture in Margot's apartment. Wes had already shucked off his loafers and Margot followed suit, unzipping her black boots and kicking them off before lining them up neatly beside Wes's.

"My name is Kelly, I'll take you back to meet Yvonne. She asked me to remind you that her schedule is very tight and she only has fifteen minutes to speak with you. I hope you'll respect her time." Kelly gave them a not at all subtle look, and for the second time that night Margot felt as though she was being lectured by her principal. It wasn't a great feeling.

"We'll respect her time if she respects that we are also here to do our job," Margot said, smiling with forced politeness that made Kelly recoil from her. Yeah, so the smile needed work.

Kelly stayed closer to Wes as she led them through the main floor of the house to an office at the back. The space was beautiful, painted a robin's egg blue and outfitted with lovely antique furniture and original art all over the walls. It looked like the office for a museum curator, or an art gallery owner, rather than whatever it was that Yvonne did.

But it looked like business was good, because the office *screamed* wealth, though in a less obnoxious way than Downey's mansion had.

Business was good for Yvonne then.

Kelly showed them in, indicating the two chairs facing Yvonne's desk, then ducked out, closing the door behind her.

Margot sat first, while Wes did his usual subtle pacing, looking around the space. Yvonne watched him, her eyes focused on each movement, though she didn't ask what he was doing or insist he sit down. She just made it very clear she knew what he was up to.

Margot saw Wes catch her looking but he continued to

linger by one of the bookshelves, as if too captivated by the leather-bound books to be deterred from studying them. Margot cleared her throat to bring Yvonne's attention back to her.

Yvonne was an incredibly striking woman. Not beautiful in the traditional sense—her features were a bit sharp, bordering on masculine in her jaw and nose—but there was something about her face that commanded attention and made you not want to look away. She had blonde hair that had been expertly dyed with honey highlights melting into the cooler ash tones, and her blue eyes were intelligent and intense.

She didn't smile, which made her look even more fierce, and Margot could imagine Yvonne's portrait hanging in some German mansion, staring down at her and finding her wanting, even through the paintbrush strokes.

Yvonne glanced at her watch, as if to remind them that time was ticking away.

"Ms..." Margot let the greeting drift, waiting for the other woman to fill in the blank at the end.

"Stradbroke."

"Ms. Stradbroke, we can appreciate how valuable your time is, so if it's all right with you we'll bypass the usual time-wasting nonsense."

"That suits me just fine," Yvonne said coolly, sitting back in her chair and folding her hands in her lap, now far more interested in Margot than she'd been in watching Wes.

"While I know you keep your clientele private, we know you've worked for Emmanuel Riga."

Yvonne stiffened slightly before her careful mask fell back into place. That was all Margot needed to know she'd hit the nail on the head. She was surprised, though, to see Yvonne react at all. Had Jesse not clued her in to what they were going to ask about? Maybe he thought his allegiance to Yvonne only went as far as telling her that the police would be asking her questions, not who specifically they would be asking about.

"I told you, I can't discuss my clients."

"Oh, I don't want you to tell us anything about Riga. We know plenty about dear old Manny, and we don't need more on him. Not at the moment, anyway. But we know that he likes to host parties for some very well-connected people. We know that you have employed the servers and bartenders at those parties."

"I employ staff for a lot of events, detective."

"Then you would know which staff work at which events. Which makes you the perfect person to talk to. Even more so if you know what kind of cars your staff drive. Especially if they happen to drive a Nissan."

A thin smile crossed Yvonne's lips. "Now, detective, you're smart enough to be aware I don't need to disclose any information about my staff without a warrant. Do you have a warrant?"

"No. You know perfectly well I need to know who I'm looking for in order to get that kind of information. Ms. Stradbroke, I'm not going to mince words here. You're a woman of integrity. You wouldn't have gotten as far in your business, working with the people you do, if they didn't trust you. But we have reason to believe that one of your employees might be a killer. And not just a one-off killer, a serial killer. So, if you don't mind me saying so, I don't think that's the kind of person you want to have in your employ."

"Jesus, you can't mean..."

"The Redwood Killer, yes. We believe he may be one of your employees."

This finally got Yvonne to really *look* at Margot, instead of staring her down. What Margot saw there was genuine fear, though not the kind you see on a woman in a horror movie about to be stabbed. No, this was the kind of deep-seated fear, the kind women carry with them their whole lives. It was the fear that made women hold car keys in their fingers, made them question getting into an elevator alone with an unfamiliar man.

It was an evolutionary fear, one that Margot's own father had trained her to feel.

Yvonne was experiencing, in that moment, what it was to realize that someone you *know* could be capable of something like that.

It was not a feeling Margot wished on anyone.

"Why do you think that?" Yvonne was sitting up straight, her chair pulled back up to the desk, and she seemed to lean in closer, like she needed to see Margot speak.

"We interviewed someone who had previously hosted those parties, and been in attendance at a few of them in person. He indicated that he got an uncomfortable feeling from some of the service staff that they might have gotten overly attached to some of Riga's girls after working multiple parties together. Do you have any staff you've received complaints about?"

Yvonne considered this question carefully. "I hope you don't take this the wrong way, but we train our staff to be almost invisible at these events—we don't *want* people to notice them. If someone had stood out enough to warrant a complaint, they very likely wouldn't have been asked to attend another event with that host."

"Maybe your own staff mentioned something. Someone acting inappropriately with other service staff?"

"For the safety of my staff, I'm very selective about who attends those... events. Only men are selected to work at parties of that nature. In the past we learned that sometimes guests who attend events like that begin to believe any women in attendance are available to... fraternize, and we soon determined it was safest for everyone involved to only send men. Not that it solved the problem completely, of course, but it certainly helped cut down on issues. But no, to answer your question, I've never had any of my staff complain about each other, or about something that stood out to them as being particularly worrisome."

"And you think they would?"

Yvonne nodded. "I'm very good to my employees, detective. I need to trust them, so they have to be able to trust me. Fair is fair. Their honesty is how I knew to make changes in regard to those types of parties in the first place. I want anyone who works for me to go home feeling well paid and well cared for. That's how we keep people on staff who I can rely on."

"Would you be able to see which of your staff were working for more than one of those parties? And if we're being specific about the things I know, one of the events would have been hosted by Richard Downey in Sausalito."

Again, she blanched. Margot was sure now that Yvonne had thought the detectives were bluffing about how much they knew.

It was satisfying to know that they weren't barking up the completely wrong tree. Even though this was certainly a long shot, Margot couldn't help but feel it was the long shot they had been so desperately waiting for.

Yvonne looked between Margot and Wes and then, even as her lips formed a tight line of distaste, she opened up her laptop and started a flurry of typing, her manicured nails flying over the keyboard with a loud *tak-tak-tak* sound. Margot waited patiently, barely daring to move or breathe, lest something she do spook Yvonne and make her change her mind about helping them.

After a few moments of tense silence, Yvonne sat back from her computer and withdrew a notepad from her desk drawer. Margot immediately noticed the custom monogram at the top of the pad, a stylized looping Y. She quickly jotted down two names and numbers, and then ripped the paper from the pad with an almost violent flourish before holding it out to Margot between two manicured fingers.

"I want your assurances that you will treat both these men fairly. If one of them is a killer, then the other is innocent. But

I'd prefer to believe they're both innocent and that they be treated that way."

"We understand," Margot said, taking the paper from Yvonne's extended hand and glancing at it. "Why only two names?" she asked, glancing up at Yvonne. She'd expected the woman to give her a list of everyone who had worked at multiple parties, which Margot had to assume was more than two people.

"You wanted to know who worked at specific parties. You also said you wanted to know who drove a Nissan." She gestured to the paper. "We have to keep track of our employees' cars because they are often doing work in gated communities or places where their cars might... stand out." Margot knew this meant *look poor*. "So it helps us to be able to pre-register those cars with security to avoid any issues that might disrupt events. I want to help you, detectives, but I'm only going to give you the exact information you ask for. I'm not going to volunteer complete employee schedules and jeopardize losing my entire roster of staff because the cops have showed up at their door. Start there, and if that fails you, then..." She shrugged and didn't say anything else.

"Thank you." Margot folded the paper and slipped it into her jacket pocket.

As she stood to leave, Yvonne spoke again. "If you don't mind me saying, detective... as much as I want that horrific case to be solved, I hope you don't find what you're looking for."

Margot understood her.

No one wants to think they've sat across from a killer.

FIFTEEN

Two names.

They had two names.

Back at the station, Margot was staring at the piece of paper Yvonne had given her, wondering if it was somehow possible that after all this time, after thousands of tip-line calls, after hours and hours spent with this case lurking in the back of her mind, somehow one of these two men might be the one they'd been looking for.

It felt impossible, like this was a dream Margot was on the cusp of waking from, and any moment she'd be back in Muir Woods, ferns brushing against the legs of her jeans as she stood over the body of Rebecca Watson in her bright pink hoodie. Back then, she had had no idea how far this road would take them, and how many more bodies would pile up along the way.

She'd had no idea how much of a mental load it would add to her life.

And now they had two names.

She stopped staring and opened a new email, addressing it to both Leon and Wes, and including the names and contact details Yvonne had provided. They could work on the initial background checks tonight, and then Leon could make announcements at the morning handover meeting with the rest of the task force to go over what they had learned.

If either of these men were their killer, they needed to be very careful about their next steps. They couldn't just waltz up to the door of these potential suspects, not with so much riding on the case. They'd have to walk a tense tightrope to observe both men, learn more about their habits, their cars, see if they could gather any DNA samples. You would be amazed what could be taken without a warrant simply because someone dropped a coffee cup in a public garbage can.

Margot had been able to collect DNA evidence at the station when suspects were too bold and took a drink from a can of soda or a coffee cup. People left evidence everywhere, if you knew how to look for it.

And they *would* look for it. They needed to find out if either of these men fit their profile, and then they would need to make sure they had a solid enough case to go in for an arrest.

Everything from this point forward needed to be the most flawless police work Margot and her team had ever done in their lives.

And it all started with a record search.

Margot input the first name on the list, Stephen Kramer. Kramer had no criminal record to speak of. A few parking tickets, and a note of a call to the police to report an argument he had heard his neighbors having and was concerned about. He was forty-one—a bit old to be a cater waiter—and a quick records search indicated no known spouse or children. The DMV reported him owning a 2010 Nissan Sentra. Red.

The second name was Drake Winston, he was twenty-seven, lived in Oakland, and drove a 2008 Nissan Rogue. Gray. He was far more interesting in terms of Margot's searches. He had a minimal criminal history. Margot wondered if Yvonne required background checks on her staff due to the nature of the people she worked for. That would make sense.

Drake Winston was not a remarkable criminal. He had a domestic disturbance on record—his girlfriend had locked herself in the bathroom and called the police, but later declined to press charges against him—and, like Kramer, a few parking infractions. But there was a note on his account to indicate that he had sealed juvenile records.

Margot stared at that note, knowing that she would likely never get that information, at least not until they had a better grasp on whether or not Drake Winston was their guy. But the fact that the records existed piqued her interest ferociously. It could be nothing, but Margot knew all too well what some of the notable childhood signs of a future killer were, and she was dying to know if any of them were buried in that sealed file.

There was a standard trifecta of signs that were typical for future serial killers. The first was bed-wetting. Innocuous on its own, and now somewhat contested by psychologists, but it seemed to be a common theme among killers. It was, Margot believed, related to the anxiety and stress that could trigger the bed-wetting, and also frequently related to parental response to the wetting. While not a part of the trifecta, Margot knew that many future killers had strained or abusive relationships with their mothers, which could certainly be tied to something like this kind of issue.

The second marker was animal cruelty. A child who was capable of abuse toward animals—and often the outright killing of innocent creatures—was a major red flag that appeared in the history of many killers. The early attempts to feel something by hurting others.

And last there was arson. Playing with fire did seem to be a common thing for killers in their youth.

Margot looked at the sealed record note and wondered if it was an assault, if it was an arson, if it was *something* that might point to Winston being the kind of youth who could grow up to be a killer.

Or perhaps had already killed.

Margot briefly flashed to the baby face of a boy who had once sat across the table from her in an interrogation room. She thought she'd needed to protect him from the horrible truth of what had happened to his family, but it turned out he didn't need her protection. He'd helped make it happen.

That boy had experienced his own traumas, had been a victim of Munchausen by proxy, and of repeated neglect by his parents, but who was to say what he might have become if they'd never learned the truth about him?

Who was to say who Drake Winston had been?

Margot knew where she wanted to start.

She looked up over her monitor to Wes, who was reading the same information she was.

"Winston sure looks interesting," he said, knowing she would be thinking the same thing.

"He does, indeed."

They both knew they couldn't just pick up and drive to Drake Winston's apartment, even though Margot had looked up the address and they could be there in about twenty minutes. No, they didn't have enough to go on yet, and if they went to talk to him without absolute certainty on their side, then they risked losing him completely. If he knew they were on to him, then he could make a run for it before they ever had a chance to get what they needed.

But they could talk to other people. People who might know him.

Margot input the name of his ex, the one who hadn't pressed charges during their domestic dispute.

Her name was Clea Rice, and she had a clean record, not even a parking ticket, which was a truly rare skill in the city of San Francisco. Clea was only twenty-five, and the domestic dispute between her and Winston had been five years earlier, making her practically a baby at the time.

Margot didn't like to make blanket statements, but at that age, young women were often too willing to listen to men who lied to get back in their good graces. She wondered what Winston had said to make her drop the charges, how he'd promised to never do it again. She wondered how long it had taken for him to go back on his word.

He must have, because a year after that, it looked like Clea got a restraining order against him. Whoever had granted that order had obviously believed that Clea was in some type of danger, because it was a five-year order, which was the maximum available. But Margot hadn't seen anything on Winston's record to indicate what might have made Clea that afraid.

There was only one way to find out for sure.

SIXTEEN

Margot and Wes should have been off duty for the day as soon as the morning shift started, but the nature of the work meant that oftentimes shift hours were meaningless. Unless there was a strict no-overtime rule in effect, it was pretty much fair game for how much time they put in during a given week.

She knew neither of them would be able to sleep until they talked to Clea Rice, so while some of the other members of the task force were heading home to get some much-needed rest and time with their families—Leon had made them promise to call him with any new leads—Margot and Wes took their rumpled, exhausted selves to an apartment in the Tenderloin.

The Tenderloin was surprisingly mellow at eight o'clock in the morning mid-week. It was an area of town that displayed the worst of San Francisco's societal issues, with homeless people set up in the middle of sidewalks, drug use happening in plain sight, and an air of neglect oozing out of every bit of cracked pavement in the area.

No one lived there unless they had to, so seeing Clea's address in that part of the city made Margot wonder just how bad things were for the woman.

Margot found a parking spot in front of a twenty-four-hour market, where, despite the crumbling edifices around it, the shop was well kept and a woman in a hijab was out front sweeping away used condoms and cigarette butts. She glanced up when Margot and Wes got out of their car, a curious expression on her face for only a moment before she went back to sweeping.

That was how people got by in the Tenderloin. No one's business was your business except your own.

Margot led them toward a doorway between two boarded-up businesses, where the smell of urine was pervasive and the buzzer was broken. Probably had been for years. It didn't matter since the front door was being held open with a brick. Wes held the door open for her and they made their way up three floors to where Clea's apartment was listed.

The building's old elevator was broken, not that Margot would have taken it even if it was operational. She didn't trust the older elevators in buildings, knowing there was always a very real risk of getting stuck in one, which was the last thing in the world she wanted.

No one ever got stuck walking up stairs.

The building smelled strongly of a disinfectant cleaner, and somewhere a baby was crying, but Margot was surprised to find that despite the rough exterior and broken door lock, the apartment itself was fairly well kept. The typical wear and tear of a build from the early 1900s was there, but overall, things were in excellent condition. Margot even saw signs of a warm living environment. One door had a floral wreath on it. Another had a child's art taped to the front. One person had a welcome mat.

This was definitely the kind of place where people were making the most of what they had.

When they reached Clea's door, it was unremarkable, no signs of decoration, but there was the distinct smell of fresh coffee wafting out from inside as Margot rapped on the door.

Light behind the peephole dimmed and then a soft voice asked, "What do you want?"

"Ms. Rice, we're here from the San Francisco Police Department. My name is Margot Phalen, I'm a detective."

"You have someone I can call to prove that?"

Evidently the badge Margot had flashed didn't do much in the way of assuring Clea, which was fine. Margot had met cagey witnesses before. People didn't trust the police much, and Margot had learned not to take it personally.

Thanks to Pressley Boyd, she was starting to have some trouble trusting the police herself.

She rooted through her pockets until she found a business card and held it up. "There's a number there for general calls, you can ask to speak to our desk sergeant, or the captain. If you mention my name, there won't be any issues getting put through."

There was a long pause and then the door locks clicked. Margot had assumed the woman wouldn't actually call it in, and had been correct.

When the door opened a petite woman with bleached blonde hair peered out at them. Her face was freshly washed and her hair still damp. With the door open the smell of coffee was even more potent, and Margot badly wanted some even though she knew she shouldn't. Sleep would need to come soon, and coffee wasn't going to do her any favors there.

Still, the scent of it made her mouth water.

"You guys are cops?" Clea asked, as if she hadn't already confirmed that with her questioning. Perhaps she was hoping to catch them in a lie now.

"Yes. Do you mind if we come in? We have a few questions for you." Margot tried to keep her voice soft and friendly.

"Your card said *Homicide*," Clea noted. At least Margot knew she'd read it. "What do homicide cops want with me?" Her gaze went between the two of them, but the moment she looked at Wes she immediately looked away. She seemed to shrink into herself.

Margot had seen that same behavior before in abused women. The way they tried to make themselves invisible to men, like they could avoid ever being hurt again if they could only slip through the world unseen.

How much of that was because of Drake Winston?

Or was he just the first of many bad boyfriends?

"We want to talk to you about your ex-boyfriend, Drake Winston," Margot said, and watched Clea's face to see if it changed when she heard the name.

It did. An immediate fear response flashed in her eyes and her cheeks flushed red. Her gaze darted behind them, as if she half expected Winston to be standing there waiting, like using his name out loud could summon him.

Any concerns Margot had that Clea might call Drake the moment they left here vanished into the ether. This woman wanted nothing to do with Drake Winston, and now Margot wanted to know why.

She was also looking at Clea for any signs of why Drake might have picked the victims he did. Often, killers would target women who reminded them either of an ex-girlfriend, or of their mothers. But the Redwood Killer victims had all been unique in their appearance. Different hair color, different builds, different ethnicities. The only thing they seemed to have in common was their connection to Emmanuel Riga's escort agency. And now, looking at Clea, Margot could see that at least physically she was not the trigger for their killer's actions, if their killer was Drake.

She was a little on the chubby side, her curves further accentuated by her short stature. She had one of those faces that would look permanently childlike, even into old age, with round cheeks and wide eyes.

Finally, she seemed to accept that Drake wasn't with them and she stepped out of the way, letting them into her apartment.

Much like the rest of the building, Clea Rice's apartment was slightly shabby with the wear and tear of age, but was otherwise neatly kept. It was a small studio, with an already-made daybed under one of the windows, facing an old tube-style TV that probably weighed almost as much as Clea did. The space reminded Margot a lot of her own apartment. Everything looked second-hand but well maintained. A tabby cat peered out from under the daybed before disappearing again.

The animal's skittishness reminded Margot of Clea's.

They followed Clea inside to the small kitchen that took up part of one wall. She poured herself a coffee from an ancient-looking perk, and did not offer them any. There was nowhere to sit besides the bed and an old armchair under one window, so Margot stood while Wes paced, keeping as much distance as he could in the small space.

He must have gotten the same vibe from Clea as Margot had, and known implicitly that this witness would do better talking to Margot alone. Little did Clea know that she'd likely get more of the warm-and-fuzzy kid gloves she probably needed if she had talked to Wes instead.

Clea didn't meet Margot's eye, she just looked into her coffee mug. Her shoulders were hunched, and she leaned against her kitchen counter like she needed the help to remain upright.

"Clea, we understand that you were previously in a relationship with Drake Winston, is that correct?"

Clea nodded. "Yeah."

"How long were you together?"

"About a year." A shudder made her whole body tremble, as if the memory of that year was wired into her flesh and merely talking about it brought back the kind of thoughts that made Clea want to escape her own skin.

"We noticed there was a dropped assault charge, but that you later filed a restraining order against him that's still active. When was the last time you talked to him?"

"I don't talk to him, that's part of the agreement of the restraining order."

"Then when was the last time he tried to contact you?" Margot clarified.

Clea shrugged, giving her mug a little swirl and watching the creamer inside move. "I've blocked all his numbers, but sometimes he gets a new phone or calls me from someone else's. Then I block those numbers. I think the last one was probably last week sometime. As soon as I know it's him, I just hang up."

"I know this is a difficult topic, but do you think you could explain to us what Drake did that made you decide you finally needed to get that protection order?"

Clea looked up at her then, not at the chin, but right in Margot's eyes.

"You're homicide detectives."

"Yes."

"Is Drake dead?"

The raw hopefulness of Clea's tone made Margot's heart hurt. It was the first time in her entire career she was sorry that she wasn't here to tell someone that their former partner was dead.

"No. As far as we know, Drake Winston is still alive."

Clea gave a solemn nod, then looked back into the depths of her coffee mug.

"Well, then. I guess you're here because he finally killed someone."

SEVENTEEN

1994

Ed opened the bedroom door slowly, wishing he had paid better attention to it when he had come into the house. Had it squeaked? Was there a shush of carpet on the underside of the door itself when it moved? What kind of secrets was it going to tell?

The door held its tongue, quiet as the grave.

When he stepped into the hallway, he couldn't help but hazard a glance over to the living room, where the flickering blue light of the TV danced on the walls and the empty couch.

The empty couch.

Ed stared in horror at the vacant piece of furniture. He'd only braved this move because he'd been certain that Bethenny's guest was relaxing and watching a movie. She was supposed to have her feet kicked up on the sofa, to be half-asleep, lulled into a stupor thanks to whatever nonsense was currently playing.

She was supposed to be right there.

The sound of a flush nearby got his attention and he broke

out into a cold sweat. *Run*, the voice in his head screamed at him. *Just turn around and get the fuck out of here.* But for some reason his body simply wasn't listening. This felt like one of the first times he'd ever peeked in a bedroom window at night, when the threat of being spotted was almost too real and kept him transfixed.

Almost like he wanted to get caught.

His pulse throbbed in his throat, and he knew that he had only two options: to go back into the bedroom and continue his interminable wait; or to turn around and bolt for the front door before that bathroom door opened.

He did neither.

The bathroom door opened.

For a moment, they both stood in absolute shock, both deer and car caught up in mutual uncertainty over what was happening and what should happen next. The voice in Ed's head continued to scream at him to run, but another part, a calmer part, said something different.

She's seen you now.

The girl was young, maybe eighteen, and she bore a striking similarity to Bethenny. Sister, then, or possibly cousin. But sister seemed far more likely given the obvious similarities. This girl's hair had been dyed black and she sported a nose ring and torn jeans. Ed wasn't sure if this was punk revival or that Seattle grunge movement he'd been hearing about, but either way she had managed to make herself significantly less attractive thanks to her efforts.

Her mouth hung open slightly, as if she was trying to decide if he was real, and if she was supposed to talk to him.

"Are you Bethy's boyfriend?" she asked finally.

God, she was so young. His own daughter wasn't so far off from being this age, but he knew Megan would have more common sense than to ruin her hair or face with this kind of pointless protest nonsense. What was she protesting anyway? Looking good? Congratulations, success.

Ed continued to look at her for a long moment, trying to figure out what he was supposed to do next. He'd come here to spend some quality time with Bethenny, and he'd done that. Now this next part of his night was either going to be a challenge, or a pleasant surprise, depending on whatever he did next.

He couldn't run. Not anymore, not with her looking him right in the eye. She'd seen too much, and the moment she walked into that bedroom and found Bethenny's body, the girl would remember his face down to the finest stubble, to the little scar on his forehead. She would be able to pick him out of any lineup.

So, no. He couldn't run. He was going to have to see this through. And thanks to the simple miscalculation of going to the bathroom when she did, that meant the girl in front of him had to die.

He didn't *want* to kill her, not in the way he did with his other victims. He picked his girls so carefully, watched them, learned every nuance of their routine until he felt like he was truly a part of their lives. He waited, prepared, and he only struck when he knew the moment was right. That was part of the pleasure for him, understanding that he'd calculated everything perfectly, and that the final result was the effort of a job well done.

This girl wasn't part of any plan. She wasn't someone he was interested in spending time with, in luxuriating over. She was merely an obstacle he needed to tackle, something getting in his way.

So, even though he knew he needed to kill her, it wasn't something he was going to take any enjoyment out of.

"You're her sister?" he asked.

She seemed to brighten momentarily, like this was her confirmation that he was, indeed, Bethenny's boyfriend.

"Yeah!" she enthused.

Then her gaze drifted down to his hands, where the red stain of her sister's blood was as obvious as day. He glanced down at it, then back to her.

"You picked a really bad weekend to visit," he said with a sigh.

EIGHTEEN

"I always knew he was going to kill somebody someday."

Margot had guided Clea over to the armchair, worried she might lose her balance at any moment. There was something so incredibly fragile about the girl, like her bones might break if she smiled too hard.

Not that she struck Margot as someone who smiled very much.

She seemed to be the kind of person who was afraid of her own shadow. Margot thought her own fears and uncertainties made her lead a shut-off life, but crouched down in front of Clea, she understood that she *was* brave, despite being afraid of the possibilities of evil in the world.

Clea, on the other hand, was shut down because she had faced those evils head on and they'd gotten the best of her.

Margot wished she could hug the girl, but wasn't sure that she wouldn't shatter in her arms.

"Did Drake ever express violent urges to you?" Margot asked.

Clea snorted, and set the coffee down on the small table beside her. The moment her lap was vacant the little tabby cat appeared out of nowhere and settled himself in, kneading his claws into Clea's leg and purring happily. Clea absentmindedly stroked the animal, and Margot watched in awe as all the stress she'd been carrying seemed to lift.

With the cat in her lap, Clea was able to look at Margot instead of needing to avoid her eyes.

"The thing about Drake is he didn't need to *talk* about violence. Drake just acted. He'd get this look in his eye, like the person I knew wasn't there anymore and someone else had taken over, and that's when I knew it was time to be scared. Sometimes I could get out of his way, but other times... well... other times you'd do your best to make it through until he ran out of energy, or the urge went away, you know? I can't really explain it any better than that."

Margot knew the look she meant. She had seen it in her own father, the way an instant could make someone you love into something that wasn't even human. She looked for that expression now whenever she sat across from a suspect in an interrogation room. It wasn't there for all of them, but sometimes if you knew what you were looking for you could spot it.

Clea knew how to spot it.

"He hurt you?" Margot asked.

"Hurting me was the easy part, I could kind of step away from myself when that happened. I don't want to say you get used to it, but I guess after a while I got used to it. I learned what set him off, learned how to avoid it for the most part. I'm just glad Gilligan wasn't around then." She petted the cat fondly.

Animal abuse. Margot made a mental check, not that Drake had done anything to the cat, thank God, but Clea's belief that he was capable was all Margot needed to hear.

"What really got me wasn't the physical stuff, it was what he *said.* He would talk about all the things he wanted to do to me, and it was..." Clea's voice caught in her throat, choking. She took a moment, looking out the window. Her fingers worked almost mindlessly, stroking the cat, the one thing keeping her grounded.

Clea let out a shuddering sigh. "He made my life so hard. He kept me from my friends, from my family. He said if I ever left him that he would go to my father's work and tell everyone in his office that he was a rapist. He would go to my mother's office and say she was robbing them. He told me if I talked about him to my friends he would follow them home at night." She roughly swiped at her face, chasing back a tear Margot hadn't even noticed. "He made sure I had nothing, that I only had him. And then one night I just had enough. He was making dinner and he said, 'Do you know how easy it would be for me to gut you with this? You'd bleed out, right here on the kitchen floor.' The way he said it, the look in his eyes, it was like he'd spent so much time thinking about it, like it was only a matter of time."

Clea lifted Gilligan the cat and snuggled him close to her, peppering his head with kisses. The tabby squinted his eyes happily, rubbing his head against Clea's chin.

Margot wondered if the reason Clea had come here, to this terrible place, was that it was the last place Drake might come looking for her. It was the kind of place where people came to disappear.

"Clea, do you think Drake is capable of murder?"

Clea nodded, not even hesitating. "I think all it would take was someone crossing him on the wrong day."

"Did he ever talk to you about his work?"

"About the parties, you mean?"

"Yes."

"He wasn't allowed to say much. He really liked to brag about having to sign an NDA. I think he felt like it made him important, and he also loved to know things I didn't know. He would drop hints constantly. Tell me he served an actor I loved but couldn't tell me who it was. Or that a model flirted with him, but he couldn't say which one—that kind of thing. It was so frustrating. But then, on the flip side, he'd be bragging about how much he made in tips, then he'd turn around and spend an hour bitching about the wealthy, and how sick they all were, and about how all the women at those parties were whores and if I ever did a job like that he would kill me before he ever let another man look at me. I don't even know, were they actually hookers?" She looked at Margot uncertainly.

Margot gave a half-shrug. "Many of them were escorts. They worked for a pretty high-end company. A lot of them also had normal jobs on the side. Boyfriends. Families."

Clea seemed to understand what she was saying.

"Did he do something to one of those girls?" she asked.

"We don't know, that's what we're trying to find out."

"If he did, he didn't tell me."

"This would have started after you two broke up," Margot amended.

Clea thought about this for a moment. "How long after we broke up?"

Margot thought she was trying to decide if she had some blame in all of this. To Drake, if he was their killer, she might. But Margot didn't want that weighing on this poor girl's head.

"Years. At least a few years, as far as we can tell."

"Clea," Wes interjected softly. "I know you don't want to spend a lot of time thinking about that part of your life, we understand that. But do you happen to have anything of Drake's left? Maybe an old toothbrush, or hairbrush?"

Clea stared at Wes like he was speaking another language, but slowly she seemed to come around.

"Oh. You want his DNA, don't you?" She passed the cat to Margot, who hadn't been expecting a purring feline in her arms and ended up locked in a staring contest with him. Clea disappeared into the kitchen where she opened up the freezer and started rummaging around behind the ice cube trays. Margot pretended not to notice the rolled-up ball of cash that got pushed to one side, until Clea found what she was looking for and came back to them. In her hands was a small freezer bag, which she held out. Printed in tidy writing on the foggy plastic were the words, *If anything happens to me, it was Drake.*

Inside there were three items: a straw, a bloody tissue, and a condom. Margot wasn't entirely sure about the cross-contamination issues that might be present, and she didn't envy whatever lab technician needed to open that bag later, but she took it from Clea's trembling hand and for the first time the girl met her gaze head-on.

"I thought someday someone might need it."

Margot passed the cat back to Clea, once again marveling at how instantaneous the relief was that washed over the girl.

"Turns out you were right," Margot said, with a soft smile. "Though, I'm glad it wasn't for the reason you thought it would be."

NINETEEN

Margot wanted to sleep for about seven hundred years, but the first thing she needed to do was to get this new evidence to the CSI team immediately. Back in the car, she slid the freezer bag into a larger evidence bag and filled in the details on the front, before passing it over to Wes.

This had been the day that wouldn't end, but Margot was amazed that her visit to Jesse less than twenty-four hours earlier had actually managed to net them something resembling a result.

Margot was desperately trying not to get her hopes up, but their visit with Clea had her putting the cart way before the horse. But there was simply no way to tamp down the fizzy sensation of excitement bubbling in her stomach. Yes, there was every possibility that Stephen Kramer might turn out to be their guy, even though he had no red flags. Not every killer was an obvious killer. But Drake Winston had more red flags than a Chinese flag factory, and Margot couldn't ignore that.

At a certain point, when all the evidence seemed to lead them in only one direction, that direction had to be the right one. It was the homicide version of Occam's Razor. But they needed to be careful they didn't ignore things that might point them in another direction simply because they *wanted* it to be the most obvious person.

Tunnel vision could be a real issue on some cases, and in this case in particular Margot was so desperate to find the killer that a suspect—a really good suspect—was so enticing it became hard *not* to get too excited.

Still, she knew they had to be careful. This could all turn out to be circumstantial and Drake might not end up being their guy.

Stephen Kramer might not, either.

This was just one lead, after all, but it was the best lead they'd had in almost a year, and Margot was having a very hard time keeping her enthusiasm at bay.

As they drove away from Clea's apartment, neither of them spoke, though Margot could feel the same uneasy excitement radiating from Wes that she was feeling herself. His knee was jostling, something that only happened when he was especially wound up about something. They still had one stop to make before they would be able to call it a day. Margot headed toward the main CSI lab, where they would drop off Clea's bag of DNA evidence. She wasn't an expert on DNA, but she did know there was a possibility of sample deterioration because the things Clea had saved had been in the freezer for almost five years. They might not yield anything useful, but Margot— unusually for her—was trying to stay optimistic. All it would take was one match. Would it be enough to lock the guy up permanently? Hell no, they'd need way more than a condom someone had kept in a freezer to convince a jury. But it might be enough to convince a judge.

Once they found their guy, Margot hoped that he was cocky enough or stupid enough to have left more evidence for them to find. So far, the Redwood Killer had been careful, but that was at his crime scenes. People tended to get a lot sloppier in their own homes and their own lives.

Plus, there was a good chance he was keeping trophies of some kind from his victims. Not every killer did, but those who killed the way this man did were likely to. He would want to remember his crimes, want to relive them. Margot wouldn't be surprised if they learned that this killer, be it Drake, Stephen, or someone else, would have made multiple visits to Muir Woods just to walk around and bask in the environment where he'd left his victims.

Margot wished she'd asked Clea if Drake was an active hiker, but there would be time to find that out later.

What they needed now was evidence that could help them bring this guy down. The smaller details could fall into place when they had the luxury of digging deeper. Because given the two bodies they'd found that week, it seemed likely that their killer might be moving in a more aggressive direction, potentially spiraling out of control. They needed to get him locked up now before any of the other women on that website turned up dead.

Margot understood why the website used fake names, it was obviously important to protect the anonymity of the women outside their work, but it was frustrating because Margot wished she could warn every single one of those girls to be careful. To look behind them. To lock their doors.

It was the same thing she wished for every body she stood over. That she could have imparted some kind of protective wisdom that might have kept them from being there.

Margot and Wes parked in front of the police lab and she carried in the double-bagged evidence like it was something both delicate and dangerous, a time bomb, or a baby viper.

They checked in at the front and were directed to the office of the lead CSI, DeAndra Leggit.

As usual, despite Margot's own lack of enthusiasm about still being awake, DeAndra was peppy and bright, smiling at both of them as they sat down across from her desk. Her braids were worn in a thick topknot today, and her rich brown skin was glowing despite all the time she must spend inside. Margot's own complexion typically veered between deathly pale and sunburned thanks to her Irish ancestors. She was profoundly jealous of anyone she met who managed to maintain a skincare routine. Serums and salves weren't something she had the patience for.

Margot also knew she was getting close to the point of exhaustion when she started overthinking people's chosen moisturizers.

She set the bag down on DeAndra's desk, almost grateful to be rid of it, but more than anything she was anxious about what would and wouldn't be found in its contents. DeAndra held the bag up, remarkably unmoved by the sight of a used condom, and arched a brow of question in their direction.

"What's so special about this that it deserved an in-person delivery, detectives?"

As she waited for their response, she started to fill in an evidence transfer form so they would later be able to track the evidence handling chain. DeAndra might be too perky for her own good, but she was probably the best and most professional head CSI that Margot had ever worked with. Margot appreciated people who contained multitudes.

"We think those samples might belong to the Redwood Killer." She cringed at herself for using the media's name for him out loud, even though she had long ago started to use it in her own mind. She hated adopting the nicknames that the public took on for these people because she found that they tended to make killers sound like the worst superheroes alive. She vastly preferred killers be remembered by their names, but in this case, they didn't *have* a name yet, and to differentiate this killer from all the other unknown suspects they were working with it was easier to use a name everyone recognized.

Still, she loathed the ease with which it rolled off her tongue.

DeAndra's eyes widened for a moment, appreciating the gravity of the evidence. "We'll do everything we can to get a rush process on this, but I have to warn you, the labs are backed up, and they don't particularly believe that one sample has merit over another. But I think, given the gravity of what we're dealing with here, I *might* be able to pull a few strings."

"If they're reluctant, I'm sure that Pressley Boyd could get the mayor and maybe even the governor to put a little weight behind you. This case is a priority to public safety," Margot urged.

"While you know that, and I know that, I also know why the lab treats every sample with equal consideration of importance. If every front-page murder got priority, then the smaller, less flashy cases would keep getting bumped to the bottom of the queue. And I know all of us in this room believe that every victim deserves their justice, not just those who get the most press."

DeAndra smiled, though there was some tension behind it. She must have had to deal with detectives every day from across the city insisting that their case should go right to the top of the heap. Margot understood, she really did. But for once she truly believed their case *did* deserve special treatment, and she believed DeAndra felt the same.

No victim had more value than any other, but in this case the onus was on them to protect all the *potential* victims of this maniac. And that had weight.

Margot explained how they came by the samples, and she noted the disappointment flit momentarily across DeAndra's face when Margot told her how old the samples were and how they'd been stored.

"You understand we can't make any promises about the viability of the evidence," DeAndra cautioned.

"We know," Wes said, his voice calm, steady, helping soothe Margot's frayed and exhausted nerves. She gave him a grateful look. He must have known she was at risk of barking back some kind of tense retort. She didn't *want* to be snarky, but she wasn't at her best on minimal sleep and high stress.

It didn't help that her next visit with Ed was looming, as well as the deeply undesirable prospect of a day or more in court. None of that was making her any cheerier. She didn't want to take out her annoyance on DeAndra and was grateful that her partner could read her well enough to know when intervention might be required.

Wes got her.

Better than anyone.

They wrapped up with DeAndra's repeated promise she would do her best to get them results as quickly as possible. It was agonizing to be so close to a result but knowing it was still out of reach.

Margot dropped Wes at his apartment with a promise to pick him up for their evening shift that evening, then headed back to her own place, feeling like a zombie as she took Betty out for a much-needed break. The street was dead quiet, a rarity for San Francisco no matter the time of day, and it made Margot feel like she and Betty had been transported to the set of a post-apocalyptic film. But perhaps that was her exhaustion draining the life out of everything she looked at. She'd been burnt out by cases before, but this one was really starting to get to her.

Maybe she was only feeling it now because they were close. Like, her body had kept her going long enough to get to the finish line, but now that the end was in sight, everything was starting to break down.

It was more than that, though, and she knew it. The weight wasn't just the Redwood Killer case. It was Pressley Boyd. It was the injustice of it all. It was knowing that years of her life had been spent fighting the good fight, but as it turned out, she didn't even know who she was fighting for.

She wanted desperately to sleep, but she had reached a point now where she was actually too tired to sleep. Her mind was racing, though none of the thoughts had any useful substance.

After helping Betty up onto the worn-out old couch, she poured herself some gin, topping it off with no-name lemon-lime soda, and sat next to her dog. She sipped the drink, staring at her TV without comprehending what she had selected to watch, until she realized she *hadn't* picked, and her streaming service had started auto-playing one of the most popular titles.

The Ed Finch docuseries.

She didn't make the connection until her own face was looking back at her from the TV screen.

Margot watched herself, marveling at the woman she saw staring back. That Margot had been ballsy. She'd done something terrifying so she could stake a claim on her own name, her own story. She had made herself uncomfortable in order to find peace.

That Margot was inside her still, even if she didn't feel particularly brave at the moment.

She lifted her glass toward the TV. "Cheers to you, Megan Finch."

On the screen, a producer asked her, "What was your father like when you were growing up?"

Tough TV Margot stared back, and said, "The same way he is now: selfish, cruel, and demanding. It just never occurred to me back then that wasn't normal."

Margot turned off the TV.

Who the hell needed normal, anyway?

TWENTY

The world moved on as Margot slept, but she wouldn't have known it from her practically comatose state.

If it were up to her, she would probably work non-stop. She didn't have a social life, and until she'd adopted Betty by accident, she hadn't had any reason to come back to the apartment between shifts. But she was still human, and human beings apparently needed to sleep sometimes so they didn't become insane and die.

She woke feeling renewed if not refreshed, with the taste of gin still on her tongue and the smudged mascara under her eyes. She also found that there were about a dozen texts on her phone from Leon, Wes, and Andrew. Her heart was racing before she was even out of bed, but as she pulled the messages up, her pulse stilled. No one was dead, no one had been arrested.

The messages from Leon and Wes were part of a group text chain. Evidently Wes wanted to share their progress with Leon, and they'd had a brief conversation while Margot had been fast asleep. She was relieved that the conversation hadn't shed any new light on things but also felt a pang of guilt for having missed out on it.

The message from Andrew was a single line.

We are on for tomorrow.

She glanced at her phone to check the time, just after four in the afternoon. She had barely slept for five hours, and she felt it.

The week had been passing in such a blur Margot had all but forgotten how soon her visit with Ed would come and the tension it would bring with it. The meeting would also mean that she'd have time one-on-one with Andrew, and he would almost certainly want to know if she had thought about his offer.

She had. In the back of her mind it was a constant white noise, not necessarily distracting her, but ever present. She had no idea what she was going to do, but the fact that her answer wasn't an immediate *no* made her think that she might have been secretly longing for an opportunity like this for a long time.

That alone made her think she needed to talk this through with some people before she gave Andrew her final answer, but she also had bigger fish to fry before she decided to upend her entire life and career.

Solve the case, then decide.

Be finished with Ed, then decide.

Wipe the slate clean before making any crazy choices. It seemed like the right thing to do.

But how clean could the slate get if she was working every day with the same people who made her go visit her serial killer father in prison so they could close cases?

What would change once they were finished with Ed that would make them see her as a person and not just a means to an end? That was something she was really going to need to think about if she decided to take the job.

She sent Andrew a thumbs-up emoji, then threw an oversized Giants hoodie over her pajamas to take Betty out for a quick walk. Once Betty was relieved and had sniffed the new marks left behind since early that morning, Margot was able to have a quick shower and eat some leftover pad Thai that was in the fridge. It wasn't a sexy meal, but by God, Thai food could do no wrong.

It took her twice as long to get to Wes's apartment in the afternoon as it had bright and early that morning when she dropped him off, and Margot cursed rush hour and distracted drivers the whole way there. She felt like taking out her portable light and pulling people over when she saw them on their phones, veering over lines and blissfully ignoring red lights.

She never did, but the urge didn't go away.

Wes was waiting for her out front, a sight for sore eyes, two cups of coffee in hand, because he was consistent and he was wonderful.

As Margot watched him approach the car, she wondered how many coffees Wes had bought her over the course of their partnership. How automatic it was for him to think of her, how many thousands of dollars he must have invested in making sure she always stayed caffeinated.

And as he handed her the cup emblazoned with a logo for a coffee shop she could see just down the block, she realized in that moment she loved him.

It hit her as suddenly as the answer to unravel a case, as if it had been there in front of her all this time, but one small thing, something completely innocuous, was the key to making it all come together.

She took the coffee, and found that rather than saying thank you, or making a quip or teasing him like she might normally, all she could do was stare at him. He was still Wes, still unchanged. His square jaw—freshly shaved—his sandy hair and brown eyes, the way he made efforts every day to look good, a little bit like Steve McQueen or Robert Redford, and how that had become a part of who he was to her. Too handsome by far for his own good, and too smart and charming to be healthy for someone who was as attractive as he was.

Yet he'd only been Wes, her Wes, and that had meant so many things to her over the course of their partnership. It meant learning to trust someone, meant letting herself be vulnerable. She realized how much she'd changed in that respect; there was a relief to it that was unlike anything she had known before.

Being with Wes had meant confusion over her feelings, fear of losing a friend, because of the risk of giving in to a physical attraction that had been undeniable.

But now she knew it wasn't just attraction, it wasn't just friendship or loyalty.

Margot had never been in love as an adult, making it hard for her to recognize the feeling and give it a name.

The coffee had done that for her.

"Thanks," she said finally, when inside she was in turmoil over what to do with this new discovery.

Months ago, Wes had wanted to have a conversation with her, to tell her something, and she had pleaded with him not to do it at the time. She wasn't ready to hear it.

Now, instead of feeling ready, she felt even more terrified at the prospect of what he might have to say. Because the enormity of her feeling—now that she had named it—meant there was so much more to lose than just a friend.

It could mean losing everything.

She took a sip from her coffee, but even though she knew it was perfect, she couldn't taste a thing.

As they drove, he apparently noticed the turn in her attitude. "You sleep OK?" he asked. "I can always get things started when we get to the office if you need to crash on the couch for a bit."

Margot smiled, something that came as easily to her as

breathing when Wes was involved. Another thing she should have realized sooner, because she was *not* a smiley person.

"No, I slept like a rock," she lied. "I should be asking you that—you and Leon were up until the wee hours of the afternoon, gossiping like schoolgirls."

Wes snorted. "We sent, like, five messages—you're only mad you weren't involved."

"Guilty."

"Well, I gather from the complete lack of updates since that there haven't been any big breaks in our absence, so that's lucky, I guess."

"Lucky for our FOMO but not so much for the actual case," Margot reminded him.

"Touché."

Margot found a parking spot a few blocks from the precinct. She realized that in a different scenario she would have made a bigger deal of bugging him about his car and asking how long he was going to force her to be his chauffeur, but the issue was she *couldn't*.

She didn't want him to get his car fixed.

A few extra minutes together, just them, no demands from the outside world, it was marvelous. And even if the only thing they had talked about was work, it was still uninterrupted time with him, something that she now realized she couldn't get enough of.

Why didn't they spend more time together?

Sure, they spent every waking hour of their workday sitting across from each other, or in cars, or at crime scenes. But now that she did a mental inventory of the past year—the time that they'd really started to become something more than simply partners—she realized her only good memories outside of solving cases were the times she and Wes were together.

God, she'd been so stupid.

All of those concerns got pushed to the shuttered recesses of her mind the moment they stepped through their office door, though. There had been a good reason that Margot had asked Wes not to share his feelings with her, and it was because the timing was all wrong. It might be true, also, that there was no convenient time to tell someone you loved them, but right now was an *especially* bad time to start delving into feelings.

They needed to catch a killer, and once that was done, Margot would give herself the permission she was waiting for to open up to Wes, even though doing so scared the ever-loving shit out of her.

There was never going to be a perfect time, so she was opting to select a good enough time.

Lock up the Redwood Killer, *then* pretend like she could have a personal life. It seemed like a fair balance.

It was like a little reward waiting for her at the end of the road, something she never really thought about. Usually, she did the work for the sake of the work, and also out of an idea that by helping solve murder cases, she might be able to create some kind of karmic balance in the universe to counter all the evil her father had done.

She'd talked to her therapist about that idea a lot, and he'd helped her to understand that she wasn't responsible for any kind of restorative justice. But even though she knew in her heart that it didn't *work* like that, she still couldn't help but feel responsible. Someone in her family needed to do something, and it seemed like, at this point, she was the only one willing to try.

Of course, now that she'd revealed who she was, there were plenty of people in the world who had Opinions with a capital O about why she did her work. Some people on the internet understood it, and were supportive of what she was attempting to do. A few people had shared their thoughts that it was all performative. And there was a small group of people in a serial killer subreddit who seemed to think she was a serial killer herself and using her day job to help cover her tracks. If the notion didn't rankle her so much, she might almost find it funny.

Thankfully no one with an ounce of common sense gave that idea any real credence, but the whole thing did start to make Margot wonder what all of this was *for.* She had been working her whole adult life, not toward some dream or some goal, but just trying to capture the feeling that she had done some good in a world where evil seemed to be ever-present.

She settled in at her computer to review the emails that had come in during the day, and tried to focus on the task at hand rather than the seeming futility of what she had lived her life for up until now. That was a bit too morose for this early in the shift.

There was plenty to catch up on, even if none of it had hit the group chat. It looked like the day team had done quite the intensive dive into Stephen Kramer, and come back with absolutely no indication he was their man. Kramer was a regular volunteer at both a soup kitchen and an animal shelter. He was divorced, but according to the day crew it looked as if he and his ex were very amicable and shared custody of a Rottweiler named Ted. This was all easily accessible through his social media profile where he and the ex frequently left each other comments and he would post pictures of himself and the dog saying, *Picked up the fur son for the week.*

While Margot was very aware that someone could seem harmless on the surface while containing murderous multitudes they hid from even those closest to them, there were absolutely no red flags with this guy. One of the detectives had found his dating profiles on Hinge and Bumble and the best Margot could see from the screenshots was that his only questionable personality trait was his love of Wes Anderson.

Being twee didn't make him a serial killer.

Based on all the background work done in the hours she'd

been sleeping, it truly looked as if Kramer hadn't done a single thing to warrant suspicion. They would obviously continue to monitor him, try to find a more recent DNA sample to compare to their victim, but even by the tone in the emails she was reading it was clear no one thought this was their guy.

The day team had also been looking into Drake Winston. Beyond all the information Margot and Wes had been able to dig up in the early stages of investigating him, the team scouring his digital footprint had found plenty to be concerned about. They had discovered a public Instagram account for him and used that username to check better known online forums, finding his profile on Facebook, Twitter, and Reddit. The contents of his Twitter and Reddit accounts were the most alarming, as he seemed to frequently contribute video game stills to a group that only existed to look at violence happening to female characters in video games. Drake seemed to relish sharing screenshots of female characters bloodied and often mangled beyond repair.

On Twitter things were even more glaringly vile. He retweeted a lot of right-wing misogynists and anti-feminist rhetoric. Margot only knew peripherally of the internet "red pill" culture that was slowly emerging, in which men claimed they were awakening to reality and needed to establish a male-first agenda, promote alpha male stereotypes, and debase and abuse women online as often as possible.

The idea of "alpha" as an idea of the idealized male made Margot chuckle a little because it was rooted in the idea that a wolf pack was led by an alpha male, when in fact wolf packs were family hierarchies with a primary male and female mated pair typically being the top of the pecking order.

These guys couldn't even use their nature metaphors properly.

But there was nothing funny about what Drake was sharing and posting online. The screenshots and links Margot was looking at showed someone with a lot of hatred, specifically hatred toward women, and in his posts, she was starting to see the shape of a motive for his crimes.

This was a man who believed that other men, richer men, better-looking men, were dominating the pool of available and desirable women. He thought—based on his online rhetoric—that he deserved to have one of these women, but had been rejected time and time again. Margot could only assume that at least one of those rejections had come from one of Emmanuel Riga's Lark girls at a party where Drake had worked. It would make sense as an inciting incident that could have gotten this notion of retribution rolling in his mind.

His rhetoric, while hinted at in comments on Twitter and Reddit, became very clear in a lengthy Reddit post on the "Red Pill" subreddit for incel chatter as he talked about women as *bitches* and *sluts*, and opined that one day they would get their comeuppance for picking men with money over men with *real* high-value offerings. What Drake thought he had to offer that was so high-value Margot had no idea, but he seemed to believe he was chronically overlooked and under-appreciated by the women he most desired.

And most reviled.

While his posts did not explicitly mention violence or murder, there was an undercurrent of threat through most of what he shared. He talked a lot about women *getting what they deserved*—it was a key phrase that came up over and over—and Margot didn't think he meant that those women would marry a nice guy like him.

There was definitely something more insidious at the heart of his intention.

She didn't want to get too carried away with these posts; they were the musings of someone on the internet, after all, not a smoking gun, not solid proof. Later, if this went to trial, social media posts like this would most certainly be widely circulated in both the actual courtroom and the court of public opinion.

Drake only had a small handful of followers on his social media accounts; more men like him complaining about how nice guys finish last.

"You know, I'm suddenly really happy I haven't dated in the past decade," Margot mused.

"I'm betting most of these guys haven't been on a date in at least that long," Wes replied, obviously looking at the same information that had been sent to her. "Talk about a warped sense of privilege. These jackasses really think they're owed something."

"Yeah, and there's a good chance it has cost at least five women their lives," Margot replied, letting out a sigh and closing Drake's Twitter account. It was too depressing to keep reading it. Someone had already done the legwork of flagging notable posts that had gone up around the days of some of the first murders. Nothing incriminating, but plenty of veiled gloating about putting women in their place.

Asked a girl out and she said no, told her I would have been doing her fat ass a favor.

Dating apps are just for bitches who can't get a man in person. Why bother?

This one bitch who was too good for me was begging me to give her a second chance, but I said no.

Margot paused, a chill shuddering through her as she looked at the date, only six months earlier.

Was the woman he referred to begging to date him, or begging for her life?

Bile tickled the back of Margot's throat and she swallowed it down. It was hard to read these posts and not see the mind of a killer at work, but the truth was, just looking at the accounts he followed and the activity of some of his favorite Reddit boards, it was obvious there were tens of thousands of men who shared this same hatred for women, and Margot knew they weren't all killers.

It *was* possible to hate women and not kill them.

But in Drake's case Margot was getting that familiar sensation she felt when she sat across the interrogation table from a guilty man. There was something so telling about reading his own words, and hearing how frightened Clea had been of him—enough that she would keep evidence, just in case—that told Margot this wasn't all coincidental.

She only hoped she was right.

The wait was agonizing, knowing that they were this close to getting their man but not having the means to make a move yet. They needed good, solid evidence before they could arrest him, and without fingerprints or video footage tying him to the crimes, what they were waiting for was the DNA match.

Normally she could be patient while waiting for results, but this case was different. It felt so much more vital that they get what they needed to lock this guy up, and every hour they didn't have their answer felt like an eternity.

Leon came into their office and pulled up an extra chair, sitting between Margot's desk and Wes's. He still looked exhausted but at least it did seem like he'd gotten *some* sleep between the last time he'd seen them and now. Margot hadn't really taken a good look at herself in the mirror this morning, but she expected she looked equally worse for wear.

Leon scratched his dark beard, which looked as if it had been trimmed right before he came on shift, and she noticed how gray the hairs were starting to get. Same with the coloring around his temples. Leon wasn't a young man anymore, but this case seemed to be leeching the life right out of him.

She hadn't noticed till now how much it was taking its toll, and wondered what he was putting on the backburner, waiting until this case was over and he could reclaim some part of himself. Was he sacrificing his health, his marriage, his well-being? There was a reason so many cops got divorces, and died of heart disease. This wasn't an easy job.

"Seems like we missed a lot of legwork," Margot said, leaning her head toward the computer screen. The one drawback of the night shift—aside from often pulling the worst crime scenes—was that the world and its work kept ticking away while Margot slept. If her body, and admittedly her age, didn't demand that she actually needed sleep, she would have pulled twenty-hour days, catching naps on the love seat, desperate to be here for every moment.

In a way, she was disappointed to have missed any tidbits the task force had dug up on Drake, the internet history, the background checks. She knew that it was all necessary work, and she couldn't solve this case single-handedly, but everything she wasn't around for felt like something she had to catch up on.

None of it was the *thing* that would break the case wide open, but all the tiny pieces of circumstantial evidence would help prosecutors nail down their case when this went to trial. The more they could pile up against him, the less reasonable doubt.

And once they had those DNA results, the case would be rock solid.

"Yeah." Leon gave a quick nod, and for a moment he let his eyes close as he rested his head against the back of the chair. Margot wanted to offer him a quick doze on their shitty couch, but she knew he'd never go for it. He was in charge of this case, and he wouldn't rest until it was closed.

"Branson—the kid you guys went out with the other night— he and another detective took the photos of Kramer and Winston out to Richard Downey to see if he could ID them."

"Smart," Margot said with an approving nod. It had been Downey who sent them on this hunt in the first place, so he was a good place to start. "What did he have to say?"

"Couldn't confirm Winston with absolute certainty but did seem to think he *might* have been someone who gave him bad vibes. Couldn't remember Kramer at all. I'm almost willing to drop Kramer completely, but I'd really like to get a DNA sample from him so we can rule him out. We don't want any stone unturned when this goes to trial. I think everyone here is convinced that Drake Winston is our guy, but we don't want to be so gung-ho about having *any* potential suspect that we miss something. I know we're all eager for this guy to be the one."

"And not for nothing," Margot said. "His ex-girlfriend had no trouble believing it was him. She hasn't been around him in almost five years, but she was still checking the shadows like he might be hiding under her bed."

"He's certainly guilty of being a real piece of work," Leon agreed. "But let's find out if he's guilty of murder."

TWENTY-ONE

In the immortal words of the great Tom Petty, the waiting was, indeed, the hardest part.

While Margot and Wes spent the bulk of their evening following up on minor leads and digging further into the publicly available information on Drake Winston, Leon busied himself preparing a warrant request for the moment they had enough to go on to bring it to a judge. They'd want to seize his computers, and anything in his place that might point to his connection to their murders. They'd need his car. Warrants had to be very specific, and Leon wanted to make sure theirs was ready to go as soon as *something* came back for them to make a request.

In the meantime, there were cops watching both Kramer and Winston twenty-four-seven, something that was certainly eating into their available resources, but it also gave Margot a limited sense of comfort knowing that Drake Winston wasn't going to be able to hurt anyone else on their watch.

That was enough to give her the ability to leave when the end of their shift rolled around early the next morning. She had reached her off day, and however hard it was to leave when they were so close to catching their killer, she had a date with an entirely different monster.

After a trip home that allowed her enough time to walk the dog, shower, and have a short one-hour nap, Margot was back in her car—this time without Wes.

She had barely had time to think about this visit, and she was glad of that as she felt the familiar twinge of anxiety following the path north to San Quentin. How many more times would she need to make this drive? How long would it take before her brain stopped going on autopilot the moment she hit the Golden Gate Bridge? Between the Redwood Killer's hunting grounds in Muir Woods, to the bleak edifice of the prison just a few more miles down the road, there were so many bitter memories wrapped up in this one stretch of land. She was starting to wonder if there would ever be a time she could come this way and not think about death.

Andrew was waiting for her in the building where guests could come check in and pass through security to visit their loved ones. It always amazed her, the little children dressed in their best clothes like they were going to church. Mothers trying to smooth down cowlicks and clear away smudges of food on cheeks, as if the men inside were expecting some kind of refinement.

Margot hadn't even put her makeup back on after changing into her prison visitor garb.

She was going to burn these khakis once her visits with Ed were through.

She knew that was partly misguided rage directed toward Ed.

It was definitely never good to start one of these days with a bad attitude, but Margot couldn't muster any fake enthusiasm for something she didn't want to do. She should be sleeping, she should be eating takeout and watching low-stakes adult cartoons with her half-blind senior dog.

There were roughly a million things she would rather be doing with her day off than sitting here waiting to meet with her father.

Andrew sat down beside her on an uncomfortable metal bench while they waited for their escort to arrive.

"How you feeling?" he asked, his steel-blue eyes scrutinizing her from behind his signature tortoiseshell glasses. She looked at him, with his salt and pepper beard and the permanent aura of a college professor, and tried to remember who they had been when they first met. She'd been fifteen, and her entire world had just come crashing down around her. He had been in his early thirties, getting started with his BAU career with the FBI, and had managed to break one of the biggest unsolved cases in the country.

He was making a name for himself just as her name was getting taken from her.

He'd looked different then, though he hadn't changed so much as to be unrecognizable. Andrew had always had a sort of non-threatening handsomeness about him. The kind of attractiveness that people found comforting and trustworthy rather than off-putting. He still had that, though a more mature variation.

Admittedly, she wasn't the chubby teen she'd been. Life had turned them into different people, but there was something about sitting next to someone who had known you that long that made silences easy to stomach. For a long time, she didn't answer him and he didn't push her to.

"How do we know this is really the last one?" she asked, her jaw clenched so hard her teeth hurt.

"I guess we don't. He seemed very adamant last time we visited that he never lied about anything. I think he believes that. So, if he's telling us this is the last one, then part of me believes it must be."

He trusted in the honor of Ed's word far more than Margot did.

"I don't know how much longer I can do this," she admitted.

She expected him to ask why, to try to soothe her, or make some excuse about all the good she was doing, but instead, Andrew nodded his head and gave her shoulder a squeeze.

"I know. It's been a long haul. Don't think I don't see what it's taking out of you. That's the misery of this job, I'm afraid. It all chips away. But this is harder for you than the regular work is for the rest of us. I get it. I know it doesn't mean much, but I'm really goddamn proud of you."

Her gaze flicked to his, and she couldn't understand why, but a prickle of tears stung her eyes and she had to look down at her hands, because continuing to look at him became untenable.

All this time she'd never thought Andrew had noticed or cared about the personal sacrifice each of these visits required from her. She thought she was a means to an end for him, a necessary tool that would get him what he wanted.

That might have been part of it, but Margot *felt* the sincerity of his words.

He really did care.

"Andrew, I'm..." She paused, because she wasn't sure what she'd been about to say. Was she going to tell him she wanted to take the job just because he'd said one nice thing to her? There was more to it than that, but she still needed time, needed to think this through. She wasn't ready.

"I'm going to need more time to think about your offer," she said finally.

He nodded. "I won't push. I think you'd be a great addition to what we're building, and I want you on board, but we can't start a new unit until this project is done anyway. We need to finish with Ed and put that case to rest. Once this is over, you can let me know."

It seemed like an awful lot of her future hinged on the time when this was all over.

She didn't get a chance to say anything else, as the guard arrived to take them to the dining hall where they would meet with Ed. When they reached it, Margot took in the room, wondering if it would be the last time she'd be here. The space smelled of pine and lemon, but not in a good way, in a way that could barely mask the more penetrating odors of shitty food and too many bodies sweating together in the same building. There was a general feel of neglect to the space, like everyone running it would simply like it to fall into the ocean one day and weren't doing much to stop that from happening.

Margot had been to Alcatraz only once, but she could see how a place like this could easily become a place like that. The differences weren't that big.

Ford Rosenthal, Ed's lawyer, was sitting at an empty table and nodded a greeting at them as they walked in. He looked tense, beaten down. She wondered if he'd once had grand ambitions for his career, only to have them all ground under the heel of Ed Finch.

How many dreams had Ed managed to drown? He was like an infectious disease that spread far beyond the women whose lives had ended. He'd taken down families, ended relationships, cut friendships off in their prime. There was seemingly no end to the damage he could do.

Margot sat down, mentally absorbing the room, not so she would remember it, but so she'd know precisely what to forget when all this was done. The metal stools screwed into the table so they couldn't be used as weapons. The old, chipped tile floor and the half-full vending machines.

The men with guns who stood around the room, a reminder

of the danger that Ed still posed, even now that he was an old man.

The door at the far end of the cafeteria opened and Margot watched as he shuffled in, wrists and ankles shackled, jangling when he moved in their direction. He looked like he had just gotten a haircut, his auburn and gray hair now trimmed in an almost respectable cut rather than the shaggy style he'd worn for the last year.

"You got yourself cleaned up for our chat?" she asked, unable to help herself.

"One of us had to," he shot back, a barb at her bare face.

Margot was so used to Ed's shitty attitude the insult didn't even register. She waited until he was seated and took a good look at him. He was pale, as usual, a by-product of only getting an hour a day outside. Margot imagined her own skin looked about that white, because she, too, barely went out. Ed probably got more sun than she did.

She smiled at that, and could see that the reaction threw him off. His brow creased and he stared at her like she was a riddle he didn't know the answer to.

"Why are you smiling?" His tone was bitter. He was obviously in a bad mood to start with, though Margot couldn't imagine why. This whole thing had been his idea, and they had come at his request. Maybe something had happened behind the scenes to set him off. Margot found that she didn't really care. He was just harder to deal with when he was in a mood. His fuse was shorter and he was less open to sharing.

"I was only thinking how nice it will be to never have to come back here again."

He snorted, adjusting himself, the metal cuffs scraping against the tabletop, a sound that set her entire being on edge.

One last time. One last time.

She knew this might not be it, that he might do what he'd done in the past and decide to shut down before they had their answers, but she felt like this time was different. This *felt* like the last time. She wasn't sure what made it unique compared to her other visits, but even the time she had walked out swearing she'd never come back, part of her had known it wasn't true.

Margot saw this visit going only two possible ways. The first, and most likely, was that she would talk to Ed and decide he was full of shit and that the bodies he was planning to lead them to either didn't exist or had been disposed of in such a way they would never be recovered.

The second option was that he *was* being honest and, the next time she saw him, it wouldn't be in prison.

But Ed was going to have to be mighty compelling for her to believe that there was any merit to his insistence that he be given a short-term Get Out of Jail Free card. In a way, putting this decision in her hands was smart, because she was the least likely person on the planet to want to give her father a way out of prison.

"Heard about your little documentary," Ed said coolly.

Margot tensed. She had a fairly good idea who had told him. Rhonda, his wife, who was now living in San Francisco. Whose own son was soon to join Ed in San Quentin, if all went well. Rhonda—who now went by Toni Willingham—was still in frequent contact with Ed, seemingly unable to resist him despite the deadly path he'd helped guide her son down.

"Oh yeah? It has glowing reviews. One of the best-rated documentaries of the year." He'd hate her bragging about it, so she decided to be a little petty. After all, if he wanted to go on a field trip he was going to need to demonstrate good behavior.

"Mmm," he mumbled. "That's one take, I suppose. They had a good subject. Heard you got a lot of screentime." This, he said to Andrew, not Margot. Margot's own screentime had been very limited. She and her brother Justin had maybe six minutes apiece in the five-hour special. Apparently, that was enough time for Ed to be peevish about, though.

Margot wasn't going to engage; this topic was already boring to her. While Justin had decided to participate because he wanted to take some power back over Ed and have his own narrative, Margot decided to do it because she was sick of carrying around a secret, as if she deserved to be ashamed of who she had been, when Ed was the one who had gone wrong.

She would never be Megan Finch again. That part of her life had ended so long ago, and she had been Margot for too long now. But Megan deserved to be unlocked from the place Margot had hidden her for all that time. That was why Margot had done it. Not for Justin, not for Ed.

So she could move forward with her life and not feel like there was anything tethering her to the past.

As soon as she'd made the decision to do it, it had felt right. Her therapist had even been supportive of the choice.

"Let's talk about the reason I'm really here today, Ed, shall we?"

"You didn't stop by just to catch up? How's your brother doing? I heard they filmed you separately."

"Well, we live in different cities, don't we?"

Ed's jaw ticked. He thought she was being petulant, and she was, but in all this time he had pretended like Justin didn't exist. She wasn't sure why he was suddenly so interested in asking about him.

"What made you pick those names?" He leaned forward on the table, looking at her intently. "What name did your mother choose?"

Margot hadn't wanted to tell him her name initially because she didn't want him to have any part of her new life. Names had power. But her mother was dead, and he already knew her and Justin's new names at this point. She didn't think her mom would care.

"We picked our own," she said, and shrugged. "Justin picked David, I'm pretty sure because of David Beckham. I picked Margot because it was a name I'd just read in a book and I thought it sounded pretty and mature. Mom picked Cathy. I honestly don't know why. She never said."

A thin smile formed on his lips. "Cathy was a friend of your mom's when she was in high school. They were close, like sisters."

While there was something unpleasant about the way he said it, Margot didn't read much into it.

Ed shook his head. "Of course your brother would pick something that stupid."

"David isn't really a stupid name," Margot said. "No stupider than Justin."

Margot didn't actually know if Ed had named Justin or if he'd simply agreed to her mother's suggestions, but she could tell he took this response from her personally.

"And you decided on a name that made you sound like you were ninety years old?"

Margot laughed. "OK, *Edgar*."

Ed stiffened. He wanted to lash out, but she saw his attention shift to the nearest guard and he inhaled through his nose as if he was counting to ten before he spoke again. It was such a familiar coping strategy she almost wondered if Ed had spoken to a therapist.

But no, that was unfathomable. Ed would never show vulnerability.

He was sure to believe himself to be smarter than any therapist, so that might put a bit of a damper on the whole process. No, this was either something he'd read somewhere or seen someone else do and adopted it.

"Look, you and I know how to push each other's buttons too well at this point. We've learned the best ways to attack. I didn't come here today to attack you, Ed. And I didn't come to talk about that stupid documentary. I don't think that's what you want either. You asked us to come here because you want a chance to breathe real fresh air and make some FBI agents go on a hike. That's well and fine. But you're going to have to convince me first."

Ed smiled, that predatory smile that made his eyes go flat and reminded her more of an animal preparing to attack than of anything human. An involuntary shudder went through her.

"Let me tell you a story."

TWENTY-TWO

1994

San Francisco

Ed thought violence was an awful lot like music.

Sometimes it could be orchestrated like a beautiful classical composition. Other times it was frenzied and organic, like jazz. But no matter how it played out, he was the one making his own symphony. The women were just his instruments.

Tonight, he'd planned for things to go differently, but a little improvisation never fazed a true master of his craft.

The girl, Bethenny's sister, stared at him in confusion. He could tell she was still trying to rationalize his presence, to make it all into something innocent that she could tease her sister about in the morning.

No part of her seemed to believe that Ed posed some kind of threat. At least not until he had his hands on her throat, pushing her back toward the kitchen counter. He needed leverage.

Choking was not his preferred method of killing, but he also had rules for himself about his knives. Bethenny's blood was still on his preferred blade, and the ritual itself wouldn't be complete until he took the time to painstakingly clean every inch of it off.

That wouldn't work the same if this girl's blood was on it, too. He knew that was a dangerous distinction to draw at a time like this, but his rules were what made all of this work. Now was not the time to start changing things up. If he did that, he was going to get sloppy.

The girl's breath wheezed, coming out thick and wet. She slapped his hands, clawed his wrists. She tried to kick out at him, but he was much bigger, much stronger. Even in her efforts to resist him, she didn't put up nearly enough of a fight.

Her socks slipped against the hardwood floor, sending her tumbling down with a *thud* and he had no choice but to go along with her unless he wanted to hold her entire body weight as he crushed the life out of her.

When he looked into her wide eyes, a piercing shade of green, he marveled at how much of someone's eye is hidden until they're terrified. He could see so much of the white around her eyes, and her pupils dark as oil, where he saw his own reflection looking back at him.

She couldn't scream, but she still managed to make noise, little squeals and gurgles, animal sounds that were undignified and ugly. Her feet scrabbled on the floor, but she couldn't get any traction thanks to both his weight on top of her and her socks shimmying across the smooth polished wood.

In movies and on TV they make it seem like choking someone to death is fast. Just put your hands around a neck and squeeze. But choking someone took strength and commitment. It could take two, three, five minutes before the fight finally ended. And that was a *long* time to exert brute force on something.

Ed's fingers were sore and cramping, his brow was slick with sweat. There was a quick ease to using a knife, something he reminded himself of over and over as the interminable seconds ticked by. Her lips started to turn purple, her skin taking on a pallid hue. The whites of her eyes were now streaked through with red as the blood vessels popped.

Still, she held to his wrists and looked him in the eye, her gaze pleading, unflinching, even though she had to know he wasn't going to stop.

"You were never part of the plan," he said through gritted teeth. "I know that doesn't mean much now, but this wasn't what I wanted either."

She squeaked and he squeezed harder, his knuckles practically white from the effort. There was a *pop* under his thumb as something in her throat caved in, and a few moments later she simply vanished from her body. One moment there was a girl full of fight, the next there was an empty shell that was nothing more than dead weight.

He let her slump to the floor and stood up, stretching out his fingers, trying to get blood flow going again while he watched to see if she might move. No, he knew what death looked like and it had covered her in its shroud. She wasn't going anywhere.

The piercing ring of a phone startled Ed, making him stumble back from the body as if the sound had come from her. The ringing continued, filling the small apartment with its shrill call as Ed waited, almost holding his breath. He should leave, get out of here, but as the phone rang, he looked down at the dead girl at his feet and the red, raw color under her nails.

He looked down at his own wrists and saw the red half-moon marks cut into his skin, and he cursed.

This was why he used the knife. It wasn't tidier... no, it was a great deal messier, but that mess wasn't *his*. When he'd started doing this more than a decade earlier, things had been easier, police had been stupider, and there were things that he could leave behind at a scene without too much fear that it would leave a trail to his doorstep.

But this was the nineties and science had started to develop and change, and he'd watched enough TV to know that he couldn't let his blood be found under this girl's fingernails.

They didn't have his to compare it to, it wouldn't lead them right to his doorstep, but he wasn't an idiot. There were precautions he needed to take to protect himself, things he needed to be smart and careful about, and this girl could be the thing to undo it all for him.

The phone stopped ringing and the answering machine kicked in with a *click* sound. "*Yo, Bethhhhh, pick up the phone, I know you're not sleeping, you little slut.*" It was a man's voice, but despite the cruel word choice he was laughing heartily. Something in the lilt of his tone and the way he used certain words made Ed sure this was a gay man speaking. A woman giggled on the other end of the phone and words were exchanged quietly before she took over. "*Beth, we're coming over. We'll be there in fifteen minutes and if you don't open up, we're going to come through the fire escape, so whatever—or whoever—you're doing, get ready.*"

Fuck.

Ed stared at the body, then over his shoulder to the bedroom.

Fuck.

He needed to leave, but this was going to be too close, too risky. If these people showed up and found two dead women, the cops would be all over this building in minutes. They'd ask questions, people might remember seeing him. He needed the gift of time. Time was a wonderful thing when it came to altering and fogging memories.

He could disappear with time.

He had to get these women out of here and that was another risk he didn't like taking. He'd moved bodies before, though not often. He didn't like to move them from where he killed them, but sometimes it was necessary.

Bethenny's apartment window faced a dark alley, that was

where he'd parked the car when he'd come in. The building itself faced a somewhat busy street if it were the middle of the day, but right now the lights of passing cars and the sound of pedestrians passing by was limited.

If he was going to do this, he had to do it fast.

He dragged the sister's body over to the living room window, marveling at how heavy such a small woman could be now that she was dead. He opened up the window and rolled her out onto the small landing outside. Then he headed back to Bethenny's bedroom where he flipped on the lights and cringed.

Ed rarely took the time to admire his handiwork in the light, but he knew from a quick glance that one look at this room was going to tell people quite the story. Blood was splattered on the nightstand, the sheets were covered in it, and there was no easy way to hide that.

He wrapped Bethenny up in the worst of the sheets, then lined her pillows up on the bed in the relative shape of a body before throwing the dark bedspread back over the whole thing. He hoped that if the lights in the apartment were off and these friends on the phone did sneak up the fire escape, that they might peek in, see the shape of a body, and decide to piss off.

The rest of the work was sloppy and hurried. He dragged Bethenny out and set her on the landing on top of her sister, then did a quick scan of the apartment. He saw a filthy-looking backpack near the couch and decided at the last minute to grab it. Something about the girl and her unexpected appearance here made him think Bethenny hadn't expected her. And if Bethenny hadn't expected her, then there was a chance no one else knew she was here.

He turned off all the apartment lights then ducked out the window.

Bethenny's apartment was on the third floor, and there was no way he was going to be able to haul the bodies down on his own, but he wouldn't need to. His car was parked next to a dumpster that was loaded to almost overflowing with stout garbage bags. Should be enough to soften the sound of a falling body, anyway.

He tossed Bethenny first, using the sheets he'd wrapped around her for additional grip, but still struggling with her weight as he lifted her over the fire escape railing. When she fell, he held his breath, watching her go, worried she would hit the metal edge or go right to the ground, where the sound might attract attention he didn't want.

She fell into the waiting bags, making little more than a rustle when she landed.

He repeated the process with the sister, though by now he was feeling almost spent from all the exertion and lifting her felt about as easy as lifting a car. Still, adrenaline was a remarkable thing, and he managed to get enough leverage to push her over the side.

She landed next to her sister.

Now he just needed to get them out of the dumpster, and into his car.

TWENTY-THREE

"Bullshit," Margot said, trying her best not to laugh right in Ed's face. "You can't expect me to believe you—that story is insane."

"How is that any less believable than anything else you've ever heard of me doing?" Ed asked, his eyebrows raised and his tone genuinely curious. "Rhodes, would it surprise you?"

He looked over at Andrew. This was the second time this visit he'd spoken to his old nemesis, and that alone was surprising to Margot. He usually liked to pretend Andrew wasn't in the room unless he found a good opportunity to lob insults at the man. But now he seemed keen to pull him into their conversation.

"You want my professional opinion, Ed?" Andrew asked.

Ed made a scoffing sound. "Let's hear it. You're the Ed Finch expert, aren't you?"

Margot was pretty sure that title might now be held by Gregory Howell, but for some reason she would prefer Ed not know that Greg existed. Greg, however, would probably have been over the moon if he learned she had mentioned him to Ed.

It wasn't that Greg was a *fan*, but he was obsessed with Ed, in a way that made others a little wary, but not in a fawning, idolizing sense. Greg had spent most of his career with the FBI so far being the foremost expert on Ed Finch besides Andrew, and you don't spend that much time thinking about another person without it warping your brain the tiniest bit.

Margot would know. She'd spent her life with Ed's words in the back of her mind, and she would be the first to admit that she wasn't a great example of a mentally well-balanced individual.

Ed and Andrew were still locked in a staring contest, neither one noticing that Margot's attention had drifted away.

"Sure, Rhodes, tell me what you think. I'm curious." Ed shifted his position so he was facing more in Andrew's direction, and while this adjustment made all the guards a bit wary—Margot could see their bodies get tense—no one moved to stop him.

He did seem to be genuinely curious what Andrew might have to say next, but Margot knew this kind of focus and feigned interest was a hallmark of psychopaths who wanted to mirror someone to make them feel more comfortable. There was really no way to ever trust that Ed's intentions were honest.

"I think it *is* possible that what you're saying is true. There's a potential that you were overconfident in your original plan to attack the first girl, and that you felt you had to respond in kind with a second victim. That would be new for you, though, in terms of your MO. You never killed two victims at the same time before, not even when you worked with a partner."

Margot gave an involuntary shudder at the mention of Jimmy. Ed hadn't asked them what had happened after they'd gone to find the man who had helped him with a handful of his kills. The man who had blown out his brains in front of Margot and Andrew rather than join Ed in prison.

It was like Ed didn't care what happened. He'd sent them

on a hunt, just for fun, and it didn't matter to him what the outcome of that had been.

"What I have trouble believing," Andrew continued, "is that you would go to all the added risk of moving both bodies when you could have simply left them behind and split."

Ed shook his head, looking at Andrew like he was stupid. "I think I explained that, didn't I? The one girl, she had blood under her nails. That might point back to me. There was too big a danger in leaving them both there with someone else about to arrive."

"If that answering machine message hadn't come through, would you have left them there?" Margot asked.

Ed looked over his shoulder at her. "Of course. Time is both the best friend and worst enemy of a killer, Buddy. You should know that. What do they say about homicide, that the first forty-eight hours is the most important? I was always careful with my kills, lined them up for weekends, or times when the women wouldn't be missed for a few days. That time does a lot of favors. People forget things they've seen. Footprints get erased. Those things make it harder for the police—and no offense, kid, but that's how I liked it. Now, it was obviously trickier with your mom breathing down my neck. Weekends were for *family* time." He said the word *family* like it disgusted him. "Didn't want me going anywhere. So that made it a little more complicated, but I just had to learn people's habits. Made it easier to pick good weeknight candidates. But honestly, my favorite time to hunt was when you and your mom and brother went off to New York. The world was my playground those days."

Margot already knew this. She'd come to know a lot about her father's activity during the times they'd been away from him. She knew her mother had never quite overcome the suspicion that he was having an affair, because the truth of what he was doing was too awful to contemplate. But Kim had also needed a break, she needed time with her parents, where she didn't need to be the bad parent all the time, just... a break. And Margot and Justin had loved those summers. Her grandparents lived on almost two acres of land in upstate New York and they had spent almost all their waking hours outside. She hadn't realized it back then, but part of the joy of those summers was being out from under the oppressive weight of Ed and his temper and judgment.

It felt good to be away from him.

Apparently, he had felt the same.

"Why take such a huge risk?" Margot asked.

Ed turned back to her, his interest in Andrew forgotten.

"Because I always did what I needed to do to protect myself."

"And you buried them somewhere you can't tell us about?" Her tone was incredulous, letting him know precisely what she thought about this proposition of his. "They have to be somewhere reachable by car. I'll get a map, you point to the spot."

He had just admitted himself how exhausting the efforts of moving the bodies out of the apartment had been. After all that, there was no way he'd taken two bodies that far off the beaten path.

Ed shook his head, though.

"Well, you tell me. Do you have any dual Jane Does on your list?" He arched a brow at her first, then aimed it in Andrew's direction. His smug expression told Margot that he already knew the answer to his question.

No, the team had spent more than a year going over every possible victim of Ed's, including almost all known Jane Doe victims who had died during his active years, and there was no known *pair* of victims.

Though, it might be possible they could have been overlooked because two-for-one wasn't Ed's MO. Margot looked across at Andrew, since he would be the one to know if there were any cases that could fit the bill. He gave her the slightest shake of the head.

This would need a little more research. He'd given them at least a first name—Bethenny?—and that was somewhere they could start looking, at least in terms of missing persons reports. Certainly, two sisters going missing at the same time would have raised some alarm bells, and for Bethenny to have up and left her apartment—especially with a bloody crime scene likely left behind—there *had* to be some information they could dig up that would help them narrow down who the victims were.

Perhaps if they knew more, they might be able to link the young women to some unidentified remains.

Except, from what Andrew's headshake indicated, there were no remains that had been found that might belong to the sisters.

Ed was trying his damnedest to convince them that there was no way these bodies would be found without him. The problem was, Margot was starting to think he might not be lying. Ed was an outdoorsman. He loved hiking, and took Margot and her brother on overnight camping trips all over California. He taught them about survival and hunting—lessons that stuck with Margot now for reasons that had nothing to do with the wilderness—and Margot knew that, even worn down and exhausted, Ed would have been capable of finding a spot no one else was likely to reach, and hiding bodies so that no one would find them.

She thought of poor Theresa Milotti, the first of his previously unknown victims, who had been mere yards away from a road, but no one had found her for decades. Ed had an uncanny ability to utilize the places that people simply didn't look.

Places a body would never be found.

It pained her to admit it, but there was a very real possibility he was telling them the truth.

That didn't mean his reasons were noble; he obviously had ulterior motives for wanting to get out of jail—even for a day—but if it meant finally closing the Ed Finch story once and for all, then wasn't that worth it? No more unsolved crimes where families and friends would be wondering *what if?*

No more visits to this prison.

"What makes this place so impossible to find, so special that you can't just give us directions like you did with Theresa? With Marissa?" She leaned in a little closer, trying to gauge his response, to catch him if there was any hesitation or sign of a lie. "Why is this place different?"

"Because it's not on land, Buddy."

She stared at him, confused, and her confusion seemed to delight him.

"Two, if by sea," he sing-songed.

Margot sat back. She imagined the massive area of the Northern California coast. The jetties, the inlets, the islands, and craggy edifices.

Millions and millions of places to put a body.

Miles of coastline where a skeleton might or might not be waiting.

"How do you know they're still where you left them? The ocean is a volatile place. Lots of things can happen to a body."

Ed smiled, lifting one shoulder. "Well, I can't say that I've been in a position to go check on them recently. But I tucked them in. Safe and sound. I think they'll be right where I left them."

She stared at him, wanting nothing more than to reject this idea, not wanting to give him the satisfaction. But a needle in the ocean was about a thousand times worse than a needle in a haystack.

The last Ed Finch victims.

She had to bring them home.

"You remember how to get there?" Margot asked.

Ed's eyes brightened for a moment. She knew then that he hadn't believed for a second she was going to buy into this, and his surprise was evident on his face.

He gave a slow smile. "Guess you're just going to have to trust me."

TWENTY-FOUR

Getting Ed out of prison, even for one day, wasn't going to be an easy task. For one thing, it wasn't the sort of event that anyone wanted getting publicized, at least not until after it had been successfully managed, and Ed was safely back behind bars.

While he might be an old man, that didn't mean he wasn't still dangerous, and even if he had been truly feeble, there was too much weight to his legacy for people *not* to be afraid of him being out on the loose.

This wouldn't be the first time a prisoner had been given supervised leave to help with an ongoing investigation, but it did require coordination between the prison, the supervising agency—the FBI in this case—as well as local law enforcement in order to keep things as safe and running as smoothly as possible.

Margot was grateful that none of that coordination fell to her.

She would go. There was no question of that. If she'd been asked months before whether she would want to meet her father face-to-face outside the confines of a prison, she would have said no in a heartbeat. But now, she knew she needed to be present, to see those two women found, and to look into his eyes one last time knowing she'd never have to do it again.

She'd thought her brother was foolish for needing some kind of closure from Ed, but it turned out Margot needed it, too.

And she needed him to know that she was the one who had helped find those last victims. It didn't matter that the whole thing had been his idea, his insidious plot to get her back into his life, and vice versa. In the end, she would wipe her hands clean of him. And she would have done the one thing she set out to do when she became a cop all those years ago.

She would have found justice for Ed's victims.

That *had* to be enough.

Margot left the prison feeling the strangest sense of ease. As Andrew walked her back to her car, she didn't say anything to him—not about the plan, not about her future career. She breathed in the salty air coming off the Bay, and when she breathed out, she *knew* she was never coming back here again. This place that had existed like a monster's keep in a nightmare, with its sickly smells and the sound of too many men with too much evil done among them. This place with its perfectly dressed children being ushered in by mothers' trembling hands.

She never had to come back here again.

Margot felt lighter than she had in years. While this ordeal wasn't over—the most difficult part was still ahead—she had the sensation of being free from something. She'd long known that her relationship with her father and the guilt she carried from it were holding her back from living a normal life. And she had accepted that was the price she had to pay. That in order for there to be balance in the universe, it made sense that she would suffer and feel lost and alone because of what her father had taken from others.

She'd made penance by helping others find peace, but she had never really believed that she would get to release herself from the burden of what Ed had put on her. It had been a burden that her mother couldn't carry, that Justin could look at only with the haze of substance abuse to dull the edges. But Margot had been shouldering it since the day she watched her father jump out of a moving car in the middle of teaching her to drive so he could run from the police and FBI.

She had watched him go while the car continued its slow crawl up their street, and even though she hadn't understood what was happening at the time, she had known her life would never be the same.

Now, as she took one last look at San Quentin, she felt like the little bits of that fifteen-year-old girl inside her were finally able to let out a breath that had been held for twenty-four years.

And that release felt euphoric.

Margot almost thought she could cry, but it wasn't time for that, not yet.

When this was over, and Ed was back behind bars for whatever years were left in his life, she would raise a toast to the end of the worst chapter in her life, and she would finally, *finally* move on.

Today was the first step of her freedom walk, and it was almost too perfectly symbolic that it was happening in the parking lot of a prison, because she felt like she'd just been released from a prison of her own.

"You look happy," Andrew said when they reached her car. "I don't think I've seen you smile like that in a long time."

She looked at him, unable to school the expression on her face. "I'm never coming back here again."

Andrew smiled back, though his own expression was a bit more guarded. "You know, we couldn't have done any of this without you. And not because you're his daughter. I think there are plenty of people in your shoes who would have shown up once and never again. Or showed up and not been able to do the work you did. You're the only reason we were able to solve all those cases. Theresa. Marisa. All the other women who no one ever thought would find justice. Or find their bodies. You did that."

Margot nodded. A different woman might have deflected the compliment, insisted it was a team effort. But he was right. If she hadn't been willing to sit across from her demons, then none of this could have happened.

She'd struggled with it, wondering if any answers were worth all the agony it had put her through.

And now that she was standing here, on the other side, she knew the answer.

"It was worth it," she said honestly. "It was all worth it."

TWENTY-FIVE

Margot slept.

She slept hard, and she did not dream.

When she finally woke, it was dark outside and her stomach rumbled its complaint, having been left unfed for the bulk of the day. She got out of bed, showered, and made a beeline for her kitchen, with the intention of getting Brody at the front desk downstairs to call in an order for her, so she could replenish the Thai she had finished off in her fridge.

But with the phone in her hand and a memorized menu sitting in front of her, she had a different idea.

She dialed Wes's number instead, and though a pit in her stomach worried that he might be out, that he might be spending his free evening with a woman less complicated, less... difficult, she tried not to let that train of thought derail her sudden boldness.

Wes answered after only two rings.

"Detective Phalen, patron saint of No Rest for the Wicked. What can I do for you this fine evening?" His voice was light, teasing. Margot felt a flush of relief.

"I want to go out."

There was a long pause, but from his intake of breath, she knew he was still there.

"Well, be still my heart. Are you asking me out?"

Despite Margot's own realization of her feelings for him, she was relieved that this was asked in a joking tone. She wasn't sure what she would do if he had sounded sincere. "I'm too good for you, Wes, we know that," she bandied back, and he laughed.

"No arguments here. What did you have in mind?"

"You're not busy?"

"God no. I was watching a documentary about a self-sustaining farm and getting a little too invested in their ongoing coyote problem. Poor chickens. You'd be rescuing me from a mindless evening of googling the finer points of having a hobby farm."

"Well, that sounds downright fascinating. I'm hungry, thought you might be willing to be seen in public with me if I offered to feed you."

"Perhaps the only way I'd risk such an association. I could definitely eat. You have a particular craving?"

Margot knew what she liked, but what she liked was the stuff that was available for easy delivery. In a city that was packed to the gills with amazing restaurants, she didn't know what was out there outside a six-minute radius around her apartment. The truth was, the only time she'd set foot in an honest-to-God restaurant in the last few years was when she'd been with Wes.

She didn't want to be afraid of experiencing things anymore.

Just having Betty had forced her to form routines, and what she'd started to realize was: routines were not a direct pathway to disaster.

Routines were actually kind of nice.

"I'm in the mood for Mexican, but I don't want to pick the place." If she picked, she'd just be doing the same things she always did.

"Mexican, eh? I can do Mexican. How about I pick you up in about twenty minutes, that work OK for you?"

And though there was the faint lump of nervousness in her throat, she was aware of another sensation as she said yes. A faint flutter in her stomach, distinctly different from anxiety, and far less familiar. Excitement.

Twenty minutes later, her phone buzzed with a message from Wes. *Downstairs. Bring Betty.*

Bring Betty? Margot read the message a few times, trying to determine if she was misunderstanding, but there was no other way to read it. He wanted her to bring the dog.

She attached Betty's leash, which made the old girl's tail thump with enthusiasm, then took herself and the dog down to meet Wes. He got out of the car when he saw them emerge through the front door, and without a moment's hesitation, plucked the little Maltese off the ground and helped her into the back seat, then held the door open for Margot. There it was again, that unexpected flip in her tummy.

"Why am I bringing my ancient dog with me?" she asked, hoping her voice didn't sound funny as she asked.

As he got in his own side he smiled slyly, but wagged a finger at her. "No, you asked me to pick, I picked. Now you need to see what I have in store for you."

The sensitive, nervous part of her that had such a hard time with trust lurched, but she tamped the nauseating feeling down. This was Wes. Wes would never do anything to hurt her or put her in harm's way.

This whole exercise was about proving to herself that it was OK to go with the flow. That nothing bad was going to happen just because she stepped outside her rigid, hyper-protected world. Perhaps it was too hopeful to think that she could go into things blind, but she *had* shared meals with Wes in public spaces before, and nothing bad had happened.

She had been fine.

This would be fine.

Margot hadn't dated when she was in high school. Not before things with Ed had gone down. For one thing, he'd been adamant that she couldn't date until she was at least eighteen. But the truth was, she had been a chubby, insecure girl, and there hadn't been a long line of guys beating down the door to take her out. After Ed's arrest, she hadn't trusted anyone enough to try. She worried about the motives of boys in her school, and then, when she was an adult, she selected partners based on how short-term they could be.

Margot hadn't ever really *dated*. She didn't know how any of it worked. Not that this was a date... but it had the shape of one.

She knew she was still riding the high of leaving San Quentin earlier that day, but for once, and despite herself, she tried not to overthink this. Wes took them on a route she didn't recognize, which was the point, until he found parking near Dolores Park, and she shot him a quick, uneasy look.

"Where are we going?"

He turned off the car and angled himself toward her. "Look, I know that you're stepping outside your comfort zone with this, and I want you to know I recognize that. I am really touched that you trusted me with this, and I'm not going to push you further than you think you can go." He looked for all the world like he was going to take her hand, but then seemed to think better of it.

"OK," Margot said.

He nodded. "So we're going to try something, and if you

hate it and want to leave, we can do that. But I want you to give it a chance."

She couldn't help but smile at him, because he was trying so damned hard to make this work for her, and if she hadn't known she loved him before, she would have known now.

"OK," she said again.

He offered up a balled fist and for a moment she looked at it, unable to understand what was happening, then realized to her own foolishness he wanted a fist bump. She tapped her knuckles against his and he grinned, obviously proud of himself. "All right, let's take brave new Margot out for a spin, shall we?"

He got out, opening her door first, then the back door to retrieve Betty, who had completely fallen asleep during their drive.

Betty seemed both enthusiastic and confused about their new location, and she walked ahead of them, her tail wagging as she sniffed the ground every few steps.

Margot soon understood their destination. There was a little taco truck set up near the entrance of the park with a line of about eight people queued up. Those who had already gotten their orders were seated up on the nearby rolling hills of the park that looked out over San Francisco. With the lights, it was bound to be quite the view, one Margot had never seen despite all her years in the city.

They lined up and Margot once again tamped down the internal voice that told her she was too exposed, that this was an unnecessary risk. There were couples ahead of them laughing and chatting easily, and Margot wondered if she would ever be able to be that relaxed.

Maybe not, but she was here. That was a promising first step.

Betty made easy friends with a nearby terrier, and by the time they got to the front of the line, Margot felt more confident than she had in a long time. She ordered a trio of street tacos, and while they waited, she reminded herself she didn't need to check behind her, nothing bad was going to happen if she just talked to Wes and people-watched.

"How you doing?" he asked, an earnest expression on his face, letting her know that this wasn't a surface-level question. He really wanted to know.

"Not bad," she replied honestly. "It's more open than I would have picked for myself, but that's probably a good thing. If I let myself get too used to small spaces, I'd probably be borderline agoraphobic by the time I turned fifty."

"Perish the thought."

"Of me being agoraphobic, or me turning fifty?"

He chuckled. "Don't be silly, Margot, women stop aging at forty-five. There simply are no women older than that."

"Just because you don't date women older than that doesn't mean they don't exist," she shot back, collecting their orders while he held Betty's leash.

He led her up a nearby hill to where people were clustered together in small groups all over the grass. While he hadn't brought a blanket, there hadn't been any rain in several days, and the grass was dry. Betty contented herself with doing a peripheral sniff of the area before she settled down, rested her head on her paws, and closed her eyes. It was a lot of excitement for both pup and owner in one evening.

Wes took a bite of his birria taco, making use of the ample wad of napkins he'd grabbed to get consommé off his chin, then asked, "So, do you want to talk about what happened today? You were visiting Ed, weren't you?"

She nodded, taking a fallen pickled red onion from her plate and putting it back on her taco. "He wants to show us where he hid his last victims."

Wes paused mid-bite. "What do you mean, *show*?" he asked around a mouthful of taco.

"I mean today's visit was for me to determine if I thought he was being honest about these two victims, and if it merited allowing him out to show us where they're buried."

"And you said no, right?" He cocked an eyebrow at her.

"I approved it. I think his story isn't totally right and that he's leaving things out, but I also think he's being as honest as Ed is capable of being. I think there are bodies out there, and they're clearly in a difficult-to-reach spot. Once we find them, then his story is done."

She could feel the weight of Wes's gaze on her and it took her a moment to feel up to looking at him. When she did, she tried her best to smile. "I know you don't agree with it, but I think we have to do it."

"He's setting you guys up," Wes said.

"Maybe. No doubt he has his own objectives in all this. Though whether that's just to force us to make a big spectacle of him, or if it's a ploy of some kind, I don't know. He's not going to escape. There will be too many safeguards against it. He's an old man."

"Now you sound like you're trying to convince yourself," Wes replied, and bumped his shoulder against hers. "You really think this is a good idea?"

"A *good* idea? No. A necessary one? Probably."

"And you're going to go?"

She nodded. "I think I need to."

"Was that what brought this on?" He gestured to the park and the tacos she was holding.

"Probably. I walked away from that meeting feeling... I don't know, I felt *free*. Between that and knowing how close we are to wrapping up the Redwood Killer case, and after that... dealing with what we know about Boyd... I know this isn't over yet, but I really wanted to hold onto that feeling."

He watched her carefully, his eyes warm, and so kind it made her chest hurt.

"Well, I gotta say, I'm not complaining."

"Me either," she admitted, realizing that she felt *good*, and hadn't had to quiet the voice in the back of her head for several minutes now.

"Here's to new beginnings." He lifted his taco in her direction and she tapped her own against it.

"To new beginnings."

TWENTY-SIX

Two days off was both too much time away from work and not enough all at once. Margot felt refreshed and optimistic heading back into the precinct, in part because of all the sleep she'd been able to catch up on, and also because she felt like she'd taken such huge personal strides on her days off that it was almost inevitable her work life should follow suit.

Being back on the day shift helped. They'd be right back in the thick of things, which would keep her from feeling like a ghost who was following in the day shift's footsteps.

The first thing she found after she stepped into her office—where Wes was already present—was that while they were gone the task force had managed to get a DNA sample from Stephen Kramer. He had evidently gone out to meet someone for a coffee and left his cup behind at the table, letting the officers who were tailing him get both his DNA and fingerprints in one fell swoop. It was a big get.

Drake Winston was being a bit more cagey, as if he knew there were eyes on him. He stayed in most days, and when he went out it was only to work and then home again immediately after. He hadn't had any social interactions during the days he'd been followed.

It seemed now like it was all a waiting game to see which DNA would come back as a match for their unknown sample. Margot wasn't great at waiting, but there was little else they could do in the meantime except continue to go through both men's social media presence. They wouldn't even be able to request cell phone records until they had more solid evidence to submit the warrant there. It was frustrating to be so close yet so far.

As it turned out, the free time was going to come back to bite Margot in the ass, because she'd only been at her desk an hour when a knock sounded at the door.

She turned around and her face fell.

"Morning, Hildy," Wes greeted the lawyer brightly.

Margot couldn't even pretend to be happy to see the assistant DA.

"Morning, Wes. Pleasure to see you as always." This sounded genuine, then Hildy turned her attention to Margot. "Margot."

"Hildy."

"I won't take up too much of your time, but I thought you should know that we're expecting to call you next week, so you'll have to be at the courthouse. I've already cleared it with your captain, and I'll give you a clearer time frame when we get closer."

Margot chewed the inside of her cheek, fighting against an impolite response. It wasn't Hildy's fault. This was just a part of the job. And while this particular trial was one she wished she could pawn off on Wes, she was at least grateful it would soon be over.

"I might have something going on next week, so just make sure you check in ahead of time," Margot replied tersely.

"Something more important than testifying in a murder trial?"

"I suspect the FBI would think so, yes."

Hildy bit her lip to keep from saying whatever was on her mind, then gave a nod.

"You feel prepared?" Hildy asked.

"To get skewered? Yes, wouldn't be the first time."

Hildy sighed. "All right then. But if you could do me a favor and try to come across more..." She searched for a word.

"Human?" Wes offered.

Hildy restrained her smile, but Margot looked over her shoulder and shot him a deadly look.

"I was going to say *approachable*."

"I will leave my *Fuck Off* T-shirt at home."

"I'd appreciate it." Hildy didn't stick around for additional chitchat. She turned on her very practical high heels and clacked her way out of their office. Margot must have been engrossed in her emails not to have heard the approach of such a distinctive sound.

"Court day." Wes shook his head in pained commiseration. "If I hadn't had to do my own yesterday, I'd have offered to take it for you, but I'm going to need a break from defense lawyers for a bit."

"Ugh," Margot groaned. "It's Lloyd Crowther's case, too."

Wes winced.

Lloyd Crowther was an old-school defense lawyer, the kind who wasn't afraid to play dirty and mean if it meant giving the jury even the slightest shred of reasonable doubt. Margot *knew* this wasn't going to go well. She knew he was going to try to convince the jury she had a conflict of interest on the case, so in a way it was probably better that she was facing him directly rather than forcing another detective—namely Wes—to answer for her ongoing presence on the case.

She just wished it was anyone *other* than Crowther. She could already hear that Southern drawl that he kicked up a few notches in court like he was Atticus Finch, ready to slay the wicked prosecution to fight for the rights of his client.

Except his client was a baby-faced killer, and Margot didn't mind a little humiliation if it meant that Ethan Willingham never set foot in public again.

But man alive, she would rather be hunting killers than going through the song and dance of convincing twelve random people that those killers should be behind bars.

Margot knew their work on that case was impeccable. All they had to do was play the tape of Ethan *hypothetically* sharing his confession with her, and that would be enough for anyone with a lick of common sense. The problem was common sense wasn't so common, and a jury of Ethan's peers might look at the kid and see someone he was pretending to be rather than who he really was.

He was awfully good at pretending.

That was sort of a trademark gift for psychopaths.

It was going to be up to her to convince that jury that the honors student and shy persona he adopted was nothing more than an act, and ironically, she would need to do that by pretending to be someone she wasn't. Someone warmer, someone more inviting, someone the jury liked. Because if they liked her, then they were more likely to believe her, and that was just an unfortunate truth.

She wasn't looking forward to seeing the kid again, but it would all be worth it to send him away for the rest of his life.

"Let's get out of here," Margot said, pushing her chair back and grabbing the coat she had hung up when she arrived.

"Where are we going?" Wes looked up from his screen.

"I want to go see if we can find any of the Larks alive, and find out what they might know."

"And how do you propose we do that?" He was putting on his jacket, so it was obvious he had no complaints about this mission, only questions about how it would be pulled off.

"It's a long shot, but I want to go talk to Fiona Thibodeaux."

TWENTY-SEVEN

Fiona Thibodeaux was not a Lark.

She wasn't an escort.

However, her sister Angela had been an unusually rough case that had landed on Wes and Margot's desk earlier in the year, and though Angela had not died immediately at the scene of the crime, she had unfortunately succumbed to her immense injuries a few days later.

Margot was fairly certain that Emmanuel Riga had Angela killed so she couldn't point the finger at his son Roberto.

It had worked, because Roberto was still a free man.

Margot didn't know how long that would last when she finally pulled the pin on the grenade that would see Pressley Boyd go down, because it was all connected. And she was hoping they would all keep each other company on their way to hell.

But while Fiona wasn't directly under Riga's thumb, she was peripheral enough to his world that she might be able to help them. She had been able to ID a few of the other Redwood Killer victims as having spent time at the Odyssey—the same bar Jesse owned—because she worked there as a dancer.

Margot didn't know if she was still working there, but she had never considered the idea of showing Fiona the Lark website. Her sister had been one of Riga's girls, so it was very possible that some of the other escorts could have been Angela's friends. Fiona might be able to give them their real names.

It was a very long longshot, but it sure beat sitting around the precinct hoping DNA results would come back.

It would also distract Margot from thinking about the trial.

They arrived at Fiona and Angela's house, and though months had passed since the murder, the exterior looked much the same. The only major difference now was the addition of a bird bath in the front yard with an angel statue perched looking into the water. Margot felt she could confidently assume this was a tribute to Angela.

It was sweet, and it also told them Fiona hadn't moved away in that time.

When they rang the doorbell, it only took a moment before the girl opened the door. She was petite, with a lithe dancer's frame and bright blue eyes. But where she had previously worn her hair in wild curls that haloed around her head, she'd gotten a drastic haircut, the curls now in a close-cropped pixie cut.

Fiona had the delicate features to pull off such a severe style.

It was obvious that she recognized them right away, but her expression still slipped into confusion almost instantly following recognition.

"Detectives?" Then after a beat her eyes widened. "Did they finally make an arrest in Angela's case?"

Margot should have expected this question and kicked herself for not thinking of it sooner. Of course Fiona would jump to that conclusion, why else would they come in person?

"I'm sorry, no. We're hoping for something soon, though.

We need to be in a position where the prosecution will be willing to... well, prosecute."

"That son of a bitch," Fiona said through gritted teeth. "He gets to go on living his life, but Angela is gone. It's not fair."

Margot couldn't help but nod. "It isn't. But we're doing everything we can to make it fair eventually. It's just going to take a little longer. I'm sorry."

"Then why are you here? Sorry if that sounds rude, or whatever, I just... Why are you here?"

Wes interjected, turning up his natural charm with a warm smile and friendly tone, neither of which Margot had ever learned to fake well. "We were actually hoping you might be able to help us with a different case."

"Oh Jesus, did Jesse do something?" She opened the door to show them in and they followed her into the living room. She sat down in an armchair while Margot and Wes sat side by side on the couch.

"Jesse?" Margot asked once they were seated. "What makes you think we're here about Jesse?"

Fiona picked up an enormous water bottle off the coffee table and cradled it like a baby as she nestled into the plush armchair. "I'm not sure. Guys like that always seem like they're on the cusp of getting into trouble for something, though, you know what I mean?"

Having met Jesse, Margot did, in fact, know what Fiona meant.

"No, we're not here about Jesse. We actually wanted to know if you might be able to help put names to a few faces?"

Fiona gave her a confused look while taking a sip from the water bottle's straw. Margot briefly mused if it was possible for a person to be *too* hydrated, because the bottle looked almost as big as the petite dancer's torso.

Margot gave Wes a quick look, wondering if, perhaps, this

whole idea had been a mistake, but since they were here, they might as well see if Fiona knew anything.

Margot handed a thick folder she'd brought with her over to Fiona. It had printed pages featuring all the headshots they'd been able to find from the Larks website, not only currently, but also previous iterations using the Internet Wayback Machine, a website that allowed them to view past versions of the site.

Fiona opened up the folder to the smiling, pretty women staring back at her, and then gave Margot and Wes another perplexed look. "What is this?"

"It's from a website that is currently being used to advertise escort services, but it has been designed to look like it's for a women's recreational soccer league. That 'team' is the same group of women your sister belonged to, and also the same group of women we believe are currently being targeted by a serial killer."

A complex array of emotions moved over Fiona's face in quick succession.

"You think the guy who killed Angela is a serial killer?"

Wes shook his head. "No, the fact that your sister was killed while her colleagues were being targeted is just a really unfortunate coincidence. But we do think her colleagues are at risk, and we're wondering if you happen to recognize any of these women and might know their real names. All the names listed online are pseudonyms."

Fiona seemed dubious about their approach, but she dutifully started to look over each page with an intensity and focus Margot hadn't expected.

"I recognize these two," she said, showing them the sheet. "But only because you showed me their photos at the club. I remember seeing at least one of them there." She didn't wait for Margot or Wes to say anything, and went back to studying the sheets.

It wasn't until the third page that her body language changed. She stiffened and tapped the paper. "I know her."

She handed the page to Wes, who was closest to her, and pointed to the photo of a blonde woman with a sleek, chin-length bob.

"You know her from seeing her at the club?" Margot asked, almost not daring to hope it could be better than that.

Fiona shook her head. "No. That's Cassie. Cassie Templeton. She's... she was one of Angela's closest friends. I'm pretty sure she was the one who helped Angela get that job. She was also one of the only people Angela worked with who came to the funeral. She was *crushed* when Angie died."

"Do you know how we could get in touch with her?"

"Sure." Fiona got up from the couch and padded into the kitchen, then returned a moment later with a Post-it. She had mentioned in one of their previous visits that her sister loved to leave her Post-its to communicate because both girls were notoriously terrible about keeping their phones charged.

The little orange square said, *Party at Cassie's! Come!* And there was an address scribbled underneath.

"Do you mind if we keep this?" Margot asked.

Fiona seemed to debate this for a moment, and Margot understood why. These notes were the last pieces she had of her sister, and losing any of them could mean losing what little of Angela she had left. But she shook off the hesitation and nodded. "Of course." She looked from Margot to Wes, her brow knit in deep concern. "Is Cassie in danger?"

Margot thought about all the girls they had found in the woods, about all the death and horror that had led them to this place, and these moments that would hopefully be the last hours and days of the Redwood Killer's freedom. She thought about the police who, even now, were watching Drake Winston's every move.

And even with all that, she couldn't be totally sure of Cassie Templeton's safety.

She smiled softly at Fiona.

"I hope not."

TWENTY-EIGHT

Cassie Templeton lived about a twenty-minute drive from Angela and Fiona's place, in a North Beach apartment that was walking distance from Margot's apartment. It was a nice building, newly renovated, and with its views of the water, must have cost a pretty penny.

What Margot was learning in all of this was that escorts could make a *lot* of money, depending on who they worked for, and those who worked for Emmanuel Riga seemed to be nicely set up financially.

Of course, the flip side of that was working for Riga and being in forced proximity to his murderous son, as well as men in power who didn't care who they hurt if it meant getting their rocks off.

They pressed the buzzer labeled C. *Templeton,* and a moment later a soft, drowsy voice came over the line. "Hello?"

Margot noted that, much like in Wes's building, this apartment had a video camera set-up so that tenants could see who was buzzing them. She held her badge up to the camera. "Ms. Templeton, we're here from the SFPD, we'd like to have a quick chat with you, if possible?"

After a long pause where Margot felt almost certain that Cassie had hung up the line, the door buzzed.

New buildings meant new elevators, so Margot had no concerns about skipping the stairs and taking the fast track to the sixth floor. The entire apartment complex looked and smelled as if it had been built the previous week. The carpet in every hall was pristine, and rather than the familiar scents of cooking that came from most apartment buildings, this one still smelled like fresh paint and plastic residue. None of the doors had any kind of adornments on them, and there wasn't a single welcome mat in sight.

It looked more like a boutique hotel than a place where anyone actually lived.

They found Cassie's apartment with no difficulty, and she answered on their first knock. Unlike with Clea, Cassie didn't bother with the chain, she just opened the door and ushered them inside. Margot wondered if this was because she had already seen their badges, or because she was a naturally trusting person. She hoped it was the former.

Cassie's apartment felt as new as the exterior halls did. All the furniture was in varying shades of white and beige, and the couch filled half the living room with its luxe, plush seats. A large-screen TV mounted on the wall seemed to be paused in the middle of a YouTube video showing a makeup tutorial, and a little nest of blankets on the large couch showed them precisely where Cassie had been when they interrupted her.

"Can I get you a coffee?" Cassie asked politely, gesturing to an expensive-looking coffee maker on the counter that appeared to be freshly filled.

Margot smiled and shook her head. "No, but thank you. I'm Detective Phalen, this is my partner, Detective Fox. We wanted to talk to you about a few of your former colleagues."

Cassie's bright expression collapsed. She was a pretty girl, and the transformation was remarkable, turning her happy, open face into something shuttered and miserable, adding almost ten years to her age in the process.

"You're here about Angela?"

After what Fiona had told them of Cassie and Angela's relationship, it was no surprise that Cassie would jump to this conclusion.

Margot gestured Cassie toward a small dining room table and they sat across from each other while Wes leaned casually against the kitchen island. He looked natural here, like it was somewhere he could belong. Margot tried to imagine him in her own apartment, with its used furniture and bachelor pad vibes, and while she liked the idea of it, she had to admit the two things didn't exactly mesh.

"Cassie, we know you and Angela were working for an agency owned by Emmanuel Riga."

Cassie's already dark expression clouded over even more.

"I work for a social media management company," she said tensely. "I do social media for a major soft drinks company."

Margot glanced around them to the overly opulent apartment, the view of the Bay beyond the large sliding patio doors that led to a balcony. Then she looked back to Cassie.

The woman's expression hadn't changed.

They must have all been trained not to talk about their work. Paying for dates wasn't illegal, but paying for sex was, and these companies toed a very fine line. With a guy like Emmanuel Riga at the helm, Margot had no doubt that the fear of God had been instilled in all these women from the very beginning, and God was Riga.

"I'm not talking about your day job, Cassie."

The girl didn't speak, she merely set about refilling her coffee, pouring in an ample amount of a flavored creamer and stirring it so slowly that the *tink-tink* of the spoon against the mug started to grate on Margot's nerves.

Finally, when she was done, she looked back at Margot and sighed.

"I know you're not stupid, detective, I do. I know why you're here. At least, I have guesses. We would be fools not to have noticed what was happening. We do talk to each other."

"You and the other Larks?" Margot asked.

A momentary flash of confusion crossed Cassie's face, until she realized what Margot meant, and then she let out a genuine laugh. "Is that what you're calling us? The Larks?"

"Because of the website."

"Of course. And the stupid fucking tattoos, no doubt."

"We *had* wondered about the tattoos," Wes said, taking the open seat next to Margot at the table.

"Do you have one?" Margot asked Cassie.

"We all have them," Cassie said. "It was from one of the parties. All the girls working ended up getting them because we'd learned about the *team* designations on that stupid website. We thought it was hilarious at the time. Someone suggested matching T-shirts, but then this party had a tattoo artist, so we all got them."

"So, Riga didn't force you to get them?" Margot confirmed.

"We're not *slaves*, Detective Phalen. We're not being trafficked. This is a job. It's a job that pays very well in a city that costs too much money to live in as a single person. We can quit whenever we want, but most of us don't because we're treated fairly and we make a lot of money. And despite how it's perceived, quite a few of these clients really *don't* want sex. The different team names, they're for the type of girl a client is looking for."

"I assumed, but we couldn't draw any direct correlations."

Cassie's expression shifted into something almost robotic as she began to explain, her face losing any animation, like she wanted to distance herself from what she was saying. "Larks were *girlfriend experiences*. We're the ones you call in when a client—usually a very famous or wealthy client—wants to be able to show off some arm candy at an event but doesn't want to have to worry about a girl getting too drunk, or too distracted by A-list partygoers, or be lured in with offers of cocaine or pills, or whatever." She took a sip from her coffee and Margot wasn't sure if she just needed to gather her thoughts, or if she was actually thirsty. "Larks were the most trustworthy, the most reliable. We were the ones that clients could trust not to say anything about what we'd seen or done. I know one of our girls has been the public girlfriend of a famous pop singer for almost four years. Guy is as gay as the chorus line of a Broadway musical." This made Cassie smile, obviously feeling genuine warmth toward the man. "But he needs to maintain appearances because his fanbase is largely female. So she goes with him to awards shows, on vacations, and she's basically being paid to be his beard. *That* is the sort of thing the Larks were good for. That's why we were the ones brought to parties with billionaires, politicians—"

"Police commissioners."

Cassie didn't say anything, but there was a sharpness in her expression that Margot couldn't miss.

"We keep quiet."

"We're not here today to get you to spill secrets on Riga or his clients. That day might come, and I hope it does, but we're here because we believe that the women in your *team*, for lack of a better word, were all being targeted by a killer. Not Angela's killer."

Cassie nodded. "When Rebecca and Leanne died so close together, we started to wonder if that was just a coincidence or not, but after Freddie, we knew it was something else. We would always leave events together. We made sure someone knew when we were out on dates. But you can't stop living your life or doing your job, you know? And we had no idea who it was. Em... Our boss told us not to worry, that we were all safe, but it was obvious he didn't have a freaking clue what was going on either. This was going to keep happening."

"We think we might know who did it, and I was hoping if I showed you a few photos you could let us know if anyone looks familiar." Margot pulled open the folder that she'd brought to Fiona's house, but instead of showing her the Lark headshots, she pulled out four photos of men. A photo lineup needed controls in place, so besides the pictures of Stephen Kramer and Drake Winston, there was a candid photo of a random man from Instagram, and another that was a photo of Margot's own brother. She had it in her desk drawer and it was the easiest thing to grab on her way out of the office.

She had felt a little guilty adding it to the pile, because during a particularly difficult period between her and Justin she had briefly managed to convince herself he might be a killer. Putting him in a lineup felt like giving credence to that, even though she no longer believed it was true.

But she'd made do with what she could find easily before they'd come here. Margot laid the photos out on the kitchen table in front of Cassie. "Do any of these men look familiar?"

Cassie didn't look at the photos immediately. She gave Margot a long, pleading stare, as if hoping she might put the photos away and not ask her to do this. Begging her not to make this necessary. As badly as Cassie must want justice for those women—for her friends—she didn't want to be involved in this.

Margot had met Emmanuel Riga only once, but once was more than enough for her to understand why the women working under him would do anything to avoid drawing unnecessary attention to themselves.

"He's not going to know you helped us." Margot wasn't sure if she meant Riga or the killer, but both were true. They had no need to make Cassie's involvement in this public at all.

The young woman let out a little sigh and then pulled the photos closer. She didn't simply cast a quick glance at them, either, which was what Margot had expected her to do. She looked at each one in turn, carefully examining them. The random internet man was quickly pushed aside.

Cassie paused at Stephen Kramer's photo, at first unsure. It could actually be quite difficult to recognize a familiar face out of its known setting. Like seeing a beloved barista anywhere except a coffee shop; their face might not immediately make sense to you.

She tapped Stephen's photo. Her expression only belied recognition and nothing else. "I've seen this man at a few of our parties. He was a cater waiter. Very nice guy, he made sure that all the girls got first dibs on the good snacks, and he'd bring us water through the night if he thought that the clients might be buying us too many drinks. I mean, we knew how to avoid drinking booze through the night, but he didn't know that. He was looking out for us. Kind of guy where you just know he's got sisters."

Margot gave Wes a quick look and caught him smiling at this remark. Wes had two sisters, and Margot had seen the impact it had left on him.

Cassie continued to look through the photos, so Margot held off on any follow-up questions about Stephen, but she didn't really think they would matter. Unless Stephen Kramer was the world's greatest actor, it was very unlikely he was going to turn out to be their man. Everyone seemed to love him, and his online presence had shown zero red flags.

Cassie didn't spend much time on Justin's photo, which was a relief for Margot and assuaged some of her guilt about including it. But when Cassie got to the photo of Drake Winston, her entire body went rigid. Her fingertips paused mid-air, hovering over the photo like she wanted to recoil but couldn't manage to move.

Her breath came out in a short little puff, and she finally

composed herself enough to slide the photo back across the table, turning it to face Margot.

"This guy. He worked our parties, too, but the attention he paid wasn't nice. It was scary. The staff weren't supposed to talk to us, not beyond offering food or drinks. But this guy would always—and I mean *every party*—try to ask one of the girls for their phone number, and then he'd get really moody when they said no. After the second time it happened, we all stopped accepting drinks he made. I think Leanne even complained to Rebecca. But then he'd be there at the next party and the next."

"Do you think he might have had anything to do with what happened to your friends?"

Cassie's lower lip trembled for a moment as the inescapable guilt of wondering if there was more she could have done to protect the other women she worked with washed over her. It was something everyone wondered when a friend or loved one died. *Could I have stopped this?*

She squared her shoulders, regaining her composure. "I don't know if he's guilty of murder, but if being a really unsettling creep was a crime, this would be your guy."

TWENTY-NINE

1994

Fuck.

What the fuck was he doing?

This whole plan—and calling it a plan felt like too kind a phrase for what it was—stank to high heaven.

Ed had not one but *two* dead women in his trunk, and not the faintest fucking clue what to do with them. At the moment he'd acted, he'd simply understood that he couldn't leave them in the apartment. It was too much of a risk.

But how was this any less risky?

He was about twenty minutes outside San Francisco, not really sure of where he was going, just driving until something clicked. There had to be a good place to get rid of them.

He considered the pond where he had put that girl from the bar, but he knew even as the thought crossed his mind it wasn't going to work. That body hadn't been found yet, but that didn't mean it *wouldn't* be, and three bodies in a pond in the town where he lived was going to bring too much attention.

No, he couldn't use the places he'd been.

He thought about Jimmy.

It had been years since they'd spent any time together, having made the mutual decision that it was simply not a beneficial friendship anymore. But Ed still knew where Jimmy kept his boat. He knew where the key was kept on board and all the little tricks to getting the boat out of the marina.

As long as the boat was in the water, he could probably figure it out well enough to get out into open water. Where he could toss them overboard.

No.

No, when he and Jimmy had dumped women in the past, they'd either been in much deeper water than Ed was willing to venture out into alone, or they'd weighed them down. Contrary to popular opinion, you couldn't just throw a body into the ocean and hope it would vanish completely.

The ocean had a funny way of returning its gifts if you weren't careful. Ed had gotten lucky in the past, but he didn't feel like this was going to be the time that the fates smiled kindly on him. He'd really shit the bed on this one.

He tried to be so careful in his life, knowing that one wrong move, one small mistake, could be the thing that undid him completely in the end. But he had also gotten complacent. He had gotten so *good* at this over the years that he took his own carefulness for granted.

How had he ended up here? How had he let something so stupid happen, something that could push him to the point of ruin?

There wasn't supposed to be anyone else in that apartment.

He'd watched her for *days* beforehand. He'd been sure he had known her routine. Her ad had specifically indicated she was single, and hadn't said a single goddamn thing about a nosy sister showing up at random intervals to make life difficult.

He smacked his hand on the steering wheel of the car several times and let out a guttural scream. In a car, you are free to be whatever you want to be. No one can see you let go of your humanity when you're going sixty down a California highway at night.

He wondered if he should just find a dirt road to pull down and drag the girls into the woods. A loose covering with leaves and debris, and it could be years before they were ever found. The woods were a great partner in crime because they were so dense, so wild, that unless someone went off the beaten path there were acres and acres of space that would remain untouched for Ed's entire life.

It was a good place to hide a body. As good as any other.

But he worried about the time. Getting two bodies from the road into the woods, making sure to leave nothing behind, and getting it all done before sunrise... it was a beast of a task. Anyone could drive by, there was a lot of risk in pulling off to the side of the road.

There was equal risk in taking them to the marina, but at least there was less passing traffic. At this time of night, the place should be deserted. And Jimmy had assured him they didn't have any cameras installed because no one wanted to stump up the extra fees that would be required for the maintenance and paying someone to actually look at the things from time to time.

Jimmy had explained once that while some folks opted to shell out extra money for their peace of mind, the reason everyone at his marina liked it so much was because no one cared. No one paid attention. Ed had gathered that a fair bit of illegal activity was being run through that marina, and that was what he needed.

Some place that, if anyone happened to spot him, they would know to look the other way and keep their mouth shut, because he would be doing the same for them.

See no evil, speak no evil.
Ed had a plan.
It might not be a *great* plan, but it was what he had.
There was no turning back now.

THIRTY

Everything takes longer when you want it to move faster.

Likewise, something can come together in a heartbeat when you want it to take its time.

It took only five days for Andrew Rhodes to secure Ed's temporary release from San Quentin. Putting the team together and coordinating with law enforcement on the other end was going to take a few days more, but the tentative date for Ed's little field trip had been set for the following Tuesday morning.

Only a few days away.

Meanwhile, every time Margot got a text or email notification, her heart was in her throat waiting for it to be from Leon or DeAndra, confirming that Drake Winston was their guy.

Everything was ready, the warrants, their whole team, all ready to go on a moment's notice when they finally got the confirmation that it was him.

All they could do in the meantime was wait.

And Margot wasn't very good at waiting.

The moment the case broke wide open, Margot was sitting across from Wes at a diner in Russian Hill. It was a place that

Andrew had taken her once, somewhere that felt trapped in time, with an older waitress who called her hon, and bacon that was cooked so crisp it was almost burnt, but tasted like heaven.

The last time Margot had been here, she'd learned that Ed had remarried while in prison, an unbelievable blow to her at the time, and something that would come back to haunt her not long after.

Fucking Rhonda.

Fucking Ethan.

Margot and Wes were finishing up their breakfast when a message buzzed on both their phones at the same time. Barely taking the time to wipe her hands on a napkin before she grabbed her phone, Margot read the message—from Leon—and in three simple words knew that day was going to be one they never forgot.

It's a match.

The DNA checks had come back.

Drake Winston was their man.

Margot glanced up to see Wes staring at his phone, before he looked up and met her gaze, his face shining with relief. There is a staggering difference between knowing something to be true in your heart, and finally having the evidence to support it. Margot sat back in the creaky vinyl booth and let her breath out in a *whoosh*. She'd been waiting for this, for this exact moment, since she'd first seen that tiny trace of evidence on their last victim. Now she hoped against hope that this was it.

And Diana Prince *was* their last victim.

The last victim found, anyway.

Whether Sabine or Diana had died first was irrelevant. They *would* be his last victims.

The rest of the Larks would be able to rest a little easier

tonight, because very soon the man who had been a specter in all of their nightmares, who had lurked in every shadow, would no longer be a threat to them.

Margot tossed some cash on the table and she and Wes made a beeline for the door. The whole time her pulse was hammering in her ears so loudly she could barely hear a thing that was happening around her. As they stepped outside and headed to her car, she was sure Wes was trying to speak to her, trying to get her attention or ask her something, but she could only hear the general tone of his voice, the words weren't getting through.

"Margot?" he said, after his initial attempts had failed. "You with me?"

She snapped out of her hyper focus as she closed the car door behind her and looked at him.

And then, without thinking, she said, "I love you."

Wes, who was buckling himself in behind the steering wheel, paused so suddenly the seat belt slipped from his fingers and slid back to the door.

"What?"

She felt like an absolute moron for saying it in that moment and her mouth went bone dry. This wasn't at all how she had wanted to have this conversation. She'd wanted them to be free of the burden of this case, she'd wanted to be finished with Ed, but it turned out that with all of those things now on the cusp of being a reality, her subconscious had decided *enough* and just let it all come out.

Was there ever really a good time, or a perfect time, to say something that might change your whole life? Margot had believed there was, but maybe this was as good a time as any.

"I..." Her cheeks felt flushed, and she was suddenly too shy to look him in the eye. "Fuck. I didn't mean..."

"Don't you dare say you didn't mean it, Margot." His voice,

usually so full of humor and much-needed lightness, was now totally serious. "You don't get to do that." This last part was almost a whisper.

"I don't want to take it back," she said, looking at the glove compartment like she might find her spine in there alongside Wes's registration and some spare fast-food napkins. "I just meant to say it at a better time."

Wes laughed, then, resting one hand on the steering wheel. Margot wasn't sure if he was laughing at her or the situation. She *knew* deep down he wasn't mocking her, but she wasn't accustomed to exposing herself emotionally. The only person she had said *I love you* to in the last twenty years was her brother. Her mother before she'd died. But no one else.

It hadn't felt right with anyone else, but the words themselves, even though she meant them, still felt so strange coming out of her mouth she didn't know what to do with them now.

They hung in the car the way a perfume can linger long after the person wearing it has left.

Finally, Margot looked at Wes and found that he was patiently waiting for her.

He had been patiently waiting for her for a long time.

There was a sweet earnestness to his expression that was unusual for him, yet it managed to make her heart clench because of what she wanted to believe it meant.

"Say it again," he said, his tone light but commanding.

Her cheeks warmed and she tried to look away, but he placed a thumb and forefinger under her chin and forced her to look at him.

"Say it again," he repeated.

"Wes..."

"I want to make sure I heard you right."

"You heard me just fine."

"Then say it again."

Now she was both comforted and annoyed, familiar territory for the two of them, and so she said, with no small amount of crankiness, "Fine. I love you, you giant idiot."

His expression shifted then, a smile practically breaking his face in half, and he released her chin only to place his hand against her cheek, his thumb grazing her cheekbone, his eyes never leaving her face.

"Now that's more like it."

She thought he might kiss her then, but he didn't. Instead, he gave her one excruciatingly long look, like he wanted to memorize her face, then he dropped his hand, did up his seat belt, and started the car.

"That's... that's it?" She stared at him. While she wasn't an expert in declaring her feelings, she thought that there was supposed to be more to it than this. Some kind of reciprocation. Or if not that, a polite rejection? But there was supposed to be something.

He put his arm behind her headrest as he checked for traffic before pulling away from the curb. When they were on their way to the station—a pause that had likely been no longer than a minute, but to Margot felt like a decade—he let his hand slide down and cup the back of her neck, fingers giving her ponytail a gentle tug.

"Margot, if you didn't already know that I have been in love with you since the moment I first saw you, then you aren't half as good a detective as I thought you were."

"Oh." She felt foolish for how much she was blushing, because in that moment she felt like a teenage girl instead of a woman inching towards forty. But *damn* it felt good to feel so out of sorts. "Well, OK then. I'm glad we sorted that out."

His hand tensed on the back of her neck.

"As soon as all of this is over, you and I are going to have a very real conversation about this. And once we've had that conversation, I plan to do some very unspeakable things to you. But that's going to have to wait. Just a little longer."

An unexpected shudder of pleasure went through her when his voice darkened with that promise. But she could wait.

They'd waited this long, dancing around it, pretending it didn't exist.

Just a little longer wouldn't kill either of them.

THIRTY-ONE

Margot was damned if she was going to die on the day she finally opened up and shared her feelings with someone.

She knew that was a stupid thing to think, but as she and Wes arrived at the muster point to take down Drake, she couldn't help but think: *I can't die after saying I love you for the first time.*

It would simply be too clichéd, like the veteran cop in a movie talking about how close he was to retirement and then walking straight into gunfire.

No, if anyone deserved a happy ending, she figured it was her.

Or at least a happy for now.

There would be time to figure things out later. Right now, they had an arrest to make.

Margot was no stranger to peril.

While her job was not one that put her in front of gunfire on a regular basis, she had still faced things in her tenure that had rattled her to the core. She had seen the impact of a sniper in person. She'd been in the midst of a tense armed standoff where it hadn't looked like she was going to walk out at the end.

She had been in a house as it was peppered with bullets intended for only one thing: to kill.

She had faced death and every time it had taken a look at her and said, *not yet.* While she knew that every person alive was working with borrowed time, she knew, deep in her gut, that today was not her day.

But she was no fool. She and the rest of the task force donned their bulletproof vests. They wore their department-issue windbreakers, and they weren't going to rely on their service weapons alone.

Going in to arrest Drake Winston, there would be no short-cuts, no unnecessary risks to personnel. Because a man who had spent the last two years killing was also a man who might be willing to take a few people down with him when he was caught.

He might be willing to take himself down, too, something that they wanted to keep from happening at all costs. This was a man they wanted alive, because he was owed the full weight of punishment that the justice department could bear down upon him. He would hopefully join Ed on Death Row soon enough. And while Margot knew that he was likely to never get that injection and would spend the rest of his days rotting in a cell, that was going to have to be enough for her.

Knowing he would never be able to hurt someone else, that was her reward in all this. The women he had tormented, the city he had held in a tight embrace of fear that it hadn't known since the serial killer heyday of the 1970s, they would all be able to sleep a little better tonight.

Margot, too, would put her head to her pillow and sleep well knowing that all her work hadn't been for nothing. That she had done the job she'd set out to do.

Her borrowed weapon felt heavy as she checked it to ensure that it had been properly cleaned and unloaded the last time it was taken from the tactical locker. She made sure she had a fresh clip and that everything was working, then stepped out of the way so the next member of the team could be prepared.

In all, including SWAT, there would be close to sixty police officers descending on Winston's home in under an hour. He lived in an apartment building that could not be evacuated without raising alarm, so the plan was to move in from all angles at once. Police would be prepared outside in case he tried to make an exit through any of the building's doors. Before moving in, a team would be set up on the roof of his building to rappel down the front and go in through his apartment's windows, barring his ability to try to escape either by using the fire escape, or a more permanent escape by jumping.

That team would also throw in the flash-bangs that would hopefully disorient Winston enough that the team waiting outside his door in the hallway could move in and arrest him.

Since he was being considered armed and dangerous, their approach had to be to subdue him first, then prioritize asking questions once they had him in custody. A polite knock on the door wasn't going to work here.

During their time watching Drake, it was clear he was living alone, and there was no one else in the apartment with him. No girlfriend that came to visit. No roommate to offset the steep local rents. Which made sense, because he wouldn't have been able to pull off the things he'd been doing if there was anyone else living with him, wondering what he was up to.

The women he'd killed, many of them had died before they'd been dumped, meaning he was killing them somewhere else. Margot hoped that once they had a chance to thoroughly scour his apartment, they would either find their crime scene there, or an obvious path to it. A rental slip for a storage locker, something along those lines.

Now that they had their DNA match, a whole new world of investigative options opened up. Requests to access his phone data had already been submitted. If he had a FasTrak tag on his car and had been stupid enough to leave it on while transporting bodies, they would soon have that information as well. They'd needed to wait a long time to get access to all the things they would need to put this guy down for the long haul, but now that the first domino had tipped, the rest would fall a lot faster than expected.

Margot, Wes, and Leon would not be on the front line of officers heading into the apartment. There were officers with more tactical training who were better suited to that job, but Margot knew it pained Leon especially not to be the one to slap the bracelets on this guy once he'd been subdued.

They *would* be the first in line to check the apartment once he was under lock and key. And provided he didn't immediately lawyer up, they would also be the first ones to get a crack at him in the interrogation room when they returned to the station.

Margot could already feel the thrill of sitting across the table from this guy. She wanted nothing more than to be the one to get him to admit to what he'd done. While she knew it was unlikely that a guy who had gone this long without getting caught was going to say something stupid just because he was in cuffs, she *loved* a good interrogation, and she wanted very badly for her chance to take a crack at this man.

But first they needed to bring him in alive.

By the time everything was coordinated, it was already late afternoon. The process of organizing a task force that large, so everyone knew who was acting when and who needed to be where, was no easy song and dance, and Margot was glad that it fell to Leon to choreograph and not her.

For a moment, as their cars moved toward Hunters Point, Margot couldn't help but think of the last time she was part of an operation like this, with a well-oiled machine heading in to bring Jimmy to justice, only to have him take his sentencing into his own hands.

She was hoping things wouldn't go that way this time. She

didn't wish that kind of memory on anyone else, and she also didn't want Winston to slip away before they had a chance to talk to him.

While she had a pretty good idea of his *why* after reading his online posts, there were other things she wanted to know. And one was tied to a lingering case that would have happened well before Drake was old enough to have committed it, but it had come to her attention while researching murders in the Muir Woods area, and she was dying to know if there was some kind of connection.

Probably not. Plenty of killers would have looked at the deep woods and seen a good place to hide a body. But these murders were different. The bodies weren't hidden to avoid detection. They were left behind with the obvious hope that they *would* be discovered.

In some capacity, this guy had been waiting a long time for today to happen, because he had wanted to get caught. There was no other reason to make your kills so easy to find.

The late afternoon sun was dropping low over the horizon and as they moved toward the apartment complex, various cars in their entourage peeled off, heading to park on different blocks, to set up near the end of alleys, to make sure the entire area was covered and everyone was where they needed to be.

Hunters Point wasn't a particularly cozy part of San Francisco. It was home to shipyards, projects and other low-income housing, and unlike the Tenderloin, which was a blight in the middle of downtown San Francisco, the location of Hunters Point meant it didn't get as much attention, and the crime in the area was the worst in the entire city.

There weren't many tall apartment buildings here, but Winston was in a newer low-income development, which at five stories tall was one of the biggest buildings around. It was a modern, ugly bit of construction which was at odds with a lot of the existing housing around it. Too fresh, too clean-looking, too new, as if it had been transported directly from an architecture firm's office and no one had ever taken a glance at the actual neighborhood before putting together something quite so unpleasant to look at.

They parked down the block, unmarked cars finding spots that would be inconspicuous to anyone looking out their front window.

There were three similar apartments all in a line, with Winston's situated in the middle. The first wave of officers who would go through his window were climbing up the furthest building at the end of the block where they'd be able to move across rooftops and make their way through Winston's front-facing window.

Margot had been wrong, he had no fire escape. The building had a clean facade. And it was also so squat that if he jumped from his third-floor window he'd most likely only break his bones instead of dying, unless he went head first.

None of it looked like what Margot had imagined, her own visual landscape so well-defined by the area immediately around her downtown. This wasn't the same at all.

Still, she needed to readjust her expectations so she could prepare herself for what was to come.

Margot's radio crackled with voices, people announcing their locations and readiness. And at last, when she looked up, there were three men on the top of the apartment's roof wearing all black and standing on the ledge, ready to drop off the side when Leon gave the word.

Leon, who was sitting in the front seat of the car with Wes beside him, Margot in the back, seemed to wait for a beat, as if he needed a moment to truly believe this was happening. That the work he'd put into this was finally going to be worth it.

"I told my wife that once we're done with this case, I'm handing in my resignation," Leon admitted, almost to himself rather than them. "I think when I promised her that, neither of us really thought we would come to see the day it happened. It felt too impossible. I thought this case might end up outliving me."

He held the radio tightly in his hand and Margot noted the slight tremble there. She reached up from the back seat to squeeze his shoulder.

"We're going to get him," she promised, even though she had no control over what happened inside.

She closed her eyes for a brief moment and said a silent prayer that all of this effort was going to pay off. Then she watched as Leon lifted the radio to his mouth and said, "On three. One, two, three—all units go!"

Outside, Margot could hear the melee begin, even though she couldn't see what was happening inside the building. The three officers on the ledge of the apartment jumped backwards, making her hold her breath at the audacity of ignoring physics and defying gravity. They bounced easily down the side of the building until they were just over Winston's apartment windows. Then she saw one of the three hold up his hands and give his own countdown with his fingers. Three, two, one.

They took the hop simultaneously, feet going through windows, glass shattering, but rather than diving in through the broken glass, they tossed canisters through instead.

A second later there was a bright flash, like an explosion, followed by the deafening *crack-crack-crack* of three flash-bangs going off. Smoke billowed out through the window and over the radio someone said, "Bangs are a go. Move move move!"

More sounds, more shouting, all muffled from this far away. In some of the nearby houses, people had come outside to see what was going on, phones out, recording all the action. Normally in this area the presence of police would make people hide away to avoid the attention turning to them, but it was obvious from the scale of the operation this wasn't your standard drug bust.

So the neighbors were coming out to enjoy the show.

"Let's go," Leon said, and they followed his command, getting out of the car, guns drawn but angled low, no one wanting to get too amped up and make any mistakes.

Other officers were exiting nearby vehicles. Margot recognized many of them from task force meetings, but their names and faces had all started to blend together after a while. She spotted Branson, his expression intense, focused, and she followed the rest of the crew toward the building. As they got closer, she could hear the yelling from upstairs with more force, and she braced herself for the sound of gunfire, but it never came.

After a few tense moments of shouting and curses from upstairs, the radio clipped to her vest crackled.

"We've got him."

THIRTY-TWO

As the din died down somewhat and they were able to make their way into the building, Margot felt an unexpected flood of relief when they got to the packed third-floor corridor and she saw Winston being led out of his apartment door, head hung low, a defeated expression on his face.

He knew he was caught.

Margot watched as he passed them, wondering if there might be a moment of awareness, of acknowledgment that he'd known they had been the ones following his every move. But he didn't look up, he stared at his shoes the whole time as the arresting officer nudged him toward the stairs.

They would have plenty of time to chat with him later. For now, they had an apartment to look over. The crowd of officers involved in the arrest started to thin out, receiving pats on the back from Leon and new instructions from over the radio. Their work was done, and they would have to move on to other things for the rest of their shift. The core members of the task force remained behind, while a few others who had been working the case headed back to the office to prepare themselves to go through the evidence that would soon arrive, and see if any of their informational requests for phone and pass data might have come in yet.

Leon was the first one into the apartment, the smell of smoke still lingering in the air and the last of the fumes trailing out the door and broken windows, making it briefly hard to see inside.

It was a small apartment, and unlike some of the others Margot had recently been in, wasn't nicely kept. Drake Winston was a slob. The sink was piled high with dishes, while the bed visible in one corner of the studio unit was unmade, and dirty clothes were heaped in a pile on the floor.

Some of the mess could be excused from the way the cops had burst in. The glass all over the floor, for one, and the table that had been knocked over by the entrance when the police had come through the door. But the rest was all evidence of someone who didn't spend a lot of time or thought in keeping his surroundings tidy.

It was funny, because from the cleanliness of his kills and his crime scenes, Margot would have expected someone a little more meticulous in their day-to-day life.

But no one ever fit the profiles perfectly. People were full of quirks.

There were six of them in total in the apartment, which soon felt like too many, given how compact the space was. But in a way, Margot was glad there were extra eyes that would follow behind her, because she wouldn't want hubris to be the reason she missed something vital.

Things got overlooked all the time at crime scenes, and that was why a scene wasn't released until it had been checked over by a number of different people. But they were the first wave here. CSI would be right behind them to bag and tag things.

They were all sporting latex gloves, but since it wasn't a crime scene, technically, they weren't wearing boot covers. There wasn't any blood evidence for them to potentially mess up. Still, they were treating the apartment with the same reverence as if a body had been found here.

Margot also knew that it was Winston's car, which would be getting towed to the CSI lab even as they spoke, that had the strongest likelihood of having physical evidence left behind from some of their victims. And they would need to match the carpet fibers they had found on Diana to those in the car. If those matched it would be one more nail in Winston's coffin, though the DNA evidence was what would be the biggest slam dunk in court.

Juries loved DNA evidence.

But Margot knew the more they had, the better.

A photographer had arrived and was snapping photos of the general interior of the apartment, awaiting their command to capture anything specific. Much like a crime scene, they wanted things in situ before they moved them. You never knew what the position of a thing might mean after the fact.

The space might be small, but it was full of a lifetime of Winston's crap, and with things piled in heaps or organized haphazardly, there was no rhyme or reason to what they were looking at or looking for.

His laptop and phone were collected, and Margot suspected he would be a more frequent visitor to the Larks website than even she was. His hair and toothbrush were taken; further means to tie his DNA to their victims in case the samples Margot had collected were called into question.

Margot inspected Winston's bookshelf, stocked only with titles from so-called alpha-male self-help gurus and washed-up celebrities, as well as stacks of violent video games that reminded Margot of the bleak forums Drake had associated with online. There was a glass bong on the shelf as well as a little metal container of weed and weed paraphernalia, but that was hardly something to write home about. Weed had been legal in the state for a few years already and though it still made *illegal* warning bells fire off in Margot's head, she had learned to stop looking at it like anything special.

Ignoring the smell while out in public was a lot harder for her.

A cop's brain had a hard time unlearning things.

Everything on the shelf was covered in a thin film of dust, and she suspected the apartment itself hadn't been thoroughly cleaned since Winston moved in. It had that unpleasant, stereotypical bachelor pad feeling to it, like Margot might want to wash all of her clothes as soon as she got out of here just in case there was semen or bed bugs on the things she was touching.

She glanced up and noticed something unusual.

"Can someone grab me a stool?" she asked. She'd seen a little folding ladder in the kitchen, likely owing to how ridiculously high the kitchen cabinets went up the wall.

Branson appeared at her side with the ladder and even unfolded it for her, a surprisingly chivalrous gesture for someone his age. She nodded and thanked him.

"You find something?" he asked.

"Not sure yet." She took the small flashlight from his hand and angled it up to the vent over the bookshelf. "Anything about that look odd to you?"

Branson shook his head. "Screws all look attached, nothing out of the ordinary."

"Mmm." Margot climbed up the two steps of the small ladder. "What I see is streaks. Streaks in the dust, here and here." She pointed to the areas by the screwheads, and then on the bottom lip of the vent cover. "Like someone moved this. Often enough that it didn't have dust on it." She ran her free hand over the shelf that was now below her and held up her fingers so Branson could see how dusty they were.

"Interesting," Branson replied, though she wasn't sure if he understood yet what she was implying.

She stuck the small flashlight between her teeth and twisted the screws at the corner of the vent. With slippery gloves on it wasn't easy, but it was still easier than it should have been. The screws had been regularly loosened and left that way, like it had become too much of a chore to get a screwdriver out after a while and he preferred to just use his hands.

Margot removed the vent cover and handed it down to Branson, then took the flashlight from her mouth and pointed the beam inside.

There was a simple shoebox within, the bright orange cardboard catching her eye immediately. She needed to stop herself from pulling it out, calling the photographer over and letting him get some pictures first, before taking the box from its hiding place in the wall and bringing it over to the island in the kitchen.

Everyone paused what they were doing, all six detectives and a photographer eager to see what was waiting inside the box.

When Margot lifted the lid, she knew that any doubts that might have lingered about Drake Winston's involvement in this case were long gone.

Aside from an assortment of Polaroid photos of their victims, seemingly captured in the minutes before they were killed, there were assorted trinkets in the box as well. Margot immediately recognized the bird necklace she had seen Rebecca Watson wearing in an old photo.

The other earrings and necklaces and bracelets were going to take longer to identify, but looking at them, all Margot could think was, *Thank God he left Diana's bracelet behind.*

She picked up one of the Polaroids gingerly, and the wide, fearful eyes of Leanne Wu looked back at her.

She took out the rest of the photos, laying them side by side on the countertop, every one of their victims accounted for.

Margot had half expected to find a photo or two telling

them there were still bodies left to be found, but she was grateful that didn't seem to be the case.

He'd left all the women there for them to find.

Unlike with Ed, there would be no wild goose chases after the fact.

Margot looked up at Leon, who was staring at the photos like they represented a puzzle he'd been trying to solve for over a year, and almost couldn't accept that it was now assembled.

"What do you say, Leon? Want to go talk to this guy?"

Leon looked pale and exhausted but there was a fire lit inside him unlike anything Margot could recall seeing before.

"You bet your ass I do."

THIRTY-THREE

The thing about serial killers is, despite their monstrous actions, they are just men.

Margot was thinking about this as she looked through the two-way mirror that showed the interior of the precinct's main interrogation room. Drake Winston was still handcuffed and sitting in one of the chairs, adjusting his weight to try to get comfortable. Since the chair had one leg that was shorter than all the others, every time he moved slightly the chair would rock, knocking him off-center and forcing him to adjust all over again.

He wasn't a large man, maybe a hundred and eighty pounds by the look of him. And though he'd been slouching when he passed Margot at the apartment, she got a fair read on his height at about the same as her own five-foot-eight. He had dark, mussed hair that could have used a haircut but was probably intentionally shaggy, and his skin was tan, like he spent a lot of time outside.

Margot already knew he had a passion for hiking.

Leon had been talking to him for about twenty minutes, and

the guy wasn't saying much of anything. No surprises there. Margot had assumed it would take a while for him to break, but she was surprised by his behavior.

Margot didn't know many serial killers, but she knew *one* very well, well enough to have observed a lot of the behaviors typically found in someone who was capable of doing something like that. And most killers had a brashness, a confidence in the way they spoke to authorities. They wanted attention, recognition, and more than anything they wanted to prove that they were the smartest person in the room at any given time.

But Drake Winston wasn't flaunting his intelligence. He wasn't being smug. For the most part he quietly offered up one-word answers. And while he hadn't yet asked for a lawyer, it wasn't doing them much good anyway because he wasn't *talking*, and that was driving Margot crazy.

Leon left the room, coming into the observation area where Margot and Wes had been sitting in uncomfortable folding chairs, watching the entire thing unfold. There was also a video camera in the room, recording everything as it happened, but Margot liked to watch things in person.

"This guy it starting to get on my nerves," Leon admitted, sagging into a chair nearby. "He's not giving me anything."

"You want me to take a turn?" Margot asked.

"Knock yourself out, kid." Leon waved a dismissive hand toward the mirror. "If you can get more than an *I dunno* out of the guy, I will buy you the nicest bottle of Scotch money can purchase."

"Margot's a gin girl," Wes said absently, still watching Drake through the window.

"Also, the most expensive Scotch money can buy is well outside any of our bankrolls," Margot said with a smile. As she got to her feet, she wasn't sure if the chair groaned or she did. She squeezed Leon's shoulder and picked up a plastic evidence bag she had requested they be allowed to keep for the interrogations.

She also grabbed a paper cup and filled it with coffee from the nearby kitchenette. The coffee at the office was repellent, and this cup was not for her. But she suspected this guy was going to require a little rapport-building before he said anything to anyone.

Margot thought about Andrew's job offer, and how this sort of situation was precisely the kind of thing he wanted her to come in to handle. In a way, she was treating this interrogation not just as vital to their case, but also to prove to herself that she deserved the position Andrew was offering her.

She opened the interrogation room door and noted with some pleasure that Drake was surprised to see her. He had likely anticipated Leon would be returning for round two. Margot liked to be unexpected, because it put the suspect off their guard. The more upper hands she could have in an interrogation, the better.

After placing the coffee in front of Drake, she settled into her own chair, the wooden legs scraping loudly against the tile floor, and made herself comfortable across the table from a killer.

Not her first time, by any metric.

"Drake... you mind if I call you Drake?" she asked, keeping her tone light, almost friendly. Sometimes it was best to dive right in with the bad cop routine, something she was fairly adept at, but in other situations it was better to play nice, build rapport. She would try that angle first before she jumped into being mean.

Drake already had opinions about women, and it would be interesting to see how he responded to sitting across the table from one in this situation.

"Sure," he mumbled, then tugged the hot coffee toward him, the sound of his cuffs on the table startlingly loud in the otherwise quiet room. "You can call me whatever you want, I guess."

From someone else it might have been lascivious, or a come-on, but from him it was a matter-of-fact acceptance that she *could* call him whatever she wanted.

"Drake, my name is Detective Phalen. If you like, you can call me Margot. I know this has been a pretty interesting day for you so far. For us, too. I wanted to see if there was anything I could get you before we started to chat."

He lifted the coffee in a semi-salute. "This is good, thanks."

"That just tells me you haven't tried it yet," she said with a smile.

Dutifully, Drake sipped the coffee and made a suitably disgusted face. "This is garbage."

"It certainly is, but unfortunately that's all we have available to us right now. I can assure you that quality levels aside it will certainly jack up your heart rate and keep you awake for a whole night shift, though, so it isn't without its redeeming qualities."

Drake sipped again, trying to hide his expression and then nodded to her. "Thanks."

"Look, let's you and I just get to know each other a bit better, and if that goes well, I'll have someone go out and grab a Starbucks, maybe a bite to eat, OK?"

He shrugged, something she'd watched him do with Leon several times, not a yes or no, nothing committal. It was frustrating, but at least she'd gotten him to give her a full sentence, so it was better than nothing. The kindness approach seemed to be working. She'd continue with it a little longer.

"I think maybe this will work best if we start from the beginning. Why don't you tell me about yourself growing up?"

Drake chuckled but didn't look at her. "You're making it sound like we're on a first date or something."

"Well, respectfully, Drake, I don't really care if you're an

Aquarius or where you went to college. I want to know if you hated your mother."

His hands, which had been fidgeting against the side of the Styrofoam cup, paused. He continued to stare pointedly at the table, but he had definitely heard her.

"I guess a lot of people hate their moms."

"Tell me about yours."

One shoulder lifted in a familiar shrug. "Not much to say. Some people want to be moms, some people don't want to be moms. I think it's safe to say what kind I had."

Margot made a small *mmm* noise, then sat back in her chair, letting her hands rest in her lap. Calm, cool, casual.

"Was your mom the first woman you wanted to hurt?"

This time Drake did look at her. He lifted his head slowly, like the effort of looking straight forward hurt his neck, but when he finally met her gaze, she wasn't surprised by what she saw.

Dead eyes.

Killers, or people emotionally and mentally damaged enough to become killers, all seemed to have the same eyes. Flat, empty, completely lacking in any kind of warmth or friendliness.

She always thought of a shark when she looked into Ed's eyes, but that probably wasn't fair to sharks.

There was no human animation to Drake's eyes.

Margot didn't like to editorialize, but she couldn't help thinking to herself, *It's probably because he has no soul.*

"What do you know about it?" he asked coldly.

"About you and your mother? Not much, not yet. But I would know more if you told me. Is she still alive?"

"Yeah."

"Not for lack of trying on your part, though, right?" She chuckled at the end, and continued to hold her relaxed pose, letting him know she was chill, she didn't mind this conversation.

Drake let out a huff, somewhere between a scoff and a laugh. "Can't start with your ma. Too obvious."

"I don't think so. Not unless you wait too long. If you're an adult, maybe. Then there's time for a long history, lots of people can share that the relationship was fraught. But no, you plan it early, pull it off before anyone looks at you like there's something wrong with you? Well, then you've got something."

Drake sipped his coffee again, this time showing no sign whatsoever that he had any opinions on its quality. "Wish I'd met you when I was twelve," he said. "Might have saved me a lot of frustrating years."

"Might have. So, what was she?"

"What do you mean?"

"People who hate their moms usually hate them for a specific reason, but it boils down to two things at the end of the day. Either she didn't pay enough attention to you, or she paid *too much* attention to you. Which was it?"

Drake arched an eyebrow at her, really looking at her for the first time since she'd come into the room. She hated the attention, but she was ready for it. She'd sat across from Ed while he scrutinized her, and somehow that would always be worse than the killers she met for the first time.

The devil you know, and all that.

"You're a strange lady cop, you know that?"

"I'm just a strange lady, Drake. Nothing to do with me being a cop."

"You hate your mom?" he asked as he leaned back in his own chair, the leg rocking while he tried to mirror her posture.

"No. Wasn't too thrilled with her for killing herself, but I didn't hate her. But it's different for me, I'm a woman."

He smiled knowingly. "Daddy issues."

She fired a finger gun at him. "Bingo."

He nodded, and this time there was more enthusiasm to it.

"That explains a lot. I've noticed with chicks who have daddy issues it usually goes one of two ways, like you said. Either they turn into sluts, or they take on a really masculine job. I think it's because deep down they figure their dad wanted a son."

"Interesting philosophy."

"You think your dad wanted a son?"

Margot pondered this, then gave him her own shrug. "Maybe. But I think he probably didn't want kids at all. I think we were his way of pretending he was living a nice, normal life." She hadn't changed her posture at all. "You didn't answer my question about your mom, though."

"My mom, same thing. She didn't want kids. Wanted to make sure I knew it. Every time I fucked up or even when I didn't, she would tell me that she never wanted to have me anyway, least I could do to thank her for skipping the abortion was to not make her life any harder."

Margot let out a whistle. "I can see why you wouldn't be her biggest fan. Let me guess, the older you got, the more you realized that all the women you met just wanted men to make their lives easier. Like your mom."

He stared at her for a moment, and she wondered if she had taken things a step too far, but instead, Drake smiled. "I don't know if I ever thought about it that way, but *yeah*. Women say they want nice guys, but they don't, you know? They'll put up with the shittiest boyfriend in the world if he drives a nice car, or takes them to expensive restaurants, or on trips. I swear to God you could be Ted Bundy and as long as you have a penthouse apartment you could still pull hoes. Women want things to be handed to them, they don't care how nice a guy is."

"You a nice guy, Drake?"

"I used to be."

"And now you're Ted Bundy. But without the penthouse."

He rolled his eyes, lifting his cuffed hands as if he wanted to make some kind of gesture, forgetting he was still holding the coffee, and some sloshed on his sleeve. "Aw, fuck," he grumbled, setting the cup back down again. "That sucks."

Margot waited a beat, not responding to the interruption.

When Drake realized she was still waiting for him, he adjusted himself in his seat again. "I'm not Ted Bundy," he said, with a tight growl at the back of his throat. "Ted Bundy wishes he was as smart as I was."

THIRTY-FOUR

1994

Ed Finch was smarter than this.

But it seemed like tonight, all his smarts had gone out the window.

As it turned out, piloting a boat was not as easy as it looked, and given his only previous experience had been watching Jimmy do it, he realized very quickly—and with some minor damage to Jimmy's boat and the one behind it at the marina—that it wasn't as simple as driving a car.

He knew it had been a mistake even as he pulled the boat away from its slip and headed into open water, the collected group of sea lions at the end of the pier calling out their warnings as he went. But once he was in the actual ocean, he understood how foolish this had all been.

The water off the coast wasn't as menacing as it would be much further out, but all the same, for an inexperienced sailor who was already running on adrenaline and madness, it was enough to make for a very rough ride.

Jimmy's boat was a forty-five-foot cabin cruiser, for which

Ed was grateful, because if it had been a sailboat he would have scrapped this idea completely. It was bad enough that he needed to fight against the choppy waves, if he'd had to contend with the wind as well... He had a feeling that would have been the moment a vengeful God would seize the opportunity to wipe Ed from the planet.

Ed wasn't a religious man, but he did sometimes wonder if there was a world-class smiting waiting for him. It was almost like every new kill he made was challenging some higher power to prove itself, to come down and stop him.

No one ever did, which further convinced Ed there was no God to fear.

If there was a hell, he wasn't worried about that either. Whatever was coming, was coming.

Tonight, he just needed to make sure he could keep this boat afloat long enough to figure out where to dump the two bodies, and then get it back into the slip. He hoped any of the new damage to the hull would be written off as the unfortunate side-effects of recent storms.

He also knew Jimmy wouldn't say anything if he figured out what Ed was up to. They might not be friends anymore, but the mutually assured destruction of the secrets they shared was enough to keep each of them tight-lipped about the sins of their former pal.

Sometimes fear was better than friendship.

Ed barely noticed the change in the landscape around him, it was too dark. But when he heard the grind of rocks under the hull of the boat, he knew he was either too close to the coastline, or he had stumbled across one of the tiny islands that littered the ocean just offshore.

It was one of those islands he'd been hoping for, because they were uninhabited, and as the boat had just demonstrated, they were hard to reach. Too far out for bold swimmers, too rocky for boaters to come to for day trips. They were mostly relegated to collecting bird shit and growing collections of spindly trees that seemed to defy the odds of all the salt air and water around them.

He cursed himself for not taking the risk of dumping the bodies in the middle of the water and hoping animals and offshore currents would do the work for him, but he had somehow gotten it in his head that this was where the girls were meant to go. Somewhere only he knew, somewhere that nature and man couldn't find them.

The boat came to a stop, rocking Ed forward against the steering wheel so sharply it felt like someone had punched him in the stomach. It took a moment for his breath to come back to him, and once it did, he knew he had to act quickly. While he was no nautical expert, he did know that none of the unpleasant sounds he'd heard so far were loud enough to be doing permanent damage to the hull.

However, if it continued to bash up against the rocks, that wouldn't remain the case for too long.

He moved to the back of the boat—was that the stern? He could never remember—and tossed the anchor over the side. It dropped only a few feet into the water before coming to a stop, so he felt confident that the universe had somehow guided him to the exact location he'd been trying to manifest. He had to hope the rocks under the boat and leading up onto the shore weren't too jagged. It seemed like the ocean only had two modes when it came to shaping rocks: smooth beach stones or deadly sharp spires that jutted out from the waves.

Once he felt sure that the boat wasn't going to drift away on him, he moved the first of the two bodies to the front of the boat. The bow? Yes, that was it.

He struggled with her weight much like he had at the apartment, but thankfully there wouldn't be much more moving around necessary. They were almost done.

He heard her splash when he pushed her over, but when he

glanced down, he could see that the body was tidily nestled among the rocks, partially submerged and bobbing in the water, but not going anywhere.

One down, one to go.

Ed wiped the sweat from his brow and got to work.

THIRTY-FIVE

Drake Winston was fully focused on Margot now, and while she was glad to have engaged him, she could have done without those soulless eyes boring into her own.

He was a truly unsettling man to sit across from once he broke out of his shell, and while that had been the goal of this entire conversation, she found herself somehow surprised by the outcome. She hadn't expected him to change so easily. Only a few minutes earlier he'd been completely shut down, but now he seemed overly keen to interact with her.

She knew that there was a *chance* her approach would work, but there was no magical interrogation formula that worked with every suspect. Sometimes they liked kindness, sometimes they reacted better to threats, and sometimes you just needed to wind them up and let them say too much all on their own.

With Drake, it seemed that he liked to be *perceived*. He liked that she asked him questions about himself and not only his crimes, and it was apparently making him more eager to speak.

Good.

Unusual, but good.

Margot wanted to look over to the mirror, to share something with Wes and Leon, to make sure they were watching, but there was no point, she couldn't see what was going on behind the glass, and she knew perfectly well she had a rapt audience.

So she kept her attention all for Drake, since that seemed to be what he wanted.

"I have a question, and it's been bugging me since all this started." She shifted her chair closer to the table, bracing her forearms on the tabletop and lacing her fingers together.

"Sure, what's that?"

"How did you get the bodies into the park? I mean, I'd guess the average weight of all our victims was between one hundred and twenty and one hundred and fifty. Not *heavy*, but that's still a lot of literal dead weight to move around. And some of them were found in such remote locations. Like, the recent girls, I get it. You just pulled over and waited until the coast was clear and then pushed them off the side. You didn't even bother covering them. You really got our attention with those." She was careful about her phrasing here. She didn't say *you really wanted our attention*. That could potentially put up some barriers, telling him what he was feeling, desiring. Instead, she gave him the outcome he'd wanted.

He'd gotten their attention.

He'd already *had* their attention, but the nuances there would likely be a moot point to Drake.

Margot knew she needed to get into specifics now, because he hadn't actually *confessed* to anything, even if he was more freely behaving like the psychopath he was. She sensed the best approach would be to encourage him to take ownership of what he'd done, to wear it with pride, because that was how she would really get him talking. At the same time, she had to be wary of saying something he didn't want to hear, as that might cause him to shut down.

"You guys liked that?" he asked, tilting his head to the side like a dog who had just heard one of its favorite words. "You like it when all the hard work is done for you?"

Margot smiled. "You didn't make any of this easy for us. You've been very clever."

He nodded, that sick smile back on his face. "You have to be smart to keep it going, you know?"

"So, tell me how you got them into the park. We have theories, but I want to know if I'm right."

Drake stared at her for a long time. She could see the internal battle over whether or not to get into the details—and thus give himself away—or to stay tight-lipped and pretend like he hadn't done it. Most men would have taken the latter option, but he wasn't most men.

"I'm going to level with you here, Drake, because you strike me as someone who appreciates it when people are honest."

"I don't like to be jerked around," he agreed.

"You know and I know that I'm allowed to say whatever I want to you if I think it will mean getting a confession out of you. I'm allowed to lie. I could tell you Diana Prince survived her attack and she told us exactly who you were."

Drake frowned, raising an eyebrow at her.

"But that wouldn't be true. And I don't think I need to lie to you to get you to talk to me. I think you've been *dying* to tell someone all about this for a very long time. I'm happy to be that person. I can even line up an interview with the *Sentinel* if you want to give them your side of things. Would be on every news-stand in San Francisco by tomorrow morning. Those are all things I can do. And I can also promise you I'm not going to lie to you because I know you're too smart to buy into that bullshit. And it's a rare treat to sit across from someone who isn't a total fucking moron, quite frankly. So, cards on the table, I'm going to tell you that you are *fucked*. We have DNA evidence. A lot of it. We have ways to tie you, your apartment, and your car to these murders. We know it was you. That's not the question I'm trying to answer here today."

"OK."

"I want to be able to tell the world how you did it. I want to know the details, because details matter, and we don't want it getting out in the media that you were a corpse-fucker like Bundy. We want people to understand the real scope of what you did here. *Why* you did it."

She smiled at him with a warmth that she did not feel. She felt sick to her stomach for the words coming out of her mouth, but he'd shown his hand already. She knew exactly how he wanted to be handled, so she wasn't going to shy away from what was working.

"I read your online posts, Drake. You're a really complicated guy, and I would hate for that to get lost in all of this. So why don't we agree to stop dancing around, and put all the bullshit aside, and we just talk like two smart people, OK?"

The silence that filled the room was deafening. Margot swore if she closed her eyes, she would probably be able to hear both her pulse and his beating in an unsteady, anxious rhythm.

Just when the silence had drawn out so long that Margot thought Drake was shutting down completely, he lifted his cuffed hands to his face, scratching the stubble on his chin.

"Let me tell you how I got the idea..."

THIRTY-SIX

More than a year earlier, when the case was still in its early days, Margot had met a retired park ranger named Wally Albright. Wally had shared something with her in their meeting that had stuck with Margot in the intervening months.

Something that had always bothered her.

A woman had died in the Muir Woods, but it never sat right with Wally as being an accident—which was what the official report called it—because the woman had been wearing the wrong shoes.

Shoes no one would ever go hiking in.

While Margot knew it was unlikely to be the same killer who had murdered that woman and her victims—the timeline simply didn't work unless the Redwood Killer was a senior citizen—Margot never forgot that little tidbit.

It turned out Wally had been right to be bothered.

"First time I ever learned what a murder was, I was in Muir Woods," Drake said, his tone almost wistful, gaze locked somewhere over Margot's shoulder, like he was picturing it in his mind's eye. "I was just a kid, you know, like *really young*, but my uncle was looking after me since my mom was too high to do it, and he took me to work one day. He pointed to a place on the trail, a good drop down, and said, 'Someone left a body here once.'"

"Was your uncle a big hiker?"

Drake smiled. "Of course. He was a park ranger."

Margot sucked in a breath. It was a connection they'd never explored beyond looking at the current staff, but it made perfect sense the moment Drake said it.

"That's how you knew the best trails to bring them in on, where to leave them." Margot nodded for him to continue.

"He showed me around the area a lot as a kid. I think he knew I needed time away from the house. He was the only adult I knew who really talked to me like I was a person and not an annoyance. He loved to explain the forest to me, take me on his favorite trails, and when I asked him if anyone had ever died there, he told me that story. It stuck with me."

I bet it did, Margot caught herself thinking.

It also didn't escape her notice that while Wally said the victim's death had been ruled an accident, Drake's uncle had called it a murder.

She had a feeling she knew why, and perhaps when all this was done, there might be one more cold case she could put to bed.

"And you thought it was a good place to leave a body of your own?"

"I thought I could do it better. They never knew if that woman died in a hiking accident, if she was killed, what the deal was."

"Your uncle seemed to know," Margot countered.

Drake smiled and lifted a finger to his lips in a shushing motion. "Uncle Isaac is a bit too dead now for that to matter much, detective. Let's let sleeping dogs lie. You wanted to know where I got the idea. Let's focus on the present."

Margot felt a flare of hatred for this man, but she was more than happy to focus on his crimes, if that was how he wanted to play this.

"We figured some of the later ones you could have gotten in from different external hiking paths, but Rebecca is the one who really baffled us. How did you manage that?" Margot's curiosity wasn't faked, here. She had been dying to know how the body had been placed right in the midst of the park's busiest area without anyone noticing it. They'd considered wagons, among other things, but they'd never been able to definitively decide how it was done.

"You liked that one?" he asked eagerly.

"It certainly raised a lot of questions."

"Paddleboard."

Margot sat back, unable to conceal the confounded expression on her face. "What?"

"I parked about a mile outside the park gates at night, then got out an inflatable paddleboard I'd stored in the trunk. Put her on the board and walked up the creek into the park. That little river, you know? The one that the main hiking path follows? Those boards can carry a ton of weight, because you're right, once they're dead, those bitches are *heavy*. From there it was easy enough to leave her in the thick of it, but I knew in that ugly pink outfit it wouldn't take long for someone to spot her. And I was right. Then I just walked out, deflated the board, and went home. You guys found her faster than the first one. Hid that one too well, had to change my approach."

"Why Leanne Wu first?" Now Margot withdrew the bag from the folder she'd placed on the table, and she laid out the Polaroids side by side on the table, facing him. She intentionally placed them out of order to see if he would make the adjustment.

He leaned forward, looking down at the pictures with the kind of smile typically reserved for looking at beloved family memories, or old wedding albums, rather than some of the last moments of these women's lives.

After a moment of staring at them adoringly, he moved his shackled hands forward and swapped the photos of Frederica and Rebecca so that the women were in kill order. He briefly drummed his fingertips on the table, then straightened Leanne's photo, which he had bumped in his adjustments.

"I liked her. I think there's this idea that I had to hate them all, and that's not true. I might not have respected them—I mean, that line of work? If you can call it work: whoring around. You can't really *respect* that, can you? But some of them must have realized they weren't God's gift, they weren't anything special, not really. Some of the others could be real goddamn bitches, like their shit didn't stink the same as everyone else's just because they came to the party in a Ferrari thanks to whoever they were fucking that week." He sniffed, scratched his stubble again. "But Leanne was nice enough to me, at the beginning. None of them really said much to us—I don't think they were supposed to—but if she was getting a drink, she'd say hi, ask if my night was going well."

Margot already knew where this was headed. She'd read so many of Drake's online diatribes that she knew the way his mind had twisted these interactions into something more than just kindness on Leanne's part. How he'd decided they were more intimate, more special.

And when she spurned him in some way, that would have been enough of an insult to make him snap.

It was obvious from the conversation they'd had with Clea, and the things he'd shared online, that Drake had harbored violent thoughts toward women for a long time.

"It must have hurt, then, when she decided to treat you differently." Margot needed to be careful how she phrased this. She didn't want to make any insinuations that Drake had been rejected for anything he had done. In his own mind, he was the victim of their relationship, and what he'd done to retaliate was justified.

"She told the older one—this one." He aggressively tapped Rebecca's photo. "She told her I was being inappropriate. Creepy. How the fuck did she figure that? Because I was being nice? Because I was asking *her* how her day had gone? So it was OK for her to talk to me but not the other way around?" He shook his head in obvious annoyance. "And I offered to walk her to her car? Isn't that just chivalry? Don't chicks always say that's what they want? The white knight, the guy with manners?" He made a scoffing sound.

"I don't think women want any one thing," Margot said, forgetting her role for a moment.

Drake didn't even seem to notice. "That's the problem. They all *say* they want something, but in the end, they only want a jacked-up jerk who treats them like shit, all because he has money or a nice car."

He was quoting himself almost word for word from his online diatribes. It was also clearly commentary he had learned to parrot from the alpha-male bloggers and podcast hosts he liked to share content from. What was most alarming about his rhetoric wasn't the misogyny. Margot expected that. It was how deeply he seemed to believe it. He shared the lines the same way someone might quote the Bible, like he had these beliefs set in his bones.

Margot had expected him to perhaps use what he had learned online as a buffer, pretend he'd been radicalized. But he *was* radicalized. She could tell from the gleam in his eye and the intensity of his voice that this was no act. This was obsession, and it was belief.

"You killed Leanne because you didn't like how she treated you? Because you felt like she led you on and then changed her tune the moment you decided to reciprocate?"

Drake's expression flashed disgust. "Because I couldn't pay

for her services, I stopped being worthy of her attention. Now you tell me what that makes her."

Margot bit her tongue, because over the past eighteen months, she had learned so much about these women she could have given Drake a TED Talk on who Leanne Wu was. She was a daughter and an aunt. But beyond who she was to other people, she was a talented painter and had almost been a professional figure skater before an injury ended her career in college.

She could tell him that Rebecca Watson was a brilliant violinist. How Frederica Mercado volunteered twice a week, walking dogs at a local shelter to try and help get them adopted. How Leanne had helped raise money for abused women to be able to stay in shelters without fear of their abusers finding them. Hell, even Diana Prince, who wasn't a gold medalist or a patron saint in training, who spent her non-work hours online gaming and ordering more takeout than Margot, was still not someone who deserved to die because of his skewed notions of women and relationships.

These women were not just escorts, and it pained Margot to realize that so much of their lives would be erased because of their jobs, and because their jobs were the reason they had died.

Drake believed these women were lesser human beings because they had earned money by dating—and yes, probably sleeping with—rich men. His disgust at his perceived rejection in favor of the Larks' clients, had pushed him over an edge, and that was why he had killed, and continued to kill, the women he had seen at those parties.

There were no *good* reasons to become a serial killer. Sometimes it was a voice in the back of someone's head, compelling them to act. Often it was a deep-seated rage toward women that extended well back into childhood.

Margot sat back in her chair, lost for the words she needed to convey what she was thinking. Drake continued to talk, complaining about women in general, but mainly about the women laid out in front of him. Margot barely heard a word of it.

Serial killers were *not* common. They were popular in books and movies, but that was because people were obsessed with the way a normal-looking person could manifest such evil into the world. There was a reason people watched Netflix documentaries and listened to weekly podcasts all about serial killers, and it was because of the *danger*. Much like with horror movies, people liked to be scared in a safe way.

Serial killers, as uncommon as they were, represented the pinnacle of human ugliness. They were as dangerous as it got, and people liked to look at them the same way they liked to look at caged predators in the zoo.

In another situation, this thing could kill me, but not like this.

People got it in their head, too, that serial killers had their reasons for killing, and somehow those reasons needed to be deep. Meaningful, at least to the killer themselves.

But sitting across from Drake as he railed against feminism and called women whores, Margot knew none of it was *interesting*. None of it *mattered*. He killed those women because a podcast host told him he deserved the sex he wasn't getting.

He killed them because they hadn't wanted to date him.

It was the ultimate manifestation of the fear every woman on the planet had when she met a date for the first time.

What if I say the wrong thing?

What if he hurts me?

Drake wasn't killing for a cause, even if he justified it to himself.

He was just like the rest of them.

Killing because he hated women.

Killing to reclaim his power.

Killing, ultimately, because he enjoyed it.

Margot waited until Drake took a pause, letting out a huff as he caught his breath.

She stacked up the photos on the table, handling each one delicately. Drake watched her intently, a little sweat beaded on his brow from the enthusiasm with which he had just confessed to everything.

He seemed, then, to recognize the change in her. The way she was no longer being friendly and open with him.

Drake sat back in his chair and let his cuffed hands drop to his lap. "Aww, hell, you're just like all the rest of them, aren't you? Play nice until you get what you want and then drop a guy like yesterday's news. All the fucking same."

Margot slipped the photos into the folder she'd brought and got to her feet. She then rounded the table so she was standing next to him, and leaned over, whispering in his ear, but not caring if anyone else overheard it.

"Maybe we *are* all the same, Drake. Maybe every woman on the planet took one look at you and decided *nope, not that one.* But you know what makes me different from the rest of them?"

He darted a quick glance at her, and while he tried to project an air of menace, his voice cracked when he asked, "What's that?"

"You were the last thing those women saw before they died. But me? I'm going to be the last thing *you* see before they put that needle in you and you never fucking wake up again. You're going to rot, and no one is ever going to care about you after today."

He stared at her.

"I'm going to be famous."

Margot shook her head, even though it was inevitably the truth. In some capacity, Drake Winston's name would live in infamy long after he was gone.

"No. After I leave this room, not even *I* will think about you ever again."

THIRTY-SEVEN

A bar wouldn't have been Margot's first choice of place to go after getting a serial killer to confess, but she wasn't in charge of deciding.

There was a little hole-in-the-wall Irish pub around the corner from their precinct, a place called O'Neill's that didn't give off the kind of vibes that drew tourists in, but certainly pulled in a constant crowd of cops.

The atmosphere when Margot, Wes, and Leon arrived was nothing short of euphoric. Cops were everywhere, and even though they were all in street clothes, it didn't take an expert to be able to spot a plainclothes police officer.

Members of the task force were at every booth and table, sipping drinks alongside the beat cops and SWAT officers who had worked adjacent to the case at every turn.

Margot had never felt more like a celebrity than when she passed through the pub's doors with her two dearest friends only to hear a massive collective cheer go up in their honor.

They didn't even get a chance to approach the bar before slick bottles of beer were being pressed into their hands and they were forced to do a victory lap of the bar before anyone would let them have a seat. Even as they settled into a booth, people would stop to congratulate them every few minutes, stealing any illusion of privacy they might have.

They'd closed a lot of cases between the three of them, but they rarely got such a hero's welcome at the end of the day. This case had felt different, it had lasted such a long time and permeated the very identity of San Francisco for so long. A serial killer out hunting in their own backyard.

Not anymore.

Margot, who felt incredibly uneasy about the attention, pushed herself into the inside corner of the booth, protected by Wes on the outside. That way she could still clink glasses and smile and thank those who were coming to congratulate her on her successful interrogation, but she didn't have to deal with any surprise touching or feel like she needed eyes in the back of her head.

After about fifteen minutes, the excitement surrounding them died down enough that they could finally hear themselves think, and could speak to each other without shouting or immediately being interrupted.

"It doesn't feel real," Leon said finally, taking a long pull of his beer bottle.

Margot wasn't drinking, but rather peeling the label from her bottle to keep her hands from otherwise fidgeting. "Does this mean you're really going to retire?" she asked him.

Leon didn't even hesitate before he started nodding. "I'm tired. I've been at this game a long time, given up a lot of time I should have spent differently. Not saying I regret it—I'm damn proud of the work I've done—but this time it took a real toll. I'm ready. Told the captain tonight. He said it was about damn time." Leon chuckled. "Going to enjoy my wife and my pension, and read a hell of a lot more romance novels."

The three of them lifted their bottles one more time to

salute Leon and a choice that was probably the hardest and easiest of his entire life.

"What about you, Margot?" Wes asked.

She jerked her head sideways, looking at him in surprise. With everything that had been going on, there hadn't been a good time to talk about her plans for the future, and how, without really sitting down to go over her choices, she had made her decision.

The two of them had so much to discuss and she was going to bring up leaving then, but now that he literally had her backed into a corner, it seemed like she had no choice but to confess.

"I got offered a job with the FBI," she said quietly, almost hoping they might not hear. "I would be working with a newly established task force helping to close cold cases that they think are connected to known killers."

"Like what you did with Finch," Leon said.

Margot nodded.

"And you want to say yes?" Wes asked, his voice low, steady, giving nothing away.

"I was going to make my acceptance contingent on them bringing you, too," she said, smiling. "But you're too goddamn old."

He bumped his shoulder against hers and took a sip of his drink. "Here's what I'm going to say, because my opinion shouldn't matter at all, but just in case it does. You are a great cop, but you would be great at anything you do. And if this wasn't something you wanted to do, you would have told the Feds to get bent the second they made you the offer. They're just realizing what I've known all along: they're lucky to have you."

He looked at her and her cheeks flushed.

"I don't want to leave you," she said quietly, unable to stop herself, even though Leon could surely hear everything she was saying.

Wes snorted. "Margot, if you think leaving SFPD means you're going to get rid of me, then you are out of your goddamn mind."

"Maybe if she stops working with you, the two of you can finally stop pretending you're not totally crazy for each other," Leon observed.

Margot's blush intensified. "I think you've been reading too many romance novels, old man."

Leon snorted. "I think that just makes me an expert in seeing when two dummies like you are being too stupid to make yourselves happy. Margot, take the FBI job. There's more out there for you than a lifetime in homicide. Trust me, it's no way to spend your youth."

"My youth is well behind me," she countered.

Leon batted the words aside like they were flies trying to get to his beer.

"You listen to me for a minute, because I know a thing or two about life, OK? You can't live for your job. I know you feel like you have something to prove—you always have. But you've proven it, trust me. Now is the time, while you still have decades left to enjoy it. Go do something that makes you feel *alive.* Maybe that's the FBI, maybe it's not. But you're staying with SFPD because it feels safe, because it's what you know, and I think you could be doing so much more." He set his beer down and really looked at her. "And for God's sake, Margot. Let yourself fall in love."

She took a sip of her beer so she wouldn't have to say anything right away, then looked over to Wes, whose cheeks were a little ruddy from the booze, the heat in the bar, and the direction the conversation had shifted.

Margot held up her beer bottle.

"To what comes next," she said.

"To what comes next," they said in unison, and the merry clink of their bottles drifted out into the celebration surrounding them.

Margot didn't know what awaited her around the bend, but she did know that, for the first time in her life, thinking about the future didn't fill her stomach with a pit of dread.

She wasn't all that familiar with the sensation of hope, but if she didn't know better, she might say that was what had been kindled inside of her as she, Wes, and Leon ordered another round.

THIRTY-EIGHT

Margot could remember the way her father had looked the last time she'd seen him as a free man. But it was hard to reconcile that mental image with the man she saw blinking into the sun as a gaggle of heavily armed guards led him toward a waiting armored truck.

She thought about a time they had all been out on Uncle Jimmy's boat. She had probably only been eight or nine at the time, but the visual was so clear in her mind it could have been something that had happened yesterday.

Jimmy was behind the wheel of the boat, wearing a goofy-looking captain's hat that had lost most of its color after years of being bleached by saltwater and sun. His cheeks were red from sunburn, and he was sipping a beer as he told terrible jokes.

Margot knew, in retrospect, those jokes had probably been too bawdy for the audience, because she recalled the pinched expression on her mother's face.

But what she was thinking about now was how her father had looked in that moment. He had closed his eyes, lifting his chin so the sun baked his skin, and *smiled*. Even then she knew what a rare and precious thing that smile was, because this was a man who took pleasure in little and found fault in much. She could recall perfectly how happy he had been in that moment, the saltwater spraying over the bow, a beer in his hand.

Even now she couldn't know what he was thinking about in that moment, but watching him squint and lift his head to the bright blue sky above, she understood that very little had changed in him over those intervening years.

He was still the same man he'd been on that boat.

Which meant he was still the same monster.

His cuffs jangled as he walked, and he was forced to take short, shuffling steps to get anywhere. While he didn't *look* like a man capable of committing so many atrocious murders, he also didn't look like a harmless old grandpa, something that Margot realized with a jolt he actually *was*.

Ed Finch was a grandfather.

Somehow that had never occurred to her in all of this, and the very shock of the sudden knowledge made her snort out a laugh. Given the scenario, where she was surrounded by armed prison guards, FBI agents, and a police escort, she knew everyone was looking at her funny.

But she also understood the grace that went along with the broad knowledge that she was looking at her own father.

Now that that secret was out, any unusual behavior on her part seemed to be forgiven. No one said anything, but her little snort had drawn Ed's attention and he was now staring at her, a look of cruel disapproval etched on his features.

She stared right back, taking in every wrinkle, every patch of gray hair. She memorized him, so that she could erase each and every line when she drove home tonight.

This would be the last day she would ever have to look at him.

He might try new methods of manipulation, make new attempts to lure her back. But once these victims were returned to the mainland, she would watch the armored truck make its way down the road, and when it disappeared from sight, she would never have to think about Ed Finch again.

This time tomorrow, she would start over.

She would stop being afraid to live her life.

She smiled at him, and it seemed to unsettle him, because for a moment he stopped walking and just stared at her, his skin paling, eyes narrowed into uneasy slits.

The guards eased Ed through the open doors at the back of the truck, and attached his cuffs to metal loops built into the base of a bench seat that stretched the length of one wall. A lap belt secured him for his own safety, and two armed guards slid in and sat across from him, while a third headed to the front seat to follow the convoy that would head up to the coast.

Looking at Ed, she couldn't help but think about Drake Winston, a man who would likely soon join Ed inside San Quentin. She also thought about Ethan Willingham, a boy who wanted to prove himself to Ed so badly that he had turned himself into a killer.

She thought about what *made* men killers, which was a nature versus nurture debate that she was in no way expert enough to make statements about. But she knew killers. She might not understand what made them who they were, or if they were born evil, but she'd spent her entire adult life learning their ways.

Casting a quick glance to her left, she looked at Andrew, whose attention was all on Ed, and further back in the crowd she saw Alana, Carter, and Greg, huddled together in a trio, also all staring at Ed.

Ed Finch, a name that would linger even after the man himself eventually died.

A name she had tried so long to escape.

It felt pointed that she was here looking at him so soon after she had told Drake Winston he would be forgotten. But the truth was, in a sense, she was right. The modern memory was much shorter than it was in the eighties and nineties. And the myth that had been created by Ed before he had been caught had become deeply entrenched in the day-to-day lives of people who lived in the Bay Area.

In those early modern serial killer years, the seventies through the early nineties, it was a time where innocence was lost in America. The freedom and love ethos of the sixties and seventies, bruised from the exhausting, soul-crushing weight of the Vietnam War, created a disillusioned population. And when serial killers started to crop up all over the country, specifically the West Coast, people learned that there were things to be afraid of on home soil that they hadn't believed possible before.

One man couldn't recreate that level of mass terror anymore. People had seen horrors since then on an unimaginable scale. In a post-9/11 world, there was simply no way for a serial killer to stir up the kind of fear they once had.

Which was why Ed's name would never be forgotten, since he had terrified a nation and taught them what fear meant, while Drake Winston would be relegated to a few hours of podcast time and then fade from the public mind, as they moved on to new fads, new stories, new tragedies.

When she saw the way the FBI looked at Ed, though, it was like watching them look at a celebrity. A horrible, monstrous celebrity, but one who existed in a different realm from normal people. He was a name most of them had only seen in books and documents. Seeing him now, as an old man, it had to be a shock to the system.

Margot paid close attention to Greg, who she knew would have sold a kidney just to have a one-on-one chat with Ed. His expression was stony, but a little perplexed, as if he was having a hard time reconciling the monster he'd studied with this old man.

The truck's back doors were shut and locked.

Andrew waved his hand in the air and shouted, "All right, let's load up."

Margot stared at the back of the truck a moment longer, then followed Andrew to a waiting SUV where she climbed in the passenger seat.

"You ready for this, kid?" he asked as soon as she was buckled in.

Margot didn't even have to think about her answer.

"I've never been more ready."

THIRTY-NINE

The ocean was in a violent mood.

While the Bay Area was largely protected from the most dangerous of the ocean's waves, when they arrived at the marina Ed had confirmed as the starting point for his journey, the water roiled with white caps and salty mist wafted up the dock, dampening Margot's cheeks and jacket.

The FBI team had arrived first, followed by local sheriff's deputies and a team of police. In all, Margot counted at least forty people who were involved in this shitshow in some way or another. She couldn't decide if it was too many or too few.

The local guys had helped clear the area, so there would be no other boat owners filming this on their phones and selling the footage to the local news. An FBI agent had been tasked with photographing the events, for posterity, but if all went well those photos would never be seen by anyone outside of an FBI office.

They had coordinated a boat through the marina's owner, and the Fish and Wildlife Service had volunteered three other boats to take agents and officers along for the ride.

In the cabin cruiser with Ed would be Margot, Andrew,

Alana, Carter, Greg, and Ed's three prison guards. It felt like too many people, but Margot couldn't imagine who she would replace or leave off. The boat was more than capable of holding nine people, though it was a snug fit. Ed couldn't be stowed away below deck, because he needed to guide them to where he'd left the bodies. Alana, who had a boating license, would be their pilot for the day, and the Fish and Wildlife boats would fall in line on either side of them with one boat trailing.

Many of the police and deputies would stay behind on shore to keep things clear and await their return. There was enough room on the Fish and Wildlife boats to bring back the remains if they found the skeletons relatively intact, but after so many years and the brutality of the ocean, it was unlikely. The most plausible outcome was that they would locate fragments of bones and send a team of forensic anthropologists out to do their best with excavating whatever else might remain or have been scattered among the sea-tumbled rocks.

Everyone was quiet as the boat pulled away from the slip and out onto the choppy mid-morning water.

"Do you remember when we used to come out here as a family?" Ed asked, his voice raised over the slap of the water against the hull as the boat fought its way through the rough swells. Even though he was practically yelling, there was something almost wistful about his voice.

Margot could sense the eyes of everyone on the boat looking at her, even as they pretended not to. While it might not be a secret that Ed was her father, it still felt strange to be reminded of it in such an apparent way.

She could have been cruel, and pretended she didn't know what he was talking about, but she found that in that moment it was easier just to be honest, even with so much attention on them.

"Yeah, I remember."

"Simpler times, weren't they?"

She glanced over and realized he was looking right at her. Despite the fact that he was still wearing his prison-issue navy ensemble, and a sweater he had knit himself, he looked different out here than he had every time she'd been to see him in prison. He looked more like the man she had thought she knew back then, and less like the man he'd turned out to be.

For a moment, instead of the killer, she saw her father, and it was such a pure shot of pain to the heart that she grimaced, then blinked back the tears that were forming in her eyes. Thank God for the stinging sea air so no one would notice.

"That was a long time ago, Ed."

"It would be nice, you know, if this is going to be it for us, if just once you might call me Dad again."

Margot looked away, because she still couldn't quite shake how badly this conversation hurt, how being here, with him, just like old times was stirring something inside of her that she didn't think still existed.

"I can't do that," she said. And though her voice was barely more than a whisper, he seemed to understand her fine. Either that, or he had already known what her answer would be.

"Well, whatever else happens, Buddy, I want you to know I've always been proud of you."

He's a psychopath, she told herself. *None of this is real, it's all part of the game for him.*

She took a deep breath, and watched the shoreline recede as they moved out through the uneven water.

"You'll want to move parallel with the coast," Ed shouted to Alana. "It was dark when I went out, but I was heading mostly north, and then a little west. It shouldn't take us more than ten minutes."

Alana said nothing, but adjusted her bearing, keeping the boat in a northwesterly direction. It didn't seem like there was much for them to find, but the whole point of this was that the burial grounds had to be well hidden.

Otherwise, there was no point in Ed being here.

He turned in his seat, squinting into the mist and smiled, mostly to himself. While his wrinkles were deeper in this lighting, his skin didn't have the same sallow green undertone that it did when Margot saw him in San Quentin. There, he sometimes seemed so unhealthy that she wondered if he might be dying. Now she could see there were plenty of years left in his tank.

Unfortunately.

Radios crackled as messages were passed back and forth, but Margot didn't hear any of what was being said. After a long silence, she turned back to Ed. If this truly was going to be the last time they ever saw each other, then she felt like there *was* something she needed to hear him admit. Just for closure.

"You never loved us, did you?" she asked.

He didn't look back at her, just kept facing out into the ocean, briefly closing his eyes.

"There are experts," he began, "who would tell you that men like me don't know how to love. We lack the capacity and empathy needed to forge that kind of connection. But I don't think you're asking me about what experts think. I guess what it all comes down to is what you think love is. Did I feel a passionate romance-novel love for your mother? No. And I think we both know that after a while I didn't feel much toward her at all but resentment. But there was a time in my life where she and I had a very meaningful connection. And your brother? Well..." Ed shrugged. "I don't know what to say about Justin, really. He wasn't a bad kid, as kids go. I can't say that I wanted a second, but your mother was so keen. But you, Megan? You were different. I knew right away that you were this little part of me, something I hadn't expected. I saw it in you the moment you were born, and I still see it when I look at you now. And I know that's not what you want to hear, because time makes revisionist historians of us all, but I think back then you saw it, too. How alike we were, how different we were to the others. So, I don't know what to say besides that. I don't know if what I carry for you is love the way greeting card companies mean it, but I know that no one else in my life ever mattered to me as much as you did. So take that for what it's worth."

The whole time he hadn't once looked at her, and she was glad of it, because her face must have shown everything she was feeling. Revulsion, horror, but also relief. The relief of knowing that at least some of her life had been real. And although it had all unraveled in an unfixable fashion, at least, for her first fifteen years, she hadn't imagined that she had been loved.

It didn't count for much now, but for whatever reason, she was glad she'd asked.

Ed glanced over his shoulder toward Alana. "It's just up ahead. You'll want to slow down soon so we don't bottom out." He pointed to a smudge of color on the horizon, and as they drew closer, Margot could make out a small trio of rocky islands.

Calling them *islands* seemed too generous, as they were barely more than an acre each, and might actually be one outcropping, with water that had risen up to cover any bridges between them. There were some scrappy trees creating the tiniest bit of an ecosystem—Margot had no idea how they were surviving this far from shore—but the islands were primarily rock.

Rock and bird shit.

Seagulls and cormorants were everywhere on the island when they got close enough to actually make out details. The gulls freewheeled over their boats, screaming their dissatisfaction at the interruption, while a few bolder birds hovered nearby to see if they had any food on offer. The cormorants kept their distance, watching the boats approach as if gauging whether or not it was necessary to abandon the island. They apparently didn't consider the boats a threat.

Alana took Ed's suggestion and slowed the boat down to a

crawl. Margot noticed little spires of rock sticking out from the water as they approached the shore.

She looked at Ed, waiting for him to acknowledge if this was it. He seemed to be considering things intently.

Then, after an arduous moment of silence, he jerked his head in a quick nod. "Yeah, this is it. I anchored as close to the shore as I could, and I pushed them into the higher rocks." He pointed out an area that was largely submerged, but where it was obvious there was quite a bit of rock below the surface. "Don't know if it was this exact spot, but it was this island."

The way he was looking at the island was almost wistful, and made Margot's stomach turn. It reeled her back into reality and dampened any of the uncertain emotions this trip had managed to bring up so far.

Ed was still precisely who she thought he was.

The boat got as close to the island as possible, and thanks to Ed's forewarnings about the terrain, they had brought along fishing waders to allow those who were going to go ashore to traverse the water without getting soaked. Margot donned a suspendered pair of waders that smelled of rubber and sweat, and then allowed Andrew to help her out of the boat.

For this part of the process, Ed's ankle cuffs needed to be removed, but the general consensus among the gathered guards and agents was that this was a fine concession to make since there was nowhere for him to run.

His wrist cuffs were briefly undone to allow him to be helped into his own waders, but they were quickly re-cuffed once he was in.

"What happens if I fall in?" Ed protested, jangling the cuffs at them and pointing his bound hands in the direction of the choppy water.

"I guess you drown," Andrew replied from the shore, where he and Margot were now standing.

A tense silence passed between the two old foes as they

both stared each other down. Ultimately Andrew handed Ed the win as he shifted position to help someone else off the boat. The water was cold, Margot could tell that even through the thick rubber of her waders, and she was glad to be on shore now, even if the compactness of the island felt like a prison of its own.

The shore was far enough away that even on a clear day it would be no more than a smudge of darkness against the blue sky, like an afterthought in a watercolor painting. Margot thought about the world on that shore, within squinting sight of this island, and no one ever being aware of the secrets kept here.

So much of what Ed had done was like that, a badly kept secret just out of sight, where no one happened to be looking. It was, somehow, how he had managed to commit so many more murders than anyone had ever believed. Because Ed's MO had been to leave his victims in plain sight, in their homes, waiting to be found by friends, family, or unfortunate neighbors once the smell got too bad.

Believing that was how all his victims had been left meant that so many other women were written off as being his potential victims. As it turned out, Ed was an opportunist, but he was also keen to protect himself at every turn. And if that meant changing his tried-and-true methods on a whim, he would do it.

Honestly, the longer she thought about it, the more foolish she realized they'd all been. His very first victim, Laura Welsh, she had been ditched in the woods. It had been written off as first-kill sloppiness, but the truth was, it was a sign that Ed would always do what he needed to do to protect himself.

One guard stayed on the boat while the other two got off to assist Ed into the water. Since every single person on this trip aside from Ed was armed, Margot watched as everyone instinctively moved their hands toward their holsters, waiting, watching. She wasn't sure if they were hoping for nothing to happen, or hoping he would give them an excuse.

Margot's hands stayed firmly crossed over her chest. She'd

worn a shoulder holster today with her personal weapon since she wasn't on duty, but she felt no immediate need to reach for it. She hadn't even unclasped the holster. While Ed was still a dangerous person, she felt unusually confident that this was all going to go according to plan.

She didn't need to have a weapon ready, because if Ed fucked up there were a half-dozen people in firing distance who would do the job for her.

After some awkward balancing and a few slips on the rocks, the guards and Ed were ashore. The final guard and Alana stayed on the boat while the rest of the crew moved further inland.

The island was small; even as a cluster of three it probably only took up about two or three acres of space. Enough room for them to move around comfortably but never really be out of sight of each other. The terrain was rough rock and lean trees, and where the ground wasn't a combination of water-smoothed pebbles and wind-sharpened rock spires, it was a soggy moss that felt like damp carpeting underfoot.

There was no brush to speak of, no dirt to bury a body, so where had Ed put those girls so that no one would find them for all this time? Even though the island was uninhabited and not a spot anyone wanted to spend an afternoon, there was no way a body had just laid out baking in the sun, swarmed by birds and picked at by crabs. Let alone *two* bodies.

Ed ambled forward, his eyes to the ground. He seemed to enjoy walking free of his ankle cuffs, periodically making a little jump from one rocky outcropping to another, which seemed to set his guards on edge every time it happened. Finally, he brought them to the space where the three islands met, where a small basin of water had formed between them.

Margot saw it almost immediately, and let out a gasp. In the water, covered in something that very much looked like barnacles, a human skull was looking up at her from under about three feet of water.

Ed gestured to the pool with his cuffed hands.

"I couldn't bury them, but this spot was there, like a gift from the gods. It was in the water, but because it was made by the different islands it formed a small... I don't know, a bowl? Water flowed in and out with the tides, but it was deep enough I could put something in it. So I dumped them in there, put some rocks on them, and split. Guess it worked."

Greg, Carter, and Margot all moved closer to the pool, which seemed shockingly calm and clear, given how rough the ocean was that morning. Just looking into the water, aside from the usual tidepool-dwellers like crabs, starfish, and a tiny octopus, Margot could see bones. Dozens of bones. A second skull was facedown a few feet from the first, like they'd been put in head to toe. Between them, arm and leg bones were jumbled with ribs and bits of spine. Whatever clothing they had been wearing had long since been destroyed by the ocean water, but their remarkably clean bones were still present.

Certainly, some of them would be missing; it was unthinkable to assume that the fingers and toes had avoided being eaten by the crabs. But there was so much of them still here.

Enough to identify them.

Enough to give their families peace.

Ed was close enough to the pool that Margot caught him staring into the water, a sick smile on his face. She'd never seen him look at anything in his life with that much satisfaction before.

He was proud of himself.

"Take him back to the boat," Margot instructed.

And while it wasn't her operation, no one questioned her. Ed was nudged back in the direction of the waiting boat.

Greg, who was acting as their scene photographer, snapped

several photos of the pool before stepping back to give them room.

Andrew came to them and stooped low, taking one of the skulls from the water. It wasn't attached to anything, and came easily. "We'll take these back to check dental records and see if we can compare any DNA. The forensic anthropologists can collect the rest."

Margot wanted to protest. She felt sick about the idea that, after all this time, waiting all these years to be found, the girls would now need to wait longer, and wait without their heads. It seemed macabre, and wrong, but she understood that Andrew was only trying to find answers to their identities as quickly as possible. She knew he wasn't being intentionally ghoulish.

So she bit her tongue.

They were coming home. That was all that mattered.

FORTY

The scene was carefully photographed, and markers were placed so the incoming crews would be able to find the bodies. Now that such a colorful marker was in place that might draw attention, Fish and Wildlife promised to have someone stationed at the island until the forensic team could be assembled to collect the skeletons.

Once all the bones were brought back to the mainland a long and difficult process of reassembly would begin, in which the experts would need to attempt to determine which bones belonged to which sister. With such similar DNA and being so close in age it seemed an almost impossible task, and Margot expected some of the bones would be muddled in the process no matter how hard they tried.

There was something almost poetic about it, the way the sisters had decayed beside one another, and would stay co-mingled even into their final rest.

As the boat pulled away from the small island, the two skulls safely stowed away in plastic evidence bags and then stowed again in the smallest body bags Margot had ever seen—

while also being wrapped in bubble wrap—they began the trip home.

Margot felt suddenly exhausted, the weight of this entire day pressing down on her more than she had anticipated. The euphoria she'd felt earlier in the San Quentin parking lot over the knowledge that this was the last time she'd ever have to see Ed was dampened now, both literally and figuratively. She was cold, tired, and sad. All she wanted to do at this point was get back to the city and spend a good twenty minutes in her shower, then eat some Thai food and go to bed alone.

Normally she might consider unloading some of this grief and unease on Wes, but after what she'd confessed to him, she knew their next private discussion would need to have more involved. And as much as she *wanted* to start that next chapter with him, she also knew this wasn't the night to take that step.

She needed to process this day, and what it meant. Needed to feel sad for these two women, but relieved for their families.

And a small part of her knew she needed to mentally say goodbye to her father for the second time. It wasn't *this* Ed she missed, it was the complicated, often cruel, but also sometimes loving man she had known as her father that she missed, that she was processing the loss of. And being around him again for these years, for the time it took to close all his unknown cases, it had been difficult and painful, but it had also reminded her that the man she'd loved *had* existed, even if it wasn't in the way she had believed.

She and her therapist Dr. Singh were going to need a few sessions for her to work through this later.

Tonight, it would be crab Rangoon, *Bob's Burgers*, and a nice snuggle with Betty on the couch.

Tomorrow, she had another problem to deal with as the trial of Ethan Willingham continued, and it would be her turn to take the stand.

The rough sound of the boat against the water had almost

turned to white noise as Margot contemplated her evening, but she soon realized Ed was speaking.

She was sitting next to Andrew, with Ed on Andrew's other side, and the two guards nearby, both looking a bit seasick as they attempted to keep an eye on Ed but also remain standing in the rough sea.

"—don't you think?" Ed asked.

Margot wasn't sure what she had missed, or if the question had been directed to her or Andrew. She glanced over and saw that Ed was looking at the FBI agent expectantly. If Andrew had heard the question, he wasn't acknowledging it.

"Rhodes, I asked you a question," Ed persisted.

"I don't care," Andrew replied solemnly.

"Ah, I see how it is. You're all done with me. You've wrung me dry of anything useful to you, and now you're wiping your hands clean of dear old Ed." There was very real anger in his voice, but his expression seemed almost sad.

Margot didn't say anything, because there was nothing to refute. He was absolutely correct. Once they got off this boat, none of them were going to come see him again. No one was going to waste any additional man hours on him. The Ed Finch task force team was already being reassigned, and Margot was going along with them.

Ed was destined to become a part of their past.

"You wouldn't have your career without me," Ed said to Andrew.

Andrew shifted sideways, looking at the man next to him, not bothering to hide the naked disgust in his expression. "Do you want me to say *thank you*?"

Ed shrugged, his features calm, unbothered. He was having fun now, using the time he had left to its utmost advantage.

"Just stating facts. You think you're going to write another book, Rhodes? Maybe a twenty-fifth anniversary edition with all these new kills. Your old one is probably looking sorely out of date now." He chuckled. "Sorry for messing your timeline up."

Andrew gave Ed a final sneer that spoke louder than words to express how he felt about Ed. Then he turned his body toward Margot, not wanting to even bother looking at Ed any longer.

Margot saw Ed move before her brain understood what was happening.

They had come this far without incident. Everything had been fine. All their careful planning had resulted in an afternoon that, while miserable in its own ways, had also been a complete success.

When Ed got to his feet, Margot simply couldn't process why he was suddenly standing.

When Ed draped his cuffed wrists over Andrew's head and pulled back, the chain between the bracelets going taut over Andrew's throat, she couldn't make it make sense.

It was only when Ed looked at her and said, "You know, the only reason I did any of this was because I wanted to make sure you turned out OK," that she realized with a horrible sinking sensation what was happening.

Andrew let out a gurgling sound, his face turning purple. The spell that had briefly swept over the boat making everyone freeze in place lifted and suddenly it was all action and shouting and panic.

Ed held Andrew in front of him, shielding himself from the guards, as everyone staggered to keep their footing when Alana dropped the boat down to a standstill.

Margot's gun was in her hand, leveled at Ed and Andrew, though she didn't remember even drawing it.

"Ed, you don't want to do this," she said. "Just let him go."

Despite her quavering voice, her firing posture was rock steady. The only problem was that Ed kept moving, blocking the clear line of fire with Andrew's body.

Andrew, for his part, was clawing at Ed's hands, desperately trying to loosen the grip and chain pressed against his trachea. He couldn't breathe, his lips turning pale blue, face blotchy and red.

They didn't have time for this.

Everyone was shouting demands at Ed. Everyone had their guns out.

The three Fish and Wildlife boats had realized something was wrong and were circling back. It was only a matter of time before someone could line up a clear shot to incapacitate Ed without hurting Andrew.

Margot blocked out the noise around her, everything fading into a quiet hum. All she could see was Ed and Andrew.

She kept her voice calm and steady, though she felt neither. "Do you want this to be what he writes in the final chapter of that new book, Ed? That you decided suicide by cop was your preferred way to die? That you were that much of a coward?"

Ed scoffed. "I came back to California knowing I was accepting a death sentence, Buddy. If anything, the state should thank me for saving them the cost."

"I don't think you want to die. I think you just want us to pay attention to you. Well, I'm paying attention. Let him go. Let him go and I'll keep visiting, if that's what you want. I'll come once a week."

Ed peered out from behind Andrew's head, not enough for a good shot. He practically had his face against Andrew's ear, knowing no one would want to risk the bullet if it meant killing Rhodes as well.

It was all too risky.

"You'd do that?"

"Of course I'd do that."

"You'd do that to protect *him*?"

Margot knew this was a trap, but she wasn't sure she was feeling mentally sharp enough at the moment to avoid stepping into it. "It's not about him. It's about you. I'm only trying to keep you alive. You can still get out of this, we can call it a lapse in judgment. Andrew won't press charges. No need for a trip to the SHU." Avoiding the solitary confinement unit would matter to Ed, because he loved his distractions. "What do you say?"

For a moment, it worked. Ed let up on Andrew's throat enough that Margot heard the massive breath Andrew took. But Ed still kept him close, and soon the chain tightened again. Margot could already see the mottled flesh where bruises would appear tomorrow and deepen over the week.

"You're lying to me to save him."

"Ed, listen to yourself. I came to visit you with just the *possibility* you might have something to say. I'm not lying to you now. If you let him go, I'll keep coming to see you. You remember what you told me, that you never lied to me? Why would I lie to you?"

Radios crackled in the background, but the shouting had stopped. Everyone was watching them now with tense expectation, waiting to see if Margot could talk him down. On the other boats, men stood with rifles pointed in Ed's direction, but there was no way to easily communicate if anyone had a clear shot.

"Ed, was this your goal in all this? Was this what you thought your endgame would be? You, me, and a bullet?"

He stared at her thoughtfully, though she could only see one eye peering around the side of Andrew's face. She tried not to be distracted by the very real peril her friend was in. She wanted Ed to know her sole focus in this moment was on him.

As if she could look anywhere else.

"What I wanted was *time*," he said.

"You had nothing but time," she countered. The gun suddenly felt very heavy in her hands, but she refused to let herself tremble or lower it even an inch.

"I wanted time with *you*," he corrected. "I don't have a lot of regrets about what happened, I think we both know that. I regret that this piece of shit caught me, but maybe that was inevitable. Especially after Jimmy. But I regretted you. I regretted not getting to be part of your life. Not shaping you more."

Margot thought about the things he'd said to her in the past, the insinuations, and a sharp acidic tang coated the back of her throat.

"All the time in the world wouldn't make me who you wanted me to be," she said.

"No. I suppose I missed my chance. After this one got his hooks into you, you were never going to be mine again." He tightened his grip on Andrew and, while Andrew was tough, he still let out a raspy squeak.

Margot shook her head, hoping she could distract Ed from his animosity toward Rhodes.

"Ed, I was *never* going to be like you, no matter what happened. I don't have that thing inside me that you do. There is no monster whispering in my ear."

He leaned away from Andrew just enough that she could see his sickly-sweet smile.

"Of all the things I'd hoped you would learn from seeing me, you should know we *all* have that monster in us, Buddy. He'll start whispering for you someday, just you wait."

Tears stung at the corner of her eyes, but she refused to let him see them fall.

"Let him go, Ed. It doesn't need to end like this."

Ed licked his lips, his gaze leaving hers briefly, skin going pale like he was only now starting to realize how far up shit creek he'd gotten himself. Then something in his expression clicked, like a decision had been made, but Margot had no idea what it was. He smiled at her again and her blood went cold.

"What do you want?" Margot asked, her tone pleading, worried this was about to spiral out of her control. If it had ever been in her control. "Tell me what it'll take for you to let him go."

"I told you what I want from you."

For a moment, Margot didn't understand him. And then she recalled their conversation on the trip out. What he'd asked, and what she had been unable to deliver.

A lump in her throat formed, keeping her from being able to respond, literally blocking words from coming out.

Finally, knowing it was the only thing she had to offer and the only thing that might work, she swallowed the lump down.

"Let him go," she repeated. "Please... Dad."

The word tasted so bitter on her tongue she almost gagged, but the world around them seemed to freeze in place as she said it.

She thought he might pretend he hadn't heard it. Thought maybe she'd misunderstood what he was asking her for. But after the longest ten-second pause of Margot's life, Ed loosened his grip on Andrew and lifted his hands back over his head.

Margot could have cried in relief, but the moment passed.

Ed lunged at her, and her body responded before her brain, the gun going off, the vibration of the shot radiating through her fingers.

Ed looked down at the bright bloom of red on his chest, almost black against his navy scrubs, but brighter than paint on his cream-colored sweater.

He slumped down to the floor of the boat as everyone moved toward him in a surge of bodies. But before he was tackled to the ground, he looked up at her, smiling.

"Now who's the killer?"

FORTY-ONE

As it turns out, killing your father doesn't get you out of testifying in a murder trial.

Margot hadn't expected that it would, and hadn't actually asked to be released from her duties, but now that she was in court, she was beginning to wonder if she should have tried.

Surely the FBI could have written her a note. Andrew probably appreciated her saving his life enough that he might be able to pull some strings. But Andrew was at home healing—and probably questioning his choice to hire her—and Margot was looking out over a courtroom full of the most sullen faces she'd ever seen outside of a funeral.

She glanced around and spotted Lloyd Crowther. She grimaced.

On a top ten list of things that Margot hated most in the world, defense lawyers would rank in the top three, without question.

As soon as she took her seat in the witness box, she knew today wasn't going to go well.

She believed, if she was a different person, she probably could have told Hildy that this wasn't a good time for her to be in the hot seat. That the intensity of what she had just gone through should preclude her from having to face questions that would ultimately become about Ed. But instead of feeling overwhelmed, she felt numb.

When she scanned the viewing gallery, she spotted the red, tear-stained face of Toni Willingham. Rhonda. And she *knew* those tears weren't for Ethan. She *knew* that Rhonda—as Ed's legal next-of-kin—had been told about what happened.

It made Margot sick, and in that moment, she knew that, despite how numb she felt about the case, there was still a deep rage simmering in her gut. She *despised* these people, and that level of personal anger wasn't going to serve her well. Crowther was going to sense it like a bloodhound could follow a trail, and he would pick at it like an unhealed scab.

This had been a mistake.

She took a deep breath, and used a technique she'd learned when she needed to pull herself back from a panic attack. This wasn't exactly the same scenario, but she thought it might calm her down. She scanned the room and told herself things she knew to be true.

The tables are made of wood.

The woman in the front row is wearing pink.

There is a portrait of an old judge on the wall.

The floors were recently cleaned and smell like bleach.

Lloyd Crowther is wearing too much cologne.

By the time she got to ten, she didn't feel any less internal anger. That was ever-present and she would likely feel it for the rest of her days. But she felt calmer. Like she could get through the rest of this day without screaming at someone. And that was the best she could hope for today.

Since she was Hildy's witness, the prosecution got first crack at her, which was probably best for all of them, because if Margot got plunged into the deep end with Crowther first thing, there would be no hope in hell of her projecting *likable* vibes to the jury.

Hildy took her through the basics first, asking Margot to describe the scene, the initial investigation, and all of the brass tacks to make sure her version of events aligned with everything the jury had been told so far. Easy stuff, questions Margot could answer without too much thought.

Then Hildy asked, "Could you tell us about your first encounter with the defendant, Ethan Willingham?"

Margot's jaw clenched as she cast a glance over to Ethan— or Ewan, whoever he was. The boy looked older now than he had the last time she'd seen him. Then he'd been seventeen and still had a bit of baby-faced innocence about him. He'd sat across from her in an interrogation room and used his *hypotheticals* to confess to a crime without actually confessing.

He thought he'd been very smart, but at the end of the day, not smart enough by half.

Now he looked more adult, his features chiseled to the point of his face being borderline gaunt. He no longer resembled a teenage boy who should be starting college. He *looked* as if he had spent a year in lockup waiting for this trial.

Waiting to see what his future held.

But the way he stared at Margot was the same. Still smug, still altogether too proud of himself, and not a single sliver of remorse for what he'd done.

"I first met Mr. Willingham at his high school. At his invitation, we met him there to have our first interview. He was participating in an after-school program."

"That was the robotics club?"

Margot nodded. "That's correct." She wanted to add that the robotics club had been building robots that fought each other violently, but it didn't seem necessary and Hildy would probably get annoyed with her for stepping outside her lane.

On the stand it was always better to keep her answers

succinct and avoid adding any flourish or opinion. *Opinion* was the fastest path to hearing Crowther shout *objection*, and Margot wasn't interested in that song and dance.

"Was that the same group that we've heard testimony from at this trial regarding the defendant's logic games challenge?"

"Yes, the participants were the same in both the club and the game."

"What first drew your attention to Mr. Willingham as a person of interest?" Hildy asked.

"When my partner and I did our initial questioning of Ms. Willingham about her relationship with Mrs. Zhou, we noticed that Mr. Willingham owned a copy of a book that got our attention."

"What book was that?"

"*Killer in the Classifieds*, by Special Agent Andrew Rhodes."

"That's a book about the serial killer Ed Finch, is that correct?"

"Yes, it is."

"And what made that book especially interesting to you?"

"On its own, not enough to warrant considering Mr. Willingham a suspect, but it was enough that we wanted to talk to him a little more. We find that witnesses or persons of interest who are fond of serial killers or seem to be too studied on the topic can sometimes become suspects if we feel that interest became more hands-on."

"So the book on its own didn't make you think he was a suspect?"

"No, we just wanted to speak to him."

This questioning continued for over an hour, until Margot's throat was hoarse. Finally, Hildy announced she had no additional questions, and the moment Margot had been dreading was finally upon her.

Crowther got up, his expression almost as smug as his

client's, and he approached the bench like a pickup artist sidling up to the bar. It made Margot's skin crawl.

"Detective Phalen, is that your legal name?"

Here we go, she thought. She'd hoped he might opt for a brief preamble, try to build up to this, but apparently he was going to go straight for the jugular.

She *knew* he thought that her connection to her father was a weakness he could exploit, but right now, she was in no mood to humor him.

"My legal name is Margot Theodosia Phalen." She'd kept a tiny sliver of her past life, making her maternal grandmother's first name her new middle name.

"Was that the name you were given at birth?"

"No."

"What name were you given at birth?"

Margot wasn't sure what the point of this was. This wasn't the big *gotcha* moment he was building it up to be. She'd made this revelation on her own on national television.

She restrained herself from rolling her eyes or sighing and hoped Hildy was proud of her for the effort.

"My birth name was Megan Anne Finch."

A little rustle of commotion went through the room, so apparently a few people were out of the loop. The jury, however, didn't seem moved whatsoever and Margot hoped that Crowther was already regretting the stupidity of this decision.

"Finch, eh?"

Margot didn't reply because phrasing something like a question did not a question make, and she wasn't going to give him the satisfaction of a response.

"Who is your father?"

"My father *was* Edgar Finch."

News of Ed's death was in the papers this morning, it had been quite a story, but the jury wouldn't have seen that, and it was possible the overworked lawyers hadn't either.

"Ms. Phalen—"

"Detective."

"I'm sorry?"

"Detective Phalen."

Crowther gave her a pinched look of annoyance, but continued. "Detective Phalen, are you aware of what a conflict of interest is?"

She chewed the inside of her cheek, letting the pain talk her down from saying something snarky.

"I am."

"And you didn't think, upon realizing there was a connection to Ed Finch's murders, that you should recuse yourself from this case?"

There it is.

"No," she replied.

He'd obviously been hoping for something more from her because his disappointment with her answer was written all over his face. Where Hildy had found her terseness a problem, it now seemed to be serving Margot just fine.

She highly doubted the jury was going to find *her* the unlikable one in this back-and-forth.

"Why is that?" Crowther asked, needling her.

"Because the case didn't involve Ed Finch."

"How can you say that?"

Margot darted a quick look over at Hildy, wondering if the prosecutor might want to whip out an objection here, but Hildy responded with a tight nod. It appeared they were just going to see where this led.

She looked back at Crowther, took a deep breath, and answered his question. "A case where a suspect appears to copy or mimic another killer does not mean the killer they are mimicking is involved in the case. Just because you like to talk louder than everyone in the room doesn't make you Clarence Darrow. Ethan Willingham wanting to copy the work of Ed Finch does not mean Ed Finch is involved in the case."

The judge didn't even need to hear an objection, she hid her smirk remarkably well as she said, "Detective, I'd like to ask you to refrain from personal remarks about counsel, or you may be held in contempt of court, do you understand?"

Margot nodded. "I apologize for saying unkind things about Clarence Darrow."

The judge did not add any additional censure, but Margot knew she was walking on eggshells. She would need to behave herself. Another look over at Hildy and Margot noted the lawyer's face in her palms, her shoulders trembling slightly. Margot was fairly certain she was trying to hide the fact that she was laughing.

Crowther was *pissed*, but so was Margot, so that put them on equal footing.

"And what about later, when it was discovered that Ed Finch had been in communication with Mr. Willingham? *Directing* him."

"Mr. Willingham's connection to Finch through his mother was not known to us at the time of arrest. We didn't uncover the text messages from Finch until much later, because Mr. Will-ingham was receiving those texts on a burner. None of this information had an impact on our investigation because it was unknown to us until after we had eyewitness testimony from Willingham's friends, and he had made his own confession."

"Are you trying to tell us that a case so deeply entrenched in the murders of *your father* was something you could investigate without bias?"

"Objection," Hildy said, bolting to her feet.

She didn't even get a chance to give her reasoning as Crowther waved a hand and said, "I'll rephrase."

Margot stared at him, daring him to find a way to ask this

question that wasn't loaded to the gills with objectionable phrasing.

"Detective Phalen, what was your opinion of my client the first time you met him?"

"I thought he was a teenaged boy."

"Can you be more specific?"

"I found him to be difficult to talk to, and felt that he wasn't taking our inquiries seriously."

"You didn't like him very much?"

"I don't have personal opinions about witnesses or persons of interest. I want to get information. If someone makes it difficult for me to get information, that may impact how they are treated."

Crowther looked at the jury as if he felt like he'd achieved something here, but the jury weren't biting; they looked stoic and a little annoyed.

"What is your opinion of Ed Finch?"

Hildy was on her feet again, "Objection—relevance? Ed Finch isn't on trial here."

The judge looked at Lloyd Crowther. Crowther said, "I'm simply trying to determine if there was a conflict of interest that caused my client to be unfairly treated by the investigators and pigeonholed as a killer without other avenues being explored."

"I'll allow it, but I want this to go somewhere *fast*, Mr. Crowther. Overruled."

Hildy plopped back into her seat, frustrated.

"Do you need me to repeat the question, detective?"

"No, I heard you. My opinion of Ed Finch is that he was a killer, and he was serving a death-row sentence for his crimes, as he rightly should have been, because he was convicted by a jury of his peers."

"He's your father."

"He was."

"I'm sorry, detective, why do you keep adjusting the tense?" He seemed genuinely perplexed by her corrections.

"Because less than twenty-four hours ago I shot and killed Ed Finch."

FORTY-TWO

Whatever Lloyd Crowther had been expecting her to say, *this* hadn't been it.

Behind Ethan, Toni began to sob, and Ethan's own smug expression vanished, replaced by the first genuine emotion Margot had ever seen from him: shock.

So they *hadn't* received the news yet.

The jury all had their heads dipped together, muttering, and a wall of sound began to build within the courtroom. The judge hammered her gavel and shouted for order to be restored, but Margot knew she'd rocked the boat and the waves would ripple for the rest of the day.

Margot smiled at Crowther, who had turned white as a sheet.

"I'm sorry... what did you say?" he asked.

"In the course of investigating cold cases that may have been tied to him, Finch was granted a brief pass from San Quentin. After showing the FBI task force the locations of the last of his unknown victims, he attacked a senior special agent. Deadly force was required."

"You killed Ed Finch?" No one was calling him out on how

inappropriate these questions were, everyone was too focused on getting more of the story.

"Yes."

She could see how he was trying to find a way to spin this, that it was obvious she couldn't be emotionally removed from a case involving Finch because it was obvious she had so much built-up anger toward him she'd been willing to kill him.

Margot saved him the trouble of having to think too hard. "For almost two years I've been working *with* the FBI to help close Ed's unknown victim cases. We have closed, in total, twelve cold cases, brought remains home to loved ones, brought closure to the women he killed. I know you want me to say I have all these feelings about my father that clouded my professional judgment, but that simply isn't the case. Ed Finch is the reason I became a police officer. Ed Finch is why I spent my whole life looking for justice for others. Because someone needs to. Because where there are monsters there needs to be hope. Hope that justice will prevail. You want me to say that I hated him so much it blinded me. That I couldn't be objective because of the connection. But I have gone to work every single day of my career with Ed in the back of my mind, knowing that it was up to me to make sure anyone else who became a victim would have someone to stand up for them. That what I did could help *others* from becoming a victim. So I'm sorry, sir, but if you want me to tell you that Ed Finch being my father means I couldn't fairly investigate this case, then you're going to be disappointed."

Margot hadn't meant to speak so much, but once she opened her mouth the words kept pouring out.

"But I will say this: I killed my *father* to protect the life of someone else, all in the name of bringing two of his victims home. So you tell me if you think my *opinion* of Ed Finch can change how I treat a suspect."

She stared at him for a long, tense pause. His cheeks were flushed.

The entire courtroom seemed to hold its breath, and Margot, too, wondered if she had stepped so far over the line that the judge was about to lock her up. She didn't really know what contempt of court entailed, but she had plenty of contempt for someone *in* the court.

Crowther cleared his throat, trying to decide if he could find a way to regain control here or if he should just abandon ship. Unfortunately for Margot, he wasn't the quitting type.

"Detective, did you know your father had remarried in prison?"

"Yes."

"How long did you know that information?"

"I found out over the course of our investigation. We were looking into connections to Finch after we found parts of Andrew Rhodes' book in Shuye Zhou's apartment. We thought our suspect might be enough of a fan to have tried reaching out by mail, and all of Finch's mail is cataloged. There were quite a few letters to and from Rhonda, his wife."

"He never told you about the marriage?"

"No. Ed Finch and I had no communication for the twenty-two years after his arrest. I only spoke to him recently to help close some cases. He may have attempted to tell me, but I don't accept his correspondence."

Crowther struggled here, he'd obviously been grasping at straws, and all those straws were coming up short.

Finally, he decided to just be direct.

"Detective, do you believe that your family connection to Ed Finch negatively impacted your ability to investigate this case?"

Margot sat back in the uncomfortable wooden chair inside the witness box and looked at him, her expression asking if he was really stupid enough to ask her that question.

"No, I do not."

"Why, then, did you treat my client with such hostility during your interviews?"

Margot snorted, then composed herself. This time she leaned forward so the microphone wouldn't miss a word.

"I treated your client with hostility because he murdered an eighty-year-old woman in cold blood."

"Objection, your honor," he whined.

Margot shrugged and looked at the judge. "He asked."

She glanced over to the jury and saw that all of them, without exception, were looking over at Ethan Willingham, and Margot didn't need to be a body language expert to see the way they were all reading *GUILTY* in big block letters over the kid's head.

Today hadn't gone at all as Margot had expected.

And she couldn't have been happier.

FORTY-THREE

It had taken Margot a long time to come to terms with the fact that justice was imperfect.

Sometimes people got away with things.

Sometimes the wrong people got blamed.

She had become a police officer because she believed that justice was something she could control. That she could figure out who had done wrong, and make them pay for their crimes.

But over the years, she had realized that there were more shades of gray to the work she did than she was comfortable with. Sometimes a guilty person was let go because the DA didn't want to risk losing the trial. Sometimes they didn't have the evidence they needed to say with certainty who had done something, even when she knew in her gut she was right.

Sometimes, a bad man would take death into his own hands rather than face going to prison.

It was too much to hope, she knew, that bad people would always pay the price for what they had done.

But riding high off the Ethan Willingham trial, where it seemed that she might have actually *helped* see justice done rather than hurt it, she felt like she could punch the sun itself.

And she knew there was one last thing she needed to do before she turned in her resignation to Captain Tate.

She pulled up a chair at an outside patio table, though the air was getting too cool to pretend it was summer anymore. An inner voice told her this was too exposed, too visible, but Margot had started to realize there was a big difference between playing it safe and wasting her life in a state of fear.

A few minutes later, the chair across from her was pulled out, and Sebastian Klein dropped into the spot facing her. He looked good, which was par for the course. Sebastian always looked good. He had dark, tousled hair, and slightly tinted glasses that she was convinced he didn't need but wore to look more refined.

He was wearing a suit jacket over a vintage Bon Jovi T-shirt, and perfectly tailored jeans. He set a notebook down on the table and smiled at her.

"How's it going today, Miss Margot? You finally decide to share your life story with me?"

She smiled back at him, feeling more relaxed than she had in years, despite how exposed she was. "Seb, the day I decide to let someone co-write the most boring memoir of the year, I will call you. But rest assured, no one wants to hear the life story of a dead serial killer's daughter."

He paused, something in his face showing an internal discomfort, and she realized after a moment what it was. He wanted to tell her he was sorry. It was a normal thing for friends to say to each other after the death of a parent. But this wasn't a normal situation, was it? This was so far from normal there wasn't even a name for it.

"It's OK," she told him, letting him off the hook for social niceties. "I'm OK. Really."

"Is it awful for me to tell you that you look amazing?"

She laughed, brushing her hair back from her forehead. "No. I appreciate that. I *feel* good, shockingly. I feel like everything is finally turning out the way it's supposed tc. But I need your help with something."

She had been debating this part for the last several months. How she could protect herself and Wes, but make sure that Pressley Boyd and Roberto Riga didn't get away with what they'd done?

She couldn't just turn her evidence over to the police. It was far too likely to disappear, leaving the perpetrators free to continue without consequence. She already had a plan in motion that would make sure the police couldn't overlook what Boyd had done.

What she needed now was someone who cou_d make sure the police wouldn't bury that story before it had a chance to get out.

This was something so explosive, Margot knew the only way to really get through it was to blow it up entire_y.

And that was where Sebastian came in.

He pivoted his chair so he was facing her directly, his uncomfortable expression now replaced with one of naked curiosity. "Do tell."

"You remember that case a few months back with the woman who briefly survived being lit on fire in a car?"

"Of course, that was awful. No arrests made on that one, right?"

Margot grimaced at this, even though he was merely stating a fact rather than assigning blame. "Yeah, that's the one. During the course of that case, I was given evidence, and it was some-thing so damning my partner and I knew the moment we tried to use it, our careers would be over, and the evidence would—most likely—end up 'lost'."

"What kind of evidence?" Sebastian asked.

"Video evidence. I'm not going to lie, it's pretty unpleasant stuff. Shows an assault."

Sebastian didn't say anything, just waited for her to explain why his help was needed in this. The press didn't do much to cover crimes against sex workers and they both knew it.

"The person perpetrating the assault was Pressley Boyd."

Sebastian sat back in his chair so forcefully it was like she had punched him. "I'm sorry, you have video evidence of the chief of police assaulting someone?"

"Someone who wound up murdered. And whose killer is still a free man right now because of his cozy relationship with the chief of police. Yes."

"Jesus." He stroked his jaw thoughtfully, trying to process this information and his part in it. "And there's no doubt at all that it's him?"

Margot shook her head. "None whatsoever. Clear visual of his face, no mistaking it. It's absolutely Pressley Boyd."

"Why did you sit on it? That case was months ago."

Margot explained the Emmanuel Riga connection—Sebastian, being a crime reporter, was very aware of who Riga was—and the concern that, in exposing Pressley, they might inadvertently let the Redwood Killer slip through their fingers.

With Drake Winston in jail and no longer a danger to the Larks, she could now take action against Pressley, and by extension Riga, without fear of a serial killer walking free.

"I can't open a case against Boyd—you know how this works," Margot said. "With something like this there's no way to know how deep the tumor goes. I can't trust my colleagues, my captain, or even Internal Affairs. There's only one way I can guarantee that he doesn't bury me and this evidence..."

"You want me to make it public."

"I want you to make it public."

They stared at each other across the table. The way the sun was dappled on Sebastian's face made him look more like a walking Gucci ad than a reporter, but she knew that he was the person for this job. For years Margot had slipped him harmless story leads to help his reporting, and he had kept her biggest secret. He'd figured out long before the documentary who she really was. His father had been one of the regular reporters following Ed's killings and his trial. Sebastian had grown up almost as immersed in Ed Finch lore as Margot had been. He'd been able to piece things together and figure out who she was without much difficulty.

But even though it was the kind of story that would have sold a ton of papers at the time, Sebastian hadn't shared it.

Margot trusted him, and she knew he was going to break this story and probably land himself a Pulitzer in the process, rather than turning it into tabloid fodder. That's what she and this evidence needed.

It's what Angela Gromand deserved.

"You know, if he figures out how I got this, your career is over anyway," Sebastian warned.

Margot smiled and slid a USB drive across the table to him.

"Don't worry about me, Seb. I'm going to make sure Pressley Boyd knows *exactly* where you got that footage."

FORTY-FOUR

Margot asked Sebastian to keep his story until Tuesday, which he readily agreed to, knowing the newspaper would need to be careful to vet his information before he was allowed to print something so damning. But Margot knew from the gleam in his eyes and the excitement in his tone as he took the USB and shook her hand that he was thrilled to have this story, and nothing short of the *Sentinel* offices burning down would keep him from publishing on Tuesday.

Which meant Margot had her own plan to put into action on Monday evening, just as her shift rolled back to overnights.

Wes knew everything; she'd had to go over her plan with him, because there was a chance he might get caught in the crossfire. No one would believe that he, having worked the Angela Gromand case with her, would be ignorant of such a damning piece of evidence. She could try to take all the blame, but Wes might end up as collateral damage.

Margot needed to know if he was OK with that before she made her move.

Wes being Wes had been behind her one hundred percent.

Getting Pressley Boyd to come to the precinct hadn't been

hard. He was still riding high from his press conference the previous day, where he'd gotten to stand next to the mayor and announce that the Redwood Killer had been arrested and had confessed. It was a one-two punch of success for him, and he was clearly still feeling on top of the world when Margot had requested to sit down with him and the captain.

They were back in the same conference room where he had previously seen her, only this time his assistant was nowhere in sight. Whatever he was expecting from this meeting, he obviously didn't feel like it needed to be recorded.

Margot sat down next to Captain Tate, wishing she had been able to tell him ahead of time what was about to happen, but knowing that her circle of trust couldn't be widened by even one more person.

He would know everything soon enough.

He would also find her resignation on his desk after this meeting was over. Her career with the SFPD wouldn't survive what was about to go down, and she had already told Andrew that she was accepting his offer. He had been as overjoyed as someone could be who wasn't allowed to speak and had almost been killed.

She was amazed he still wanted her on his team after everything that had happened, but it turned out saving his life had probably gone a long way toward earning his eternal gratitude. It probably had helped make her fairly popular with the whole team, actually.

Margot adjusted herself in her seat and looked across the table to Boyd, who was wearing his typical ill-fitting suit and smug smile.

She couldn't wait to wipe that smile off his face.

"Detective Phalen, thank you for asking for this meeting. While I assume you're expecting some congratulations over the work you did with the Redwood Killer case, I actually want to discuss a more pressing matter with you, so the timing of your invitation was very prescient."

It had been a busy week for Margot, so she couldn't be sure which bit of bad press he was about to lecture her about. She just smiled back at him and waited for him to get to the point.

"We've been seeing a bit too much of you in the media of late. While your work bringing the Redwood Killer to justice will go a long way to garner public goodwill, you also shot a federal inmate—your *father*, no less—and then had quite the unfortunate outburst in a criminal trial. What do you have to say for yourself? Any reason I shouldn't be suspending you while you're investigated to confirm you're fit to continue working?"

"Hey now," Captain Tate interjected. "You didn't discuss any of this with me ahead of time, and if you did, I would tell you that Detective Phalen's work is beyond reproach, and I won't allow her reputation to be sullied because of some vendetta you have against her."

His cheeks were flushed and Margot looked at him, a warm, genuine smile crossing her face. He was one of the good ones. She never should have doubted it.

She placed a hand on his forearm and gave a gentle squeeze. "I've got this."

He appeared bewildered, and Boyd looked annoyed by her casual response. He was about to say something else when Margot held out her hand to stop him.

"I don't care what you think of me, Pressley."

"That's *Chief* to you," he snarled.

"Not for long, no. See, I think you made a few mistakes when you thought that title and your position could protect you forever. You felt invincible, and I'm here to remind you that you are not. You're just a man. And soon you'll be just a man who is sitting next to every other felon we've put away."

"What absolute nonsense are you talking now?" he asked, his tone enraged but his eyes wide with fear.

Margot met his gaze. He knew there were secrets he didn't want her to be aware of. And he also knew, if she was talking like this, she had figured out at least one of them.

"Tomorrow morning, the *Sentinel* is going to print an exposé about you. I'm telling you this now, not so you have time to stop it—because you can't. I'm telling you because, when that story breaks, I want you to know that *I* was the one who did this to you. I wanted to look you in the eyes when you realized your life is over."

"This is outrageous. You're done. You're never going to be a police officer again. When I'm through with you, you'll be lucky to work as a security guard at a mall."

Margot shook her head. "I'm not afraid of you, Pressley."

"You should be."

"No. You should be afraid of me. Very, very afraid." She pulled out her phone and he flinched.

Margot smiled.

She turned her phone to face him, holding it at an angle so the captain could see. Then she pressed play.

The familiar, awful video of Roberto Riga and Boyd assaulting Angela Gromand played. Margot didn't watch it. She stared directly at Boyd, watching the color drain from his face as he aged ten years over the course of the video.

When it was done, he was silent.

Captain Tate whispered, "What the fuck?"

It was the first time she'd ever heard him swear. Well, perhaps that wasn't true, but it *felt* true.

"In about two seconds, I'm going to send that video to every single police email account in the city of San Francisco. Tomorrow morning, everyone you have ever met will know the truth about you."

"Detective, don't do this," Boyd said, his voice low and tight. "You have no idea what will happen if you release that video."

She was too busy attaching a zip file of the video to an email draft. After a beat she said, "I do. I know you'll go to jail. I know Roberto Riga will, too. Finally. I know Emmanuel Riga will have to answer some very serious questions, and while it might not be enough to take him down, it's a good start."

She got to her feet, the chair scraping loudly as it moved back.

"And I'm not worried about losing my job, *Chief*. Because, effective immediately, I'm resigning my position." She gave Captain Tate an apologetic look. "I'm sorry to do it like this, but I had no choice. I didn't know who I could trust, and I needed to make sure he didn't get away with it."

"You don't have to leave, Margot," Captain Tate said.

She smiled at him again, so grateful to him for all he had ever done for her, and so relieved to know her respect for him hadn't been misplaced.

"It's the right time," she said. "And it will make it so much harder for all the cronies he has left to make my life a living hell."

She turned her attention back to Pressley, who looked like he was trying desperately to come up with an escape plan, a bribe, anything to make her change her mind. Instead, he watched as she turned her phone back to him and hit the *Send* button on the email.

Immediately, Boyd and Tate's phones pinged with the notification.

Through the conference room glass, she watched as first one, then two, then more people opened the email and saw what it contained.

Around the city, it would be more of the same.

Margot slipped her phone into her pocket, then took her badge and department-issued gun and placed them both in front of the captain, removing the bullet clip in case Boyd felt compelled to do something stupid.

She leaned forward, palms on the table, and looked Pressley Boyd right in the eye. "The woman on that video is dead, and she died *because* that video exists. I couldn't stop that from happening to her, but by *God*, I want you to know that Angela Gromand did this to you, and I hope to hell you never forget that name, because she deserved so much better than this. And I'm glad the last thing I ever did as a cop was to bring you down."

And with that Margot straightened herself, and walked out of the conference room and the police department for the last time, stopping only to grab her bag and jacket and give Wes a nod.

She didn't have to worry about missing him.

But she might miss that stupid couch.

FORTY-FIVE

The night air was cool and damp, but Margot wasn't in any hurry to go inside.

She stood on the street corner with Betty, who was happily sniffing the traces left behind by other dogs throughout the day.

The temperature had dropped enough that Margot needed her jacket, but she still felt high off her own bravado. What she had done today had been borderline insane, and could have been—and might still be—dangerous. But she also felt more *alive* than she had... ever.

For most of her adult life, Margot had made choices for others. She'd chosen her job because she felt like she needed to make amends. She'd stayed alone because she felt like it was the only way for her to truly be safe. She had lived a half-life for almost twenty-five years without ever stopping to wonder what she could have been, and where her path might have led her, if only Ed hadn't ruined everything.

But now, for the first time, she felt as if she might actually have an opportunity to live a life for herself.

Ed was gone—something she still hadn't really come to terms with. Perhaps there would come a time when she felt compelled to grieve him, but she didn't think so. Before all this had started, she had felt like her father—the one she'd known before everything unraveled—had died the day Ed was arrested.

Now he was gone for good.

If anything, she felt only relief.

And now that the truth about Pressley Boyd was out there— along with damning evidence against Roberto Riga—she had started a tidal wave of events that wouldn't stop until they had swept the department clean.

She wouldn't be there to see it happen, but she still felt proud of herself for taking such bold action to ensure Boyd had no way to backpedal and hide from what he had done.

While she had burned her bridges with the San Francisco Police Department, she knew it was a necessary step to bring justice to someone who thought he was beyond the reach of the law. She had, in her last action as a detective, helped ensure that the police department would become a less corrupt place.

She wasn't foolish enough to believe she had rid the force of crooked cops. That would be insanity, and well beyond her abilities. But she had gotten rid of the rottenest cop of them all, and it was going to have to be enough.

A car pulled up to the curb, the headlights momentarily blinding her, and her deeply ingrained fight-or-flight told her to haul ass back to her apartment. Instead, she stood still, breathing in through her nose, out through her mouth, and held her ground.

She didn't need to be afraid of the world.

And once she was calm, she realized that she knew the car.

Wes got out of the driver's side, his dress shirt unbuttoned and sleeves rolled up to the elbows. He looked tired, but also wore a smile that was warm enough to melt butter. He came to stand on the sidewalk with her, a few feet back, his hands stuffed in his jacket pockets like he was nervous about what they would do on their own if he wasn't paying attention to them.

Betty sniffed at his pant leg, her tail wagging when she recognized his scent.

While Margot didn't fully trust Betty's opinions on men, considering she'd lived the bulk of her life with a killer, it did make her feel warm and fuzzy to see that the dog so obviously adored Wes.

Wes, likewise, seemed grateful for something to do with his hands and bent down to give the senior pup a good rubdown. Betty licked his face repeatedly.

"Careful, I might start to think you like her more than you like me," Margot teased.

"I can't help it, Margot. Bitches love me."

She let out a snort of laughter, and he got to his feet, after giving Betty one last scratch behind the ears.

"How bad was it after I left?" she asked him, shifting from one foot to the other, suddenly shy and uneasy about his response.

She'd felt like a rockstar when she walked out of the building, but she knew there would be fallout from her actions.

"Well, I'm on paid leave for two weeks while Internal Affairs try to get this all sorted out. Obviously, there were some issues about hiding evidence that impacted an active case."

"Shit. I'm sorry."

Wes shrugged, smiled. He didn't look bothered in the least. "We knew it was a possibility. To be honest, from what I've gathered about the IA investigation from the little bit they told me, this is all to keep things above board and beyond reproach. With the whole Boyd thing, they know it's going to get messy, so they're playing it precisely by the book."

"We know how that works," she said, thinking about the painstaking efforts they'd taken on the Redwood Killer case.

"We do. And we knew that when this shit hit the fan it

wouldn't just hit Boyd. It's going to take months to figure out who he had working under him, and even then, it's unlikely we'll get everything clean. But before I left, Branson was getting a warrant for Roberto Riga's arrest."

Margot let out her breath in a puff and closed her eyes, letting those words sink in. She smiled.

"Good. Good."

Wes nodded. "Who knows what they'll get to stick, but the assault charges will let us hang on to him until we can finally get him for Angela. And whatever else he's been up to."

Margot knew none of these cases were hers anymore, and it pained her to leave them unfinished, but she was relieved to know they wouldn't be forgotten now that she was gone.

"And you?" Wes asked, his eyes searching hers like he might find his answer there. "You feel good?"

She looked at him carefully, debating how to answer that question. Betty plopped down on the sidewalk and put her head on her paws, a contented sigh wheezing out of her.

"I don't know if *good* is the right word for it. My father is dead. I nearly got held in contempt of court and made a permanent enemy of Lloyd Crowther..."

"Worth it to know that little shit Ethan Willingham will never see the light of day again," Wes observed.

"Without a doubt. And a small, petty part of me is gratified to know he'll never get to spend a minute of his life behind bars with the man he idolized."

Wes chuckled. "That does sound like your flavor of petty."

"And I just walked out of my job after tanking the career of the most powerful cop in the city."

"To go work with a new, elite FBI unit," Wes said. "I think *good* can sum up all those things."

Margot nodded thoughtfully to herself. "It's been a hell of a week."

"One for the ages." He took a step closer to her, but with

Betty between them he couldn't close the gap completely. "I think there was something else that happened this week that we haven't really circled back on."

"The Giants' playoff odds?" she said, grinning at him. She felt younger and freer than she had in decades. She wanted to bottle this feeling and drink it. She felt *alive* for possibly the first time in her adult life, and it was such a magnificent, euphoric feeling she didn't know if she trusted it. But she never wanted it to end.

"There's that, but I was thinking more about the whole thing where you said you loved me."

Margot pressed a palm to his chest, not sure if she wanted to pull him in, or protect the distance between them. Letting someone in was a terrifying concept. But letting *Wes* in definitely felt right.

"Did I say that?" she said, teasing him, even though teasing felt cruel.

"Trust me, Margot. A commitment-phobic asshole knows when he hears those words. Typically, it's like our Bat Signal to run for the hills."

She leaned a little closer, enough to smell that perfect hit of his cologne, and to see the stubble on his jaw. "You don't seem to be running."

"I have no intention of going anywhere. Not if you meant it." He suddenly looked so serious, something she wasn't accustomed to with Wes. And normally it might have made her nervous, but in this situation it just made her feel seen.

"Not that long ago you wanted to tell me something, but I asked you to wait. I said it wasn't the right time. Well, the case is solved. Ed is dead. Everything I was using as an excuse is gone. I want to hear what you were going to say."

"You already know," he protested, closing the distance between them. Betty was practically wedged between their feet now.

"I do. But I still want to hear it."

His breath smelled like mint, and up close she could see flecks of green around the iris of his eye.

"Margot Phalen, I am stupidly, wildly, recklessly in love with you, and now that you're not a cop anymore, I'm hoping you'll still be my partner."

"God, Wes, that almost sounded like a proposal."

"If you want it to be, sure."

"Maybe let's wait and see if you can deal with me as a girlfriend before you decide to make it a lifetime commitment."

He looked at her, his eyes hazy and unfocused. "Now I want to hear you say it."

"You want me to propose?"

He cupped her face between two big hands and tilted her chin up slightly so she was looking at him.

"Enough jokes. For now."

Her breath came out thready, giving away her complete lack of chill. "OK. I love you. I didn't think it was something I was even capable of, but for once in your life, you proved me wrong."

He smirked. "I guess that's as close to serious as I'm going to get."

"It was very serious."

"Shut up, Margot." And with an achingly delicate press of his lips to hers, she finally let him have the last word.

A LETTER FROM THE AUTHOR

A massive thank you for reading *Out of the Woods*! I can't believe this was the last book of Margot and Ed's story! But if you have been enjoying Margot's journey, it's not over, as the next phase of her career will start in January 2026 with her joining the FBI! If you want to join other readers in hearing all about my Storm new releases and bonus content, you can sign up for my newsletter:

www.stormpublishing.co/kate-wiley

And if you want to keep up to date with all my other publications, you can sign up to my mailing list:

www.eepurl.com/ASoIz

Reviews mean the world to authors, as they can help new readers decide what to pick up next. People have been discovering Margot through word-of-mouth and with the series now complete it would be the perfect time for others to jump on board. I would be so grateful if you would leave a review. Even a short review can make all the difference in encouraging a reader to discover my books for the first time. Thank you so much!

This has been a wild ride across five books, and I feel so lucky to have gotten to tell this story the way I so badly wanted to. Margot found her readership, and to everyone who has supported the series from day one, or for those picking up the book for the first time, thank you so much for helping bring her to life.

Thanks again for being part of this amazing journey with me and I hope you'll stay in touch—I have a lot more planned, and if you keep reading, I'll keep writing!

Kate Wiley

www.katewiley.com

facebook.com/SierraDeanAuthor
x.com/sierradean
instagram.com/sierradeanauthor

ACKNOWLEDGMENTS

Wow, the end of the series. When I dusted off the manuscript for *The Killer's Daughter* (then called *In the Blood* which later became our book four title), I knew submitting it to a new publisher was a long shot. It had been turned down by agents and publishers, and while I believed in it so fiercely, I knew selling yet another serial killer story wasn't going to be easy. But, as it turned out, it was just waiting for the right home. In this industry, getting a series picked up for multiple books is never a sure thing. Getting it picked up for five is almost unheard of. Five books turned out to be the exact right amount of breathing room to give life to this story in a way that felt super satisfying (but also left enough for Margot to do that I'll be lucky enough to take her into a whole new series). For all of this, I am eternally grateful to Storm Publishing and to Vicky Blunden. The way you hype me up is like nothing I've ever experienced and I'm so lucky to get to work with you sharing these stories. To Oliver, Alexandra, Elke, Naomi, and to the astonishingly talented copy editors I've worked with on this series, thank you for everything!

To Lauryn Allman, no acknowledgment would be complete without you, the voice of my Margot. You are such a hype woman for this series and I might just have to let your compliments go to my head.

This book was a wild ride to write, and when I hit *the end* I wanted to give (almost) every character a big hug. I think I might have written this book in a fugue state because I don't remember anything about the process, but after several months there *was* a completed book in front of me, so I suppose I must have written it in between periodic bouts of impostor syndrome and occasionally leaving my writing cave to squint at the outside world.

Thanks, as always, to my mother, because she is the most supportive person in my life. To my friends, who are my chosen family and still pretend to be excited when I release new books, and to the libraries of the world for stocking them (someone sent me a photo of my book in a New Zealand library and it made my entire year).

Thank you, finally, to you reading.

9 781805 084532